Charming the Professor

Book One of the
Charm Gate Time-Travel Series

Donna MacMeans

Acknowledgements

Many years ago I spent a fabulous week in New Orleans with my good friend Sherry Hartzler. This book grew out of that trip. Thank you to Sherry and Rosemary Laurey who helped me get it started. Thank you to Jeanne Adams, Cassondra Murray and Nancy Northcott who helped me complete it. Thank you, Saralee Etter, who corrected my French and Spanish. Thanks as well to Christina Stahurski who edited the manuscript, and my husband, Richard, for his proofreading skills. Finally, thank you to Shane Riley on Jackson Square for giving us directions (grin).

I love New Orleans. If you go, I highly recommend a trip to The Court of Two Sisters for brunch. Be sure to have a mimosa for me and simply enjoy all that is New Orleans (and don't forget to stop by and grab hold of the charm gates. You never know who you might release with your touch :-)

Prologue

Madrid, Spain 1853

WHAT VALUE ARE potions and enchantments if you can't rid me of one meddlesome charm teacher?" Queen Isabella's glare burned hotter than the thick sulfurous mixtures bubbling on the alchemist's hearth deep in the secret confines of the palace.

Padre Rodriquez hid his frown, knowing Isabella had her subjects throats slit for less. He had obligations, secret obligations, that necessitated his throat remain intact.

"My queen," he said. "You have the authority to remove Señorita Charlebois from your court. You have no need of my paltry abilities."

Even in the dim light of his secret chamber, Rodriquez could see the advancing affliction on the young queen's peeling, scaly arms. Seven years of a disappointing marriage had given her an unwelcome air and a permanent frown. Try as she might, he knew Queen Isabella II would never be an attractive woman. Perhaps that was the reason she so often sought solace in his underground chamber where no one else dared venture.

"It's difficult," the queen said, opening a heavily jeweled fan. "Given her father's position in the French Empire, releasing Señorita Charlebois from court responsibilities might be construed as an insult to Napoleon III. I suspect they rid themselves of a problem by sending her to me. Still, I can't afford to strain relations with such a powerful neighbor."

Rodriquez doubted that statement. The ever-pleasant Señorita Charlebois appeared highly competent. She'd be a welcome addition to any court, yet every breath the charming señorita took seemed as a thorn in the queen's side.

"Why do you dislike the girl so much?" He carefully moved his latest concoction away from the fire to make the thick air more palatable. "Do you object that she is French, or do you find she is lacking in some knowledge of foreign etiquette?"

"She lacks compassion." Isabella spat the words as if they fouled her mouth. The caged animals set up a loud ruckus at the implied threat in her tone. She glanced at the birds hopping frantically in their confinement, then closed her eyes, seeming to compose herself.

"I am the Queen of Spain," she stated. "The señorita knows I must produce heirs to secure the throne but my husband has, shall we say, other preferences. He has forced me to seek alternatives to secure the royal line."

Even Padre Rodriquez, a representative of the one true church, had heard whispers of her husband's fondness for young men. Thus Rodriquez turned a blind eye to Isabella's flirtations and passions for dance with young men at court. Rumors suggested the captain of the palace guard and not the king-consort, had truly sired the baby princess Maria Isabel.

Señorita Charlebois was not the only one who disapproved of the young queen's promiscuity and debauchery, yet she seemed to be the only one receiving the queen's displeasure.

"You have a new cleric," Isabella said, interrupting his thoughts.

"Tomas Barreda," he replied, grateful for the change in topic. "He comes to us from Barcelona. A very devout young man."

"He did not seem so devout to me," the queen said, snapping her fan shut. "He spent all of last evening speaking with that French tart."

Ahh…the girl's beauty and popularity had generated the queen's jealousy, not any dereliction of responsibilities. The señorita was everything the queen wished to be and therefore was despised. He feared no logic or counseling on his part would sway her opinion.

"Señorita Charlebois has the ability to make a stranger feel comfortable," he said, walking a fine line. Sweat streamed down his face. The queen might attribute it to the heat of his sanctuary, but he knew better. "I believe they had some commonality, a mutual acquaintance perhaps."

Isabella's black eyes glared at him with barely suppressed rage. "She stole his attention from me. This is not the first time her simpering smiles have thwarted my opportunities. There was Gustavo and that jaunty soldier, Lucas. I should have danced last night, not Charlebois."

As a man who valued his existence, Rodriquez kept silent.

"I have tried to discourage her close association," Isabella complained. "Yet the silly girl refuses to abandon her duties. I fear stronger measures are required."

"Surely you can use your influence to persuade a man to marry Señorita Charlebois and remove her from the royal retinue," Rodriquez counseled. "There must be many men willing to court her. She's so...so..."

"What?" The queen halted her pacing at his hesitation and glared at the captive alchemist. "She's so what?"

"Charming," he said, quickly substituting for "beautiful," the word on his tongue. "I was about to say she is so ... charming."

He held his breath, waiting for the tense moment to pass.

The queen frowned, then stepped so close he could smell the Madeira tainting her breath. "I have heard whispers, Padre. It is said that you can make living things vanish."

His whole body tensed. "I am a scientist, my queen, not a magician. My mission is to transmute baser metals to release those properties that might—"

"I know about your mission, Padre, and I know that you have stumbled upon a use for your philosopher's stone that was not intended." A wicked smile tilted her lips.

He struggled to calm his breathing. How could she know? His order demanded secrecy. "Who has told you such things?" he asked cautiously.

"My sources are not important." Fire light danced in the ruby at her throat, the ruby they called the Moor's Tear. It shimmered as if tiny flames licked her neck. "Fulfilling *my* need, however, is essential to the continuation of *your* research and existence. It is not the church that has kept you well fed, comfortably housed, and able to pursue your avocation."

He hesitated, knowing these were not idle threats. The queen's malicious spirit had already separated many of his peers from their earthly confines. His next words could easily seal his fate.

"I may have had some limited success with mice and rabbits," he admitted cautiously.

Her eyes widened with an evil spark. Instantly, he realized he had confirmed her unsupported suspicions. Now he was trapped, much like the rodents he kept for his experiments.

"Where do you send them, Padre?"

"I don't know. They simply disappear," he confessed. "My experiments are in the early stages. I've yet to discover how to reverse the process." Perhaps if she understood how little he knew, she'd grant him time to perfect his art.

"Excellent." Her voice hissed. She turned her back and set her fan in rapid motion. The scent of over-ripe roses assaulted him. He captured his cough in his fist.

"Have you ever tried your process on a person?" She tapped her finger on the thin metal housing of caged pigeons.

Dread danced down his spine in an icy shiver. His stomach roiled in protest. "Your Majesty, surely you aren't suggesting –"

She charged his worktable, her eyes narrowed to daggers. "I wish for you to permanently remove Señorita Charlebois from my life. I want no more interference on her part."

"You wish me to arrange for her murder?" He prayed that was her intent. Although repulsive, especially when the victim was to be a sweet innocent as was Señorita Charlebois, a murder in Madrid could be easily arranged. Thus, his recently discovered power of transmutation would remain secret.

"No. I have enough difficulties with insurgents, I don't want them to seek aid from France if there's a suspicion of foul play." Her lips tightened. "I want her to disappear. Vanish. Make it seem as if she's run away from her duties on her own accord." She stepped closer, making it impossible to avert her cold, black eyes. "But make certain that she never returns. Can you do this?"

For a moment, Rodriquez's mouth gaped like that of a fish. What was she asking? Even in this bastion of heat, his blood chilled. "What you suggest would be a blemish on one's soul for eternity. Your majesty, I beg that you reconsider. Perhaps if I spoke to her –"

"Can your speech cause her skin to peel like this?" She held her lace mantilla away from her neck. "Can your words dull her eyes and hunch her straight body? No. I want her out of my sight."

"Please your majesty," he pleaded. "We are dealing with a human life."

"If you deny me, we will most certainly deal with a human life," she threatened. Evil portent surrounded him, suffocating in its closeness.

She stepped back, a thin smile played upon her lips. "I understand you visit a young woman on the outskirts of the city. A woman who cares for an infant." She paused a moment. "Your son."

Blood drained from his face leaving tingling in its wake. How could she know of Cristobal? They had been so very careful. Even the bishop had no idea. The queen's spies must be everywhere!

"You are extremely valuable to me, Padre," she continued with a sneer. "Too valuable to lose. But a small babe…" She shook her head. "While it distresses me to think that you will be the end of your line, if a life must be sacrificed better it be one that has barely started."

Sacrifice! Gooseflesh rose beneath his cassock. He had no wish to be the instrument of Señorita Charlebois's demise, but he could not sacrifice his infant son. His glance fell upon a nest of captive mice shivering in a wooden box. He felt a kinship.

"I will require heat," he said, defeated. "Immense heat to tap the vast quantity of required energy, and iron. I must have sufficient iron. Can you arrange such things?"

"Would a foundry suffice?" Queen Isabella smiled, victory in her grasp. "I am scheduled to tour such a facility later this week."

Rodriguez nodded, numb to the queen's glee. He turned his back so she wouldn't see him raise his hand to touch his forehead, chest and shoulders.

"I believe I shall have Señorita Madeline Allegra Charlebois herself confirm the details," she said with malicious laughter.

A shiver rippled down the Padre's spine. He bowed his head but couldn't recall a prayer for such a despicable act. Instead, he offered what would most likely be an ignored prayer for forgiveness.

May God have mercy on my soul.

Chapter One

Present day, New Orleans, USA

THE ROLL OF thunder overhead on an otherwise perfect late March afternoon chased most of the luncheon patrons out of the famed brick courtyard of The Court of Two Sisters. The jazz trio cast anxious glances to the troubled skies then quickly packed their brass instruments. Yet Professor Grant Stewart, deeply embroiled in his own personal tempest, took little notice of the dark clouds and broiling conflict above the century-old wisteria.

"I'm serious, Grant," his sister-in-law lectured, ignoring his scowl. "I grieve for Carolyn every day. She was more than my sister; she was my best friend. That's why I'm telling you, for your daughter's sake you need to get on with life."

Grant listened politely. He'd heard similar platitudes from concerned friends before. Unless they'd suffered a loss such as his, they just didn't understand. How could they? They still had hopes and dreams. All of his were sealed in a sun-bleached tomb along with his wife, the victim of a drunk driver. *It should have been me. Not Carolyn.*

"I'm trying," he said, forcing his thoughts away from all he'd lost. "You'll be pleased to know I've started seeing someone."

"Who?" Beth's fork clattered to her plate.

He thought that news might get her attention.

"My accountant," he replied. "She's very driven, very focused in her career." *And as different as Carolyn as night is to day.* "We have that narrow focus in common."

He forced a smile, hoping Beth would accept the burgeoning relationship as an attempt to bring normalcy into his life even though normalcy as he once knew it would never again be possible. Carolyn's loss had ripped a hole into his very soul that could never be truly repaired. If it hadn't been for his daughter, he might have crumbled up and died himself. It was for Kimberly's sake that he'd begun dating, not for his own. She would need a woman's influence as she grew older. He didn't hope to find love again, but companionship, someone with which to share day-to-day responsibilities, *that* might be possible.

"So while I appreciate your concern, you can see Kim and I will be just fine," he said. "We have a routine. We need each other. We'll manage." Discussion closed.

Beth leaned forward, her tailored jacket barely missing the remnants of shrimp étouffée. "Then why has Kimmy asked to come home with me?"

"She can spend the night at your place." Grant shrugged. "I don't mind if —"

"She doesn't want to just spend the night." Beth captured his gaze. "She doesn't want to live with you anymore."

That dagger bit deep. He'd already lost his wife. He wasn't about to lose his daughter.

Beth's eyes filled with compassion. "Don't you see? She says you're sad all the time and that makes her sad too."

"Jesus, Beth. She's only six. She doesn't know what she's saying" Grant grumbled, throwing his napkin on the table. "It doesn't matter what she says, you can't take her."

An ominous roar rolled across the dark sky. Beth scowled at the clouds as if even they had sided against her.

"She knows her mother is in heaven," she said. "She thinks maybe her dad has gone away as well."

"I have to work, don't I?" That was true enough. The cold numbing postulates of quantum physics kept him sane and grounded. They kept his grief from swallowing him whole. He needed to work more than he needed to breathe. "I won't make tenure if I don't publish. The tenure review was extended once due to the accident. They won't do it again."

"Maybe gaining tenure is just not meant to be. You both need more time to heal." Beth reached across the table, placing her hand on his forearm. "You've gone through how many babysitters in the last year? Maybe if Kim stays with me—"

"You can't have her." He pulled his arm away.

"But—"

"No 'buts' about it. I won't let you take Kimmy away from me."

"I'm not trying to take..." Beth abandoned her argument with a shake of her head. She pushed her chair back. "Look, just think about it, okay? We can talk more about this later. Meanwhile, I'll pick Kim up from Mom's. She appreciates spending the time with Kim, but that ball of energy wears her out."

Was that today? Had two weeks passed all ready? Perhaps there was something in Beth's counsel, but he wouldn't allow anyone, not even his sister-in-law, to take his daughter. He glanced at Beth, feeling a little guilty about his earlier tone. "I really appreciate you and your mother helping like this."

"Just think about what I said." His practical sister-in-law pushed a button on her umbrella then scurried toward the courtyard exit that led to Bourbon Street.

Grant signed the restaurant receipt leaving a generous tip for the patient waiter, took a final sip of wine, then stood to leave. A fat raindrop plopped on his plate, followed by another on his shoulder. Damn, he'd left his umbrella in his car. He dashed past the three-tiered fountain toward the interior restaurant, continuing past the unattended maître d's station to the covered passageway that led to Rue Royale. Just as the glass door separating the air-conditioned restaurant from the humid passageway closed behind him, the threatening clouds unleashed a downpour on the Crescent City.

It would quickly pass. These storms usually did, leaving the city steamier than before. He'd just wait it out here in the passageway where it was dry. The refreshing scent of the rain slipped beneath the two swinging shutters that served as doors out to the street. Puddles formed on the warm concrete just outside. Grant leaned against the wall, surprised when his shoulder scraped the edges of decorative iron placed ceremoniously against the brick. The gates! He'd forgotten about the Charm Gates. His gaze lifted to the wooden sign attached to the ornate black curves:

These Charm Gates were wrought in Spain especially for the Court of Two Sisters. According to legend, Queen Isabella had them blessed so that their charm would pass onto anyone who touched them.

For all the times he and Carolyn had come to this restaurant, he'd avoided the charm gates. Even with Carolyn's teasing encouragement to grab on with both hands to claim the maximum amount of charm, he'd just ask why should he when Carolyn had enough southern charm for the both of them? She'd laugh and squeeze their joined hands. But Carolyn was gone and he needed to find his way without her. He slipped his hand down the cold metal grating.

"I miss you," he whispered in the empty hallway. On impulse, he grasped the iron grating with both hands and leaned his cheek against the bars. "Oh baby, I miss you so much, but it's time to let you go. I need to move on. I hope you understand."

CHARMING THE PROFESSOR

A white light exploded around him as a crack of thunder split the air. His body flew backwards to the opposite wall, where he crumbled into a boneless heap, welcoming the calm dark solitude.

MADDIE STRUGGLED TO breathe, her restrictive corset hampered her efforts. Her teeth rattled. Her legs felt numb. Ice must have settled deep in her bones. Senseless shapes and unnatural colors defied clear vision. She panicked. What in the name of all things holy was happening to her?

The last thing she remembered was touring one of Madrid's premier foundries — a dirty, noisy place — with Queen Isabella and her entourage. The queen had sent her for a fan left in her carriage, well needed in that hellish place of fire-licked vats of molten ore. Even now, the stench of sulfur still lingered in her nose.

Still, that the queen chose her, a highly placed advisor, over one of the ever-present footmen, felt to be an insult. The poorly concealed laughter from the queen's ladies-in-waiting supported her impression. But Madeline had never refused a request from the queen, so off she went. Before she'd gone far, though, Padre Rodriguez had stepped in front of her. She recalled his sad, remorseful eyes. He said something, she couldn't hear him well, then he raised his hand and a blinding flash...

Suddenly she was here—wherever this may be--cast onto the cold, hard floor of a narrow corridor, half-frozen and shivering. How could this be? Where was the queen? The entourage? The noise? The stench? Only an explosion could produce such blinding light and the force necessary to toss her through the air like a discarded apple.

An explosion! *Mon Dieu!* The queen! She pulled herself off the floor, vigorously rubbing her arms for warmth. She scanned the narrow hall for more of Queen Isabella's group. But she found no one. No scattered bricks. No residual smoke. No evidence of an explosion. Her parasol lay on the floor near a discarded bundle of cloth at the opposite end of the otherwise empty passageway.

Where was she? Was this another of the queen's cruel jests? She drew deep draughts of air, hoping to slow her racing heart. Her mind struggled to sort through possibilities. Only the rumble of thunder overhead touched on the familiar.

This wasn't the first time Queen Isabella had plotted against her etiquette advisor. At least this time Madeline hadn't been shut away in a cold, dank cellar, or abandoned in the country, away from the comforts of the palace. She shifted her shoulders back, her resolve thickening. Just as she had survived those torments, she would survive this as well.

A low moan issued from the pile of abandoned clothing. Long legs, a distinctly masculine trunk, and an attractive, slightly battered head, took shape amid the cloth on the floor. Another victim of the queen's twisted humor, no doubt.

"¿Está usted en dolor?" She asked about the queen from a cautious distance. "¿Dónde está la Reina?"

The drab bundle shifted, then straightened, struggling to sit up. She was about to repeat her question when she noted the dark trail of blood down the stranger's angled cheekbone. *Merde!* Immediately, she pulled the lace handkerchief from her sleeve and hurried toward the wounded man. Kneeling beside him, she cradled his head while she blotted the wound.

"¿Qué le han hecho a usted?" What had they done to him?

His skin lacked the rich Mediterranean tones of the queen's typical couriers. He had more the look of a foreigner, a handsome foreigner, she modified. It was bad enough Isabella played tricks on emissaries in her own court, but to treat visiting foreigners in this fashion. Inexcusable.

He didn't answer, yet a warm breath slipped past his lips, bathing her wrist, chasing away remnants of their chill. At least, she wasn't trapped with a corpse. Her glance traveled the length of him, pausing at the loose shapeless trousers. He must be English. Only an Englishman would wear such unflattering garments.

Her fingers traced the line of his brows above his closed eyes. He had a kind face, a handsome face, although someone had mercilessly chopped off his hair within a few centimeters of his scalp. Another of the queen's torments, no doubt. Was there no end to the indignities she imposed on those not meeting her favor? The small dimple on his chin stole little attention from his enticing lips. Would his eyes be brown as well? She lightly tapped the man's cheek hoping to bring him to consciousness.

"Señor, despierta. Debemos buscar a la Reina." When he didn't respond to her demand in Spanish that he wake up and help locate the queen, she tried French, her native tongue. His eyes, a surprising dark blue, fluttered open but not in a focused, coherent way. He mumbled incoherently.

She hadn't his full attention; she could see that. While she hated to inflict additional pain, it would be for his benefit. She mumbled a quick prayer for forgiveness, squeezed her lips tight, then pulled her hand back and slapped him.

SOFT LYRICAL PHRASING in sweet feminine tones drifted about his head like a distant lullaby. He was content to listen to the melody until a light tap on his cheek interrupted the dream. Forcing his unwilling eyes open, he discovered the blurred, unfocused image of an angel with troubled green eyes, fringed by thick lashes and pale creamy skin. Exuberance filled his heart. Could it be? Her name slipped past his lips like a prayer. "Carolyn?"

The angel slapped him, jarring him fully awake.

"Monsieur, rèspondez-moi! Où est la reine? Qu'est-ce que s'est passé à la fonderie? Où sommes-nous?"

Every nerve ending immediately exploded in protest. This was more than a slap. Pain racked his body as if minute shards of glass had been driven into every inch of his skin. His eyes squeezed shut. "What the devil?" He arched against the wall to push back the sensation. "What just happened?"

"Il faut que je retourne à la Reine…"

"In English, dammit!" The flash of light, the searing pain…had he been struck by lightning? He'd been touching metal.

The angel reared back with an audible strange swish. Her expression shifted from shock to indignation, although it could be his vision was shifting as well. The worst of the sizzling burn passed, allowing his chest to relax with a fading tingle. The angel wasn't Carolyn. That disappointment hurt more than the residual throbbing in his head. He took a deep breath then glanced at the woman.

Shoot! He hadn't meant to scare her. She hovered about a foot away, posing in some frilly, tiered period costume straight off the set of *Gone With The Wind*. Some sort of black lace veil framed her face then rose high on her head before falling to the back, almost as if she were a medieval princess. She brandished some fancy do-da umbrella like a sword, twirling the pointed end in tiny threatening circles. Definitely not Carolyn.

"You some kind of tour guide?" He asked, rubbing the tender spot where his head had met brick. A wet viscous substance coated his fingertips.

The sky rumbled softly with retreating thunder. Rain continued to fall beneath the swinging door, but without the earlier intensity. The storm was passing.

"I won't hurt you." He held up his hand like a policeman directing traffic to ward off the threatening umbrella. "I haven't the strength to battle a fly at the moment. You needn't be afraid." Using the brick wall for support, he pulled himself slowly to his feet. "Was it lightning? I saw a flash right before I hit the wall."

Her lips parted as if to reply, but then she hesitated. She frowned, then tried again as if her lips wouldn't mold the word. Her umbrella pointed from the floor to his chest. "Who?"

"Who am I?" He tapped his shirt. The woman's face eased in relief. *You'd think a tour guide would be a bit more communicative.*

"I was about to ask you the same question." He rubbed the back of his neck. "I'm Grant Stewart."

He extended his hand in greeting, but as she didn't advance he used it to brush the dust off his pants. "Who?" He said gruffly, pointing toward her in a similar fashion.

She straightened, lowered her weapon to her side, then curtsied in a simple yet elegant bend.

"Je m'appelle Mamoiselle Madeline Rosette Allegra Charlebois. Je suis une demoiselle de la cour d'Isabella." She hesitated, cocked her head then continued, as if testing the sound, "Queen of Spain."

"Queen of Spain, huh?" *Yeah, right.* He glanced to the floor for his fallen cell phone. "Sounds like someone else took a blow to the head."

Her face brightened, her smile adding kilowatts to the dingy hallway. The phone lay at the base of the iron gate, its digital display shattered. He reluctantly retrieved the useless device and crammed it in his pocket. "A lot of good this is in emergencies."

"Monsieur. The queen? Nous avons visité…" She stumbled for the word, opting instead to puff out her cheeks and swirl her arms in wide arcs.

Just his luck, he meets an angel and she turns out to be on permanent Mardi Gras.

"We need to get you some help." His head throbbing, Grant moved to the connecting door of the restaurant. He pulled on the handle. Locked. Why had they locked the door? He knocked on the glass and tried to peer through the lace curtains. "Can anyone hear me?"

Her fingertip, clad in a leather glove, tapped on his shoulder with a soft chiming such as that from a child's charm bracelet. He turned, expecting to see the crazy woman's admittedly attractive face, but she stared not at him, but at the Charm Gates. Her eyes wide, her lower lip quivering, she pointed toward the wooden sign.

"Yes, those are the Charm Gates." He said, noting that her skin seemed more pale than it had just a moment before. He certainly didn't need a fainting woman on his hands, especially one wearing twenty pounds of clothing. That concrete floor would be hard on her head should she fall. He gently pushed on her shoulders, backing her up till the brick wall offered support.

"Perhaps you should just sit down here till help arrives." He returned to the connecting door, pummeled the wood with his fist, rattling the windows. "Hello? Is anyone inside? We need an ambulance here."

"Where is Isabella?" the woman asked slowly, every word spoken with careful enunciation. Concern darkened her eyes. "She is injured?"

"If she's injured, she'd be at a hospital...just where you should be," he said.

Something moved behind the lace curtain covering the glass. With renewed urgency, he pounded until a waiter responded. Finally! As soon as he could turn the distressed damsel over to the waiter, he could return to Tulane with just a throbbing headache as a souvenir. The connecting door opened, sending a refreshing current of air-conditioning into the humid corridor.

"There's been some sort of accident," Grant said. "Could you call an ambulance? I think the lady has a head injury."

The waiter looked past him into the hallway. "What lady?"

Grant turned. The swinging door at the far end of the hallway slowly closed.

"Damn."

Chapter Two

MADELINE LIFTED THE front of her skirts and dashed through dirty water rivulets streaming over the broken pavement. She hadn't understood all that the handsome stranger had said, her English coming back to her slowly, yet one word had struck instant terror. *Hospital.* One went to a hospital to die. No one, especially not some peasant in ill-fitting trousers, would force her to go there.

She dashed past storefronts and some odd hulking carriages that lined the street. They didn't look familiar, but she had no time to consider that now. After crossing the street, she rushed around a corner to escape notice of that threatening man from the hallway. Sheltered by an overhead balcony, she leaned heavily against a stucco wall to catch her breath.

She had no protection against the rain. Her parasol was designed to shield the harsh Spanish sun, not a downpour. Fortunately, the rain soon diminished to a sprinkle. Madeline shook out her sodden skirt and petticoats under the protection of the balcony. Her maid would be devastated to see the results of the queen's latest jest. Why Isabella harbored so much malice toward her defied reason. Attempts to appease her highness only increased her anger. One would think she'd value an instructor with her knowledge of diplomatic etiquette, yet the very sight of Madeline enraged the queen. Of course, those that referred to her as a charm teacher in the queen's presence did not help Madeline's cause as it suggested the queen was lacking in charm. She was, but she resented being reminded of that fact.

However, the queen's trickery was old news. Best to dwell upon this latest torment from the safety of her apartment on Calle Mayor. She just needed to collect her bearings.

Think girl! She could hear her father's tirade in her head. Don't be stupid. Use the intelligence God gave you.

She peeked around the corner from whence she came and ventured a breath of relief. No one had followed her. So she looked at leisure. The wrought iron balconies and storefront facades resembled those of

Madrid, but none of the buildings were familiar. Surely, she'd remember that impressive red building with the ornate railing, yet she didn't. And where in Madrid were the roads so well packed as to not produce sucking mud in the rain? This was a mystery.

A grinding noise, surging in power unlike anything she had ever heard roared from her left. She turned just in time to see a metal monster with two unblinking eyes approach her with the speed of four invisible stallions.

"Mon Dieu!" Was it possible for such monsters to exist on earth? Without a thought beyond survival, she ran in the opposite direction. Risking a glance over her shoulder, she collided chest-first into something that knocked her off-balance and flat on her back.

"Oh dear, are you all right?" A woman's voice spoke in the same language of that crazy Englishman. "We didn't realize you didn't see us."

Too frightened by imminent death to be embarrassed at her scandalous sprawl on the pavement, Madeline struggled to rise to her feet. Her corset and wet petticoats, however, made the necessary bending difficult and painful. Even as she struggled she could feel vibrations of the beast's advance through the pavement. This was it. Isabella had finally succeeded in ridding herself of her etiquette instructor. Madeline winced at the impending bloodshed.

"Help her, Harry," the woman said, obviously unaware of the advancing doom. "Can't you see that costume is weighing her down? The poor dear must be soaked."

The monster arrived in an ear-shattering screech and a foul putrid stench. Thick black wheels pulled even with her splayed form. Garish red skin of hammered steel covered its body, thin as a sword blade and probably twice as deadly. The monster paused then continued its noisy rumble down the street. As it passed, she noted a man casually seated in its innards, showing none of the panic she'd expect from one about to be consumed. What in God's creation?

"Those garbage trucks are a smelly lot." A man's bare arm appeared above her billowing skirt. She accepted his hand and was physically jerked to her feet with neither form nor grace.

"Merci," she gasped, grateful to be upright, even though she had difficulty maintaining her balance. She braced an arm against a wall for support.

Lifting her gaze beyond her filthy hemline, she gasped. Large hairy feet encased in peasants' sandals shifted in front of her. Bare skin led to naked ankles, which reached higher to hairy naked knees. She covered her eyes, afraid to follow the path farther. Had these strangers no respect for decent women?

"What's the matter, dear? Eyelash in your contacts? You didn't lose one, did you?"

Peeking through two fingers, Madeline saw a woman dressed in a colorful camisole and harsh heavy drawers, while her companion stood without shame in his smalls.

"Look at her, Harry." The woman nudged her companion. "She looks like she's seen a ghost."

"Maybe she did." He chuckled. "This *is* New Orleans."

Orleans? Did he mean the city in France? How could that be? She was in Madrid…touring the foundries…touring at the queen's invitation…

More scantily clad people appeared on the rapidly drying pavement. Some stopped and pointed as if she was the one inappropriately attired. This was not the France she remembered from her youth.

A musician played a horn in the distance, a sweet, slow melody. Another low rumble beneath her feet warned of a second encroaching monster. Above it all, a church bell tolled in familiar brilliant clarity, a beacon of normalcy. Hope sparked within. Even in the worst of times, the church had always provided answers, had always promised peace. Without hesitation, she lifted her skirts and hurried toward the sound.

"Wait! You forgot your umbrella!" The woman shouted.

Madeline gave no heed. She was headed for sanctuary.

The peal of the bells lured her to a grand white cathedral. She climbed the few steps in haste, yet paused in the church vestibule to smooth wrinkles from her damp bodice and skirts. Unfortunately, she could do nothing about the torn fabric at her elbows and waist, or her torn mantilla. The Lord would have to forgive her those indiscretions.

She stepped into the nave, averting her gaze from the scantily clad denizens standing in the rear. She had passed so many on her way to the cathedral that their lack of clothing no longer shocked with its novelty. Given the state of her own attire, she was certainly in no position to judge. Instead, she focused on the familiar scents of amber and beeswax, and listened to the melodic chanting of unseen monks. If appearances were an indication, she had certainly stumbled into a well-appointed cathedral.

She chose a pew midway down the aisle, before sinking to her knees on the padded kneeler. Her eyes closed, she bowed her head to steepled fingers.

Reverend Mother, help me in this hour of need. Give me the guidance needed to find my way safely home. Give me the strength to withstand the queen's cruel tests of my loyalty. I would do nothing to harm Queen Isabella or the Spanish government. Give me peace to perform my duties in a worthy fashion. Show me the way.

She shifted her position, earning a jab on the inside of her arm. Glancing down, she spotted the culprit, the corner of a hard covered book in a bookrack on the back of the pew before her. A Bible? Perhaps the Reverend Mother had chosen a psalm to communicate her guidance.

As a consequence of accompanying her father on his diplomatic travels, Madeline could read and write in several languages. It was this aspect of her upbringing that allowed her to be of service to Queen Isabella. The same skills allowed her to decipher the language on the missalette. But if this was Orleans, why weren't the words written in French? Why English?

Her eyes skimmed to a date beneath the words, a date one hundred and sixty-odd years in the future. She gasped. How was this possible?

She bolted upright, gained her feet and made the sign of the cross. The missalette fell to the hard floor, echoing through the nearly deserted nave. Gooseflesh lifted on her arms. She re-examined her surroundings.

The two lamps in the overhead chandelier did not flicker, nor were there any telltale wisps of smoke. No choir of monks stood in the recessed corners of the church, yet their soulful voices surrounded her as if she were gifted with a private audience.

She was dreaming. Yes, that was the only explanation. She closed her eyes, pinched her arm and willed herself to wake, but when she opened her eyes, nothing had changed and her arm hurt. So many questions demanded an answer, but who to ask? She searched for the familiar black cassock of a priest, but none could be found. A church without priests? A chill danced down her spine.

"Excuse me," a stranger said. "Can I take a picture of you standing with my little girl?" A barely attired woman with exposed limbs, chopped hair, and her similarly garbed daughter stood in the aisle by her side. "I just love your gown," the woman said. "It's so authentic. What a pity you got caught in the rain. This'll only take a minute." She pushed her little girl against Madeline's wide skirts. "Say cheese."

Lightning flashed from a tiny silver box, blinding her. Madeline stepped back, caught her heel on the torn hem of a petticoat, and lost her balance. Her arms flailed in the cool, incense-laden air. Her cry for help echoed as the monks continued their hymn. The back of her head struck the curved edge of the wooden pew and her chaotic existence turned to a comforting black.

"MR. STEWART, YOU don't have any typical symptoms of someone struck by lightning." The doctor referred to his clipboard. "I'm sorry, I guess I should call you, *Professor* Stewart." His quick smile disappeared into professional concern. "No burns at the point of contact, no internal injury or hemorrhaging that we can find, nothing stitches won't fix. It looks as if you just fell and struck your head." He glanced up, his lips quirking to one side. "Are you sure that isn't what happened?"

"There was a woman," Grant said tightly, recognizing how foolish it all must sound. A quantum physics professor unable to explain the catalyst and impact for that strange burst of energy. "She must have seen it. The force threw me across the hall."

"The paramedics said you were alone." The doctor twisted a chemical ice pack and applied it to the lump on his head. "Hold this. It will help with the swelling."

"She left before they came." Grant tried to remember her name while he took hold of the ice pack. The chill negated some of the throbbing. All he could remember was Mamoiselle something, something, something and her beautiful face, green eyes and elaborate costume. "She was a tour guide … and French. She was definitely French, but she kept talking about Spain and some queen."

"A French tour guide speaking Spanish." The doctor cocked a brow. "That's a new one."

"No. She wasn't speaking Spanish." Grant hesitated, concentrating on memories. "Well, I suppose she did at first, but mostly she spoke about Queen Isabella." He thought he was making sense, although with the percussion section pounding in his head, he wasn't sure.

"It really doesn't matter, Professor Stewart. You've suffered a minor concussion. I don't think it's any more serious than … a bump on the head." The doctor laughed at his joke. Grant winced.

The hospital privacy drapes that defined the emergency unit suddenly parted admitting Grant's sister-in-law. After an anxious glance at the doctor, she hurried toward Grant. "I came as soon as I could. Are you all right?"

"And you are?" The doctor asked with a slow smile and a discernible interest.

"Related." She extended a slim hand. "Beth Kincaid."

"Doctor Richmond." He took her hand. "Professor Stewart should be just fine."

"He says it's just a bump," Grant said. "You needn't have come." He glanced around the room. "Where's Kimmy?" He frowned. "I thought you were going to pick her up?"

"She's in the waiting room." Beth turned her attention back to the doctor. "Will he be able to—"

"You left her alone?" Grant slid off the examination table. An infinite number of things could befall a helpless child left alone in a hospital.

"She'll be fine." Beth rolled her eyes at the doctor. "That poor girl spends most of her life alone."

"I was just explaining to the professor," the doctor addressed Beth as if Grant no longer occupied the room. "He'll probably have a nasty headache, but I don't want him taking any medication for a while. I can release him from the hospital, but only if a responsible person monitors his condition. Would that be you?"

Grant thought to intercede, then reconsidered. He hadn't been the most responsible parent of late, as Beth had noted earlier. That will change, he resolved. As soon as he left this place, that will change.

"I'll send one of the nurses to go over the release instructions," the doctor continued. "Wait here for just a few more minutes." He pulled the drapes open to the busy antiseptic atmosphere of the emergency room, then offered his hand to Beth. "It was a pleasure to meet you, Mrs. Kincaid."

"Oh, that's Miss." Beth blushed, a sight Grant hadn't seen in a long time. Of course, barricading himself away in his study hadn't allowed for frequent interactions with either his sister-in-law or his daughter. "I'm not married," she added.

"Miss Kincaid," the doctor corrected with a hungry smile. "We'll have you on your way in just a—"

"Doctor Richmond," a young woman with the rich musical cadence that only existed in New Orleans, interrupted. "Begging your pardon, doctor, but do you, by any chance, speak French?"

"Not since high school," he said, still looking at Beth. "What seems to be the problem?"

"The police brought in some crazy woman in a southern belle outfit

19

who doesn't speak English. I think she's speaking French, but—"

"That's her!" Grant shouted. "That's the tour guide at The Court of Two Sisters. She saw what happened."

"What tour guide?" Beth asked. "I didn't see a tour guide at lunch."

"Calm down, professor." The doctor put a restraining hand on Grant's arm. "No need for another accident." He turned to the hospital assistant, his eyebrows lifted. "You say the police brought her in?"

She nodded. "She fell at the Basilica on Jackson Square and struck her head. The Monsignor sent her here. We can't find identification and she's not exactly helping."

"Must be my day for head injuries." He smiled. "Is she bleeding?"

The nurse shook her head.

"Mad... Maddie..." Grant stirred the air with his hand as if the action would clarify his memory of the frightened angel. "Madeline. That's it. She said her name was Madeline something – something." He glanced at the doctor. "Try calling her Madeline and see if she responds."

"Grant. What's going on?" Beth asked, her gaze narrowing. "Is this that accountant you mentioned?"

"Thank you, professor," the doctor said. "I'll give that a try. The nurse will be here in a moment to release you. Watch out for those lightning bolts." He nodded to Beth. "Miss Kincaid."

"She's not crazy, just afraid," Grant called after the departing physician who didn't acknowledge his comment. Damn. Why did he feel responsible for the woman? It's not like he forced her to run out into the street. *Just like you didn't force Carolyn to stray into the path of a drunk driver.*

"Grant?" Beth repeated.

"It's nothing," Grant said, ignoring the familiar guilt that absorbed all his emotions, all his responsibilities. *Think of Kimmy,* he reminded himself. *Stay whole for your daughter.*

He retrieved his fallen ice pack then pressed it to his head. "I think God thumped me on the head to make me take our luncheon discussion more seriously." He offered Beth a weak smile. "Let's go find that nurse and get the hell out of here. Kimmy needs to get home to bed and I need to write some more before I can do the same."

They started to leave the curtained enclosure when a wheeled cot burst through the emergency room doors demanding attention. A knife handle protruded from a vast pool of blood on the man's chest. Another cot with a second body followed with equal bloodstains. The room exploded with the chaos of doctors all shouting orders while nurses wheeled clattering machines.

Beth's smile faded. "Looks like we're going to be here a while longer."

Chapter Three

FINALLY ALONE, MADELINE slipped off the bed on wheels in the tiny room created by ugly cloth draperies. Suffering lingered thick in the air with an occasional moan or shouted protest. Unease settled deep in her bones while gooseflesh lifted on her arms. Death was common here.

If this was the world of the future, she wanted no part of it. She preferred to be in a world she understood, back with her family, trying to gain her father's respect through her service to Queen Isabella. Here, bodiless voices dropped from the ceiling, bright unnatural light flooded everything, and odd mechanical noises tolled like tiny death knells. They probably were.

Even the church, the one institution upon which she could always rely, the one institution that had always offered her solace, had sent her to this... this... *hospital*. She shivered. She could trust no one.

Her extensive experience in languages proved to be of little assistance. A dark-skinned woman in a shapeless jacket babbled some singsong gibberish while playing with a strange listening device about her neck. Perhaps a small element of English existed in the woman's lyrical phrasings, but it was unlike any English she could recall from her early years in London. The woman wrapped a device about her arm that squeezed like a snake strangling its prey.

Well, Madeline wasn't about to quietly submit to being anyone's prey, future or not. There comes a time when proper manners must be ignored, survival being one such occasion. Madeline let loose with a string of loud admonishments more suited to the gutter than any palace. The woman's eyes widened. Madeline wasn't certain the woman understood all she'd said, but she'd recognized the tone. The attendant hurried out of the room, but Madeline feared it would not be for long.

If she were to make an escape, now was the time. She crept to a break in the curtain wall and peeked at the commotion beyond. A parade of agonized souls upon teacarts burst into the common area of the room demanding attention. Recognizing that the dire events occurring before her provided a suitable diversion for her escape, Madeline quietly slipped from the cloth enclosure, into the common area then the wide hallway beyond.

To her credit, she no longer shrieked and ran at the unnatural noises and voices from the ceiling. She didn't stare at the indecent men and women roaming the hallway. She simply nodded, smiled, and continued to put distance between herself and the room of curtained bedrooms. If only she could find the way out of this house of death, however no windows existed to help with direction.

Someone tugged at her skirt. Madeline glanced down into the wide-eyed innocence of a little girl.

"You look like my dolly." She held up a bedraggled fashion doll dressed in what once must have been a fine walking dress, but both the doll and the pretty dress had been loved to the point of deterioration.

Madeline glanced at her own dress, soiled and ripped beyond reproach, yet similar to that of the doll. At least, her attire was more similar than the minimal coverings of the strangers roaming the hall. She smiled and nodded. "Oui."

The little girl screwed up her face. "You talk funny."

"Oui." Madeline sighed. "I do."

The little girl slipped her hand into Madeline's. "Will you read me a story?"

Tenderness pulled at Madeline's heart. Since her arrival in this strange world, no one had touched her with such simple kindness and benevolence. She nodded, then tenderly squeezed the child's tiny hand. The little one led her to an empty windowless room lined with chairs. With all the bustling activities beyond the doorway, perhaps no one would bother to look for a lost soul from the past in this small quiet place.

"I'm Kimberly," the little girl said thumping her chest. "What's your name?"

"Madeline." She opted for the short version. Everything appeared to be short now: short hair, short clothes, short words, and short names.

"Madin?" the young child struggled.

"Maddie," Madeline offered, believing the name her family called her would be easier for the child. She was rewarded with a shy smile.

"My daddy's hurt," Kimberly said. "I'm waiting till he can come home." She wriggled her tiny bottom onto a chair beside a table piled with periodicals of shiny paper and bold colors, so unlike the periodicals from Madeline's era. Kimberly pulled a skinny book decorated in bright paint from the middle of the pile. A smile spread across her young face. "Green Eggs and Ham. Let's read this one."

Green Eggs? Madeline's stomach roiled in protest. Just as she pondered what kind of animal would lay green eggs, she found her answer on the cover: a vile cat-like creature with human hands and a tall hat. Although tempted to make the sign of the cross, Madeline had only to glance at Kimberly's face to see that the animal posed no threat. Indeed the child appeared delighted.

Kimberly opened the book across their shared lap. Her stubby finger traced across each line of print, while she carefully enunciated each word. Madeline followed her progress, recognizing some words in English while learning new ones. Soon she was repeating the singsong rhythm along with Kimberly and expressed equal delight at their success. When they finished one book, Madeline glanced to the pile. "More?"

While Kimberly searched for another book, Madeline scanned the room for more practice material. A newspaper lay folded on the adjacent chair. She opened it, noticing a nonsensical name across the top: The Tulane Hullabaloo. Glancing at the columns, the handsome face of that peasant from the corridor smiled back at her. *Sacred Bleu!* Her breath caught. The very same man but without blood trailing down his cheekbones. The back of her neck tingled.

"That's my daddy." Kimberly pointed to the picture with pride. "Aunt Beth said he hurt his head."

"Your daddy?" Madeline stared at the child in amazement, suddenly noticing the resemblance. She tapped the paper. "He's here?"

The girl nodded.

Outside the room, a woman's voice called for Kimberly.

"That's my Aunt Beth. I have to go," she said. "I wish you could come with me." She looked as sad as Madeline felt. In those wide, sad eyes she saw the connection to the man in the corridor. How could one so small, so new to the world, have experienced the kind of pain that took residence in one's soul?

"I, aussi," Madeline replied. She pulled the little girl to her chest in a quick hug, then loosened her when the women's voice called again.

"Bye-bye Maddie." Kimberly waved, then grabbed her doll's arm from a nearby chair as she ran into the hall. "Coming!"

Madeline waited a few moments, absorbing the loss of the child's company.

How extraordinary that the first person she'd met in this strange world would be the father of the child, Kimberly. Madeline examined the paper for a name and found one: Grant Stewart, Professor of Physics at Tulane University. Which would mean that man, the one she'd threatened with her parasol, was a science scholar, a *professeur*. Could this be the work of providence? Her entreaty to the reverend Mother had asked for guidance. Could the child be the answer to her prayer?

She ripped the professor's image from the paper and slipped it into her corset before leaving the windowless room of chairs and books of cats in hats, to search for Kimberly, her father and the way back home.

But they were gone.

Ignoring the stares and pointed fingers of the people meandering the corridor, she hurried down the hallway searching for a clue. A child's voice led her around the corner where she spotted Kimberly in her father's arms. They entered a giant glass turnstile. She paused, hesitant to stride into what could be a trap. Her association with Queen Isabella had ingrained caution exceedingly well.

The panels made a hurried *fa-lump*, then the professor and his daughter appeared uninjured on the other side. A woman, his wife she supposed, or perhaps Aunt Beth followed behind. Madeline waited a moment, then dashed across the busy room, into the clutch of the glass, then was gently pushed into humid air outside.

Sound exploded all around her, clanging bells, blaring horns, hammering, engine noises, rhythmic musical patterns, they assaulted her from every direction. She stopped, stunned. Even the clear sky overhead growled as a monstrous stiff black bird glided over buildings that reached up to the clouds.

Heat rose from the pavement. Vile smells filled her lungs. Baby metal monsters raced past like thoroughbreds on a track seemingly dedicated for their use. Her quarry walked on the far side of the racetrack, but how to reach them without dire injury? People waited near a pole. At some mysterious signal, the monsters slowed to a stop, allowing the group to cross. She walked swiftly to the pole, but the monsters wouldn't wait. They sped forward at breakneck speeds.

Now that she was close, she could see people seated placidly within. *Carriages*. The word formed in her mind. These were horseless carriages that traveled in a blur of motion, sound, and smell. The book Kimberly had read to her showed the cat traveling in something similar. She had called it a car. Pleased that these were not the malevolent beasts she'd imagined, she relaxed while more individuals joined her at the pole. At some unspoken command, the cars stopped and the throng swept her along to the opposite side of the track. People pressed on either side while she anxiously searched for a glimpse of the professor and his daughter. They had disappeared, and with them, her best chance of returning home.

PANIC FORMED A lump in her throat. She felt as a lost soul wandering the rings of Dante's Inferno without even the assistance of a guide. What to do now?

The parade of pedestrians increased once the street opened to a wide boulevard identified as Canal Street. She glanced in both directions but saw no evidence of a canal, or boats. Instead, a green mechanical omnibus glided along rails down the center of the boulevard. The sheer volume of people on the streets astounded her.

She continued to be swept along, listening and deciphering little bits of conversation. Cooking smells wafted from opened doorways. Her stomach grumbled reminding her she hadn't eaten in an age. A century, she corrected with an inward grimace. Even those green eggs from the children's story would be appreciated, but she had no means to obtain them. Eventually the crowd thinned and she was again alone, abandoned, hungry and weary of walking.

The steady plod of a mule and the jingling of a harness sent her spirits soaring. She turned in anticipation to the familiar sound. Clearly, not everything from her time had been abandoned. She waved her hand at the driver and his steed. To her surprise, he pulled back on the reins slowing the open-air carriage to a halt.

"You look like you'se gonna melt right there on the pavement. You headin' for the Quarter?"

Madeline nodded, though she wasn't certain what he asked, not that it mattered. While she had no idea where this Quarter might be, she would have agreed to just about anything if it meant she could get off her feet. At least the carriage driver, an older dark-skinned man with silver hair, had a broad and sincere smile.

"Climb on up, then." He waved her forward. Madeline complied, hefting her heavy skirts to reach the high seat.

"I haven't seen you around the circuit," he said. "Who you working for?"

Grateful for the opportunity to sit, Madeline smiled her most complacent smile and shook her head.

"You don't know who you work for?" The driver asked incredulously. "Those are mighty fine duds to be handing out to a stranger."

He spoke nonsense. What were duds? Why would she work? She counseled royalty.

"I'm Louis, by the way." He extended his hand. "That there's Tootsie." His chin pointed to his mule.

"Louis," Madeline repeated. She tentatively slipped her gloved hand in his as two men might. He grasped it firmly and shook hers once.

"What do I call you?" he asked.

Madeline just smiled.

"Do you have a name?" Louis asked, a bit of the friendliness slipping from his voice.

Name! That word she recognized.

"Je m'appelle Mamoiselle Madeline Rosette Allegra Charlebois."

He laughed. "You're a frenchie. No wonder you didn't understand." He looked her up and down. "But if you don't talk the language, how're you gonna answer questions? Do you only do French tourists?" He shook his head, an incredulous grin on his face. "Man-oh-man, the things those groups do to compete."

They rode in silence, though Madeline noticed Louis stealing glances her way. Her stomach rumbled again, even more audibly this time.

"You hungry?" Louis asked. He made a motion of putting something in his mouth and chewing, then patting his belly.

She nodded and laughed a little. She understood hungry.

"Yeah. You look like you haven't eaten in a while." He kicked a brown paper sack on the floor with his foot. "Go on," he said. "Nothing fancy, just a sandwich. I can get me another."

Manna from heaven! She eagerly consumed the concoction of creamy white sauce with crunchy seafood – oysters?

Louis pulled a container of clear liquid from a box and handed it to her. "To wash it down."

She turned the cool translucent cylinder over and over in her hand. It wasn't glass, of that she was certain. How could the liquid stay in such a flimsy container?

Louis made a disgruntled sound, then removed the odd object from her hand. He twisted the top to remove a white stopper then handed it back to her.

She sniffed cautiously at the opening.

"You drink it," he said exasperated. "You know..." He held his fist and thumb to his lips.

She copied his motions and water moistened her lips. Louis shook his head, smiled, and clicked the reins. "Doc's gonna love you."

She rode with Louis in the carriage for the remainder of the day. They traveled the same path so many times, Madeline could soon name a building on command. The repetition assisted her learning other bits and pieces of the language and culture as well. To her dismay, she noticed the carriage passengers would give Louis what she suspected was currency when they left. What was she to do? She had nothing to compensate him for his kindness.

The temperatures cooled as the daylight faded. Lampposts placed along their route brightened as if lit by an invisible hand. Glancing at the padded seats in the back of the carriage with longing, Madeline hoped Louis might let her spend the night there. After a night's sleep, she would ask Louis to take her to this Tulane University so she could search for the professor. However, after the last tour of the day, Louis directed Tootsie to the line at Jackson Square. He coaxed her off the seat then led her to another dark-skinned man draped in colorful cloths and shiny beads.

"Louis. What's you got there?" The stranger had the same lyrical voice as the woman in the hospital. He sat by a small table on the pavement not far from the long line of carriages.

"This here is Madeline, and she's a frenchie." Louis smiled wide. "She's been great for business in that getup and all, but it's getting late and I think she's got no place to go. I got this feeling she just don't belong here."

"Is that so, Sugah?" The man studied her face, even though the flame from his candle couldn't have provided sufficient light. "Let's see what the bones say."

He handed her a bowl of stones, shells, and broken animal bones, cleaned of all flesh and bleached near white. He gestured that she should shake the bowl then toss the contents on a cloth with a large leering pagan skull painted on the center.

She recoiled, grasping the delicate gold cross about her neck.

"It's okay Madeline. This here is Doc," Louis said. "He ain't goin' hurt you. Those bones tell your fortune."

"Doctor Antoine," the man said, extending his hand. "My friends call me Doc."

He offered the bowl again. "The skull is for tourists. They expect a certain homage to the dark arts." He leaned in. "But we know it's all for show." This time she hesitantly took the bowl and hastily tossed the contents on the devil cloth.

He studied the pattern then looked at her with widened eyes.

"Let me see your hands."

Though she was embarrassed to comply given the state of her gloves, she held out her hands for his inspection.

He chuckled softly, which heightened his soft brown eyes. "May I?" He pulled on the tips of her gloves before holding her palms beneath the light of the candle. "You said she's French?" he asked Louis, his voice barely above a whisper.

"She don't talk much but what she says sounds French," Louis said.

Then the doctor did the most miraculous thing. He looked her in the eye then asked, in French, where she lived.

Tears welled in her eyes. Finally! Someone with whom she could freely communicate. Someone who could tell her what had happened to her. She clasped his hands and poured out her story about the queen and the foundry, and awakening in the hallway.

The strange doctor glanced at Louis. "She's a lost soul, all right. I didn't understand it all but I think she lives in Madrid."

Louis scratched his head. "Madrid? Isn't that up Shreveport-way?"

The doctor-man squinted, studying Madeline's face. He waved his hand impatiently at Louis, then continued in French very slowly. "You've been gone a long, long time?" He pointed to her clothes.

Madeline nodded enthusiastically. "Oui."

"What happened while you were gone?"

She shrugged. How could she answer such a question?

"So what's you want to do?" Louis interrupted. "You goin' ta keep her? I gotta take Tootsie back. I can drop her at the shelter, but if she can't say nothing but gibberish, then – "

She was tempted to interrupt to explain that she understood some English from the brief time she lived in London. She just didn't recognize certain words...and accents.

The doctor turned to Louis. "You go on now. I'll see that she's taken care of. I can't understand nothing anyway with you jabbering in my ear."

Louis smiled and winked at Madeline. Their discussion had apparently been settled in her favor. He lifted Madeline's hand as before and shook it. "It's been a pleasure meeting you, Miss Maddie. You can ride with Tootsie and me anytime."

A smile crept to her face. Her father used to call her Maddie when she was a little girl. Once Louis had left, the doctor sat across from her and studied her eyes.

"Madeline," he repeated. His bright white teeth gleamed in the dark. "You look tired. I have a place you can stay if you like."

Her drowsy eyes widened. "I'm not a harlot, monsieur!"

"No, I don't think you are," he said, apparently surprised by her reaction, or perhaps it was her English. "My sister lives with me. She has an extra bed in her room. We like to help out people when we can. It adds to the common good. Karma, you know."

No, she had no idea what karma was, but she hadn't another alternative for shelter. And she was so very, very tired. While he dismantled and folded his table and chairs, she found a rock to conceal in her hand. If anyone thought to violate her, she'd be prepared.

Doc glanced at her fist. "Does that mean you've agreed to stay with my sister?"

She nodded, too tired to even say yes.

"Good, because everyone contributes. You're French so you're probably a good cook, so that's what you'll do." Doc led the way and Madeline followed.

Silly man, she thought, she'd never cooked for herself. That was the purpose of servants. But she supposed she could learn. It couldn't be difficult, could it?

"One thing you should know before we get home." The doctor looked right and left then lowered his voice. "What do you know about voodoo?"

Chapter Four

"KIM, SWEETIE, YOU can't color on daddy's papers."

"But you colored on them." Kimberly said, her big eyes pleading innocence.

Remembering his promise to spend more time with Kimberly, Grant fought the urge to yell and instead took a deep breath. "No, honey. The red pen marks changes for my speech. I'd planned to input them into my computer."

Of course that was impossible now.

Kimmy left the room. For one so small, her footfalls pounded through the house. Grant glanced briefly at the red and orange cat scrawled in permanent marker across his notes, before he wadded the paper in his hand and tossed it in the trash. That speech was just two days away, yet he was taking five steps back for every one forward in preparation.

He checked his watch. "Where the devil is she?"

The babysitter he'd contracted through an agency was over an hour late. While he wasn't pleased with her punctuality, he'd be grateful for her arrival. His lunch with Beth and the subsequent trip to the hospital yesterday had robbed him of valuable time. Kim's artistic endeavors had set him back even more. If the sitter would arrive now...

The phone rang.

"Mr. Stewart?" A high-pitched voice sounded in his ear. "This is Melba from Kids Love Us Babysitters. I'm afraid Alice quit this morning."

"Alice," he repeated with a scowl. "Who's Alice?"

"Alice was the woman watching your little girl. She said your daughter was too much for her to handle so she quit."

Something crashed in the front room, shattering to pieces by the sound of it. He squeezed his eyes shut trying to recall what it might have been. "But you'll send somebody over immediately, right?"

The voice hesitated. "Mr. Stewart. Alice was the second sitter to leave after watching your daughter for one day. It appears babysitting

Kimberly will take a very special sort of sitter. We've begun interviewing but I won't have anyone till next week at the earliest."

"Next week?" he said stunned. He raised his hand to his head, but the tenderness of the stitches chased it away. Instead, he hit a bobble head toy of a scientist from a popular TV show. It bounced erratically until coming to a rest, its idiotic grin still in place. Crap!

"What am I supposed to do until next week?" he demanded, turning away from his desk and the toy. "I have work to finish."

"Daddy, I'm hungry." Kimberly had returned and tugged on his shirt.

"Not now, sweetie. Daddy's on the phone." He patted her shoulder before turning his attention to the woman speaking in his ear. "I'm sorry. Could you repeat that?"

"I said… I understand you have the ability to work from your home. Your first sitter, Mrs. Rumpole, mentioned that you stayed in your office the entire time she was there."

"Yes, but she was only here a day. Look, I have classes to teach, a very important speech to write, equations, research … I need somebody before next week to help."

"I'm sorry. We'll try to find a new sitter as soon as possible but there are ads to run and interviews to schedule. All this takes time. Perhaps you know someone that could watch your daughter in the meantime. A relative or a girlfriend?"

His mind slipped briefly to his sister-in-law, but after that lunch meeting he was determined not to ask for her assistance. He supposed he could ask Jennifer.

"Of course, if you wish to use another agency, Professor Stewart, we would certainly understand."

Grant had the impression that using another agency was exactly what they wanted him to do, but having gone through the interviewing process once, he knew finding another agency would require the same lengthy search.

"No," he said. "Go ahead with your interviews. I'll think of something in the meantime. Thank you." He clicked off.

Kimmy had settled in the corner of his office, preparing to beat on a toy drum. That toy would have to find a new home.

"Let's see what we can find for lunch." Grant swooped her up in his arms amid a flurry of giggles and took her to the kitchen. He swung her high onto a chair at the table, then raided the refrigerator for ingredients to make a sandwich. "We've got ham…pickles…cheese…olive relish."

He tossed each item on the table.

"It's too quiet here," Kimmy said. "Can we get a puppy?"

Grant sighed, the last thing he needed right now was another distraction. "How about I put on some music?"

"I don't like your music." Kim grimaced. "Will you read me a story?"

"Daddy's getting something for you to eat right now, sweetheart." He fumbled in a drawer for a knife to spread the condiments on bread. If there's one thing he knew, it was how to build a great sandwich.

"The lady at the hospital read me a story."

"That was nice of her." A little spiced salami, some cheese, a little of that olive relish...

"She saw your picture in the paper."

Grant proudly cut his culinary creation and placed it lovingly before his young daughter. Who said he couldn't care for her on his own? "Here you go, Daddy's world famous salami and cheese sandwich."

Kimmy stared at her plate, then pushed off the top piece of bread, frowning at the green relish.

"Eat up, Kim. It's good," Grant encouraged around a mouthful.

"No. No. No. I don't like that stinky stuff." She crossed her arms and scowled. "I want peanut butter."

Grant reached across the table with the knife to scrape off the olive relish. "You should have said you wanted peanut butter before I started making the sandwich. There. All the olive relish is gone. You like cheese, right?" He looked hopefully at his young daughter. She reluctantly nodded. "Then you can eat the cheese."

She eyed the altered sandwich with distaste. "No. There's stinky juice on it." She scooted her bottom away from the table. "I wish the hospital lady was here."

He hadn't a clue who the hospital lady was, but he'd appreciate her help as well. "I wish she was too."

Kim hopped off her chair and ran circles around the table shouting, "I don't want it. I don't want it."

Grant caught her on her third trip around. "Why don't you and Dolly hop back up on the chair and I'll make you that peanut butter and jelly sandwich you wanted." Once she was settled, he pulled his cell phone from his pocket and quickly accessed Jennifer's number.

"The hospital lady read to me and looked like Dolly." She held up her doll.

Cradling the phone between his shoulder and ear, Grant spread a swath of peanut butter across a new slice of bread.

"No jelly," Kim grumbled.

"Hi Grant. I was just thinking about you." Jennifer sounded fresh and professional. A smile spread across his face from just hearing her voice. "Unfortunately, I'm really swamped here at work so I'll have to call you back."

"But I really need to talk to —"

"Great," the voice said as if he hadn't interjected. "I'll see you Thursday night. Looking forward to your speech."

She clicked off before he had time to spread jelly on the other piece of bread. What was he supposed to do now?

Kimmy pulled the plate with the single slice of bread and peanut butter toward her.

"After lunch we can play dress-up," she said happily munching on her sandwich. "And then read a story and color in the coloring book and…"

At least one of them was happy.

DOC LED HER to the sort of building that, had it been maintained, would be the residence for a minor official. Yet this building wore a century of neglect. Once they'd entered the front door, she was confronted with walls and doors. Many families lived here. Doc led her up a flight of steps to a door. She kept her rock at the ready. Once inside, the tiny front parlor was lit with a steady yellowish light. The doctor called out and one of two closed doors opened.

"This is my sister, Cici. She'll take care of you." A girl younger than herself by a few years wriggled her fingers at her in greeting. Madeline did the same.

"The kitchen is over there." Doc pointed to an open area, though, there was no fireplace that she could discern for cooking, and no servants to perform such chores as food preparation and cleaning. In fact, the only fireplace was in the parlor and it appeared to serve more as a shrine than an edifice for heat. Religious statues of various saints were scattered on the mantle with candles, stones and empty bottles randomly distributed around them. When she turned to ask Doc a question, she noticed a similar display heavy with red and black cloth next to the front door.

"Don't touch!" Doc warned. "The loa don't like their altars disturbed." He placed his folded table and the box of bones in a tiny room.

Unease prickled Madeline's skin. While the Catholic Church often placed candles before statues, she'd never seen them adorned with bowls of candy, corn, stones and what appeared to be a rooster foot. Green paper currencies were stuffed throughout. Was this a common adaptation for Catholicism? It seemed pagan and sacrilegious. Could that cathedral with the unseen monks and flashing lights have been an artifact of old? Perhaps it was a museum of religion the way religion was once practiced? But no, it had a missalette with the current date. She shook her head. It was all so confusing and she was beyond tired in trying to figure it all out.

"Why is she dressed so funny?" Cici asked.

"She's a lost child from the eighteen fifties —"

"Eighteen fifty-three," Madeline corrected.

"--And she needs our help to get back home," he concluded. "Right?"

"Antoine! Eighteen fifty-three?"

The two spoke too rapidly for her to follow. The long day pulled heavy on her eyelids. Sleep. Sommeil. El stueño. It all sounded so lovely. She just needed a lady's maid to help her out of her clothes. She closed her eyes just to rest a minute. Her hand relaxed and the rock fell but the sound seemed far away and unimportant. Someone tugged on her arm. She jolted awake.

"Come," Cici said. "I'll help you undress and lend you pajamas. Antoine says you'll stay here tonight."

"HE'S BESEECHING LEGBA," Cici whispered. "The gatekeeper."

Madeline watched her first voodoo ritual. She was one of six invited for this occasion. Taught to respect another's culture, she kept her awkwardness to herself. She relaxed, however, as the ceremony began with many familiar prayers and hymns from the church. After that, however, the activities took a sharp deviation.

Doc poured rum and set it before the statute of Saint Peter. He swayed and mumbled in a language she didn't recognize.

"Legba guards the path and lets us communicate with the loa." Cici explained. "They're like the Catholic saints, powerful spirits in the afterlife who could intercede on behalf of the Great Creator and give guidance to those on earth".

"Sometimes," Louis, another of the invited attendees, grumbled. "They haven't interceded for me."

Doc removed his shirt. In the flickering light from the candles, his snake tattoos seemed to move and slither. He shook a rattle at Louis. Madeline recognized the scold. "We make these sacrifices to beseech your help," Doc announced.

It was her cue. She placed her lace edged handkerchief amidst the odd doll heads and colorful beads on the mantle. The linen still held bloodstains from dabbing the professor's head. While she certainly was not a believer in voodoo, she hoped the spirit, Ezulie-Freda, appreciated her meager offering.

Louis placed a rose on the mantle, then smiled at her timidly, while another woman placed green paper currency on the altar for Legba. Madeline had overheard her earlier mentioning that she was "between jobs." Cici explained in low tones that this meant she was out of work and looking for employment. People beseeched spiritual help for many causes, just as they did in church.

No longer dressed in her soiled gown, Madeline wore a long skirt that hid her legs but hugged her body without the benefit of layers of petticoats. She continued to wear her corset beneath the flimsy blouse Cici had provided. Her long hair was plaited and coiled. After two nights of a sound sleep and two days of watching the marvelous talking box, a "television" they called it, Madeline thought she looked and sounded like quite the modern woman.

Louis patted a rhythm on a small drum. A smoky haze from many candles filled the small crowded room. Doc danced in the center shaking his rattle stick.

Madeline leaned close to Cici. "How long does this take?"

Cici placed a finger to her lips, gesturing for silence. Madeline settled in for a long evening.

Then Cici's eyes drifted shut. Just as Madeline supposed her friend had fallen asleep, Cici's body began to violently twitch and shake.

"Ezulie-Freda is riding her," Doc shouted.

"There's a man," Cici cried out. "He calls her to this time."

Doc looked at Madeline. They both knew this message was meant for her.

"Who?" Doc demanded. "Tell us Ezulie-Freda."

"Find him. The wheel turns. Time flows." Cici gasped in a whispery voice.

"How?" Madeline asked, knowing instantly that Cici referred to the man in the hallway. The one with the blood stains on her sacrifice. "How do I find him?"

"Paper," Cici recited as if in a trance. She shivered once then collapsed to the floor.

The fine hairs on the back of Madeline's neck lifted. She'd never told Cici about the professor or their meeting.

"We need a paper," Doc said. "Louis, go out and get a Times-Picayune."

"Maybe Ezulie meant paper money?" the "in-between" woman suggested. "She wants a more valuable sacrifice than a handkerchief."

Cici's eyes flickered open and sought Madeline's.

"Not those papers," Madeline said with conviction. "She means this." She turned her back to the others, unbuttoned the top button of her borrowed blouse and retrieved the newsprint from between her breasts. She handed the paper to Doc.

"He was in the hallway when I arrived," she said, tapping the photograph. "I found it at the hospital. I don't know how to contact him."

"Cici. You okay?" Louis blotted Cici's forehead with a masculine handkerchief. "I've never seen Ezulie ride you before."

Doc studied the torn paper. "According to this, he's speaking tomorrow night at Tulane," he said. "The topic is ripped off, but the date and time are clear. Tomorrow night." He handed it back to her. "Did you know that he's a quantum physicist?"

"No," she replied, not exactly certain what a quantum or a physicist were separately, much less together. She glanced at the paper. The speech topic was indeed missing, except for one word: string..

"He studies time, matter and space," Doc explained.

"Perhaps if you explain your situation, he could help," Cici added.

Hope expanded in her chest. Like so many other miraculous discoveries in this age, time-travel must be a common occurrence. Except... "He thought I was addled."

Doc and Cici stared at her, confused.

"Crazy, lunatic." Her face brightened. "Bananas." Two days of watching that marvelous talking box had given her verbal options for insults.

"Nevertheless. He's the key," Doc insisted. "You must see him. I will take you."

"But what will I say?" she asked, embarrassed. She hadn't realized that she'd traversed time when she first met the professor. Would he even talk to her?

"Let Ezulie-Freda guide you," Doc counseled. "She has directed the way."

Chapter Five

"I DON'T MEAN to be critical, Grant, but do you really want your daughter backstage?" The dean of the quantum physics department raised an eyebrow. "I wouldn't think the distraction is wise."

Grant tightened his grip on Kim's hand as she stretched for the just-out-of-reach stage control panel. "My babysitter quit earlier this week and I couldn't find someone to watch Kim on short notice. Jennifer said she's coming tonight. I'm hoping she can keep an eye on her."

Grant peeked out the side curtain hoping to see Jennifer in the front row reserved seat, but it was empty. The rest of the auditorium, however, was filling up quickly. Unusual, he thought, for a lecture on string theory as it relates to time and everyday life.

"Jennifer? Have I met her?" the dean asked.

"No, I don't believe so. She's the woman I've been seeing. Very competent...a CPA, in fact," Grant added with a nervous smile. "I'm certain, once she arrives, she'll keep Kim occupied."

"Very well then," the dean said. "Let's hope she arrives in the next five minutes as that's when I'll give your introduction. We don't want to keep the press waiting."

"No sir," he said. This wasn't just a gathering of students. The University had invited the press and alumni to the speech in the hope of improving fundraising opportunities. Grant's stitches began to throb. Hopefully, his bandage wouldn't look too disreputable.

"How're your publishing credentials coming?" the dean asked. "That tenure meeting will be here before you know it."

Just as he was about to reply, his daughter tugged his hand.

"Maddie!" she cried.

Grant turned to see a black man and a beautiful woman with blonde hair coiled in a bun. She immediately slipped to one knee and held her arms out to Kimberly as if they were old friends. Kimmy pulled free of him to run to her extended arms.

"Kim. Wait!" This was not the time for his daughter to run wild. He went after her and pulled her away from the attractive stranger. "Are you supposed to be back here?"

The moment she glanced up, recognition rocked him. He knew those green eyes and that nose with the jaunty tilt. But she looked different, normal.

Kim smiled up at him. "It's the hospital lady, Daddy. The one that read to me."

"That was you?" he said, stunned. She'd exchanged her voluminous skirts for a dignified pants suit and abandoned the silly lace thing that had covered her hair, but he knew that face, and remembered the sight of her threatening him with an umbrella. "What are you doing here?"

"Antoine Johns, pleased to meet you," the man said, grabbing his hand in a firm handshake. "We wondered if we might have a chance to talk with you after your speech tonight. Given your specialty and the mutual experience shared by you and Miss Madeline, I thought you might--"

"I'm so sorry I'm late." Jennifer swooped through the side entrance to the stage, whispering loudly as she pressed a kiss to his cheek, then rubbed the spot vigorously with her thumb. "Terrible traffic. I just wanted to pop back here to wish you luck."

Behind him, James Chen, dean of the quantum physics department, stepped to the podium to offer a microphone-enhanced welcome to the audience. The amplified sound boomed through the auditorium.

Jennifer frowned at Madeline, but Grant had no time for introductions. "Jenn. Thank God you're here," he said, keeping his voice low. "I hate to impose, but I need you to watch Kimberly while I do this. The sitter didn't show and I can't leave Kimmy alone."

Jennifer hesitated then she smiled extending a hand to the child. "Of course, I'll watch your precious daughter. She and I will become good friends, won't we, Kimberly?"

"No." Kimmy pushed her way out of the restraint of his arms and ran to the more-reasonably-dressed crazy lady. "No. I want Maddie!" Her young voice rang clear and loud.

The amplified introduction paused. "It seems even Professor Stewart has women difficulties just like normal people," Dean Chen said. The audience laughed before he continued citing Grant's academic achievements.

"Kimberly," Grant warned.

"Please Monsieur. I would be happy to mind Kimberly while you conduct your talk," Madeline whispered in a delightful French accent.

She smiled down at Kimberly. "We have much to discuss."

"You speak English," Grant said surprised.

"Oui. And French and Spanish. But Mr. Johns and his sister have reminded me of my English."

It was a shame she hadn't been "reminded" of her English when she was babbling like she was bona fide bonkers.

"Grant, who is this?" Jennifer hissed. "She's not that lunatic you told me about? Do you really want *her* to watch your daughter?"

The microphone boomed. "Join me in welcoming, Professor Grant Stewart…"

Applause signaled the time for his entrance.

"She's not crazy." Antoine frowned at Jennifer "She's just misplaced." He nodded at Grant. "If it'll make you feel better, I'll stay with them."

"I don't know you either," Grant said, exasperated.

"I know Maddie," Kimberly said establishing her preference.

"Professor Grant Stewart…" the dean announced again from the podium.

Damn! He didn't want to send his daughter off with strangers, but Kimmy had a fierce grip on Madeline's hand.

"Jennifer, stay with them, okay?" he said. "I need to know at least one of the people watching my daughter." He turned and walked to the podium. When he glanced back, the two women, a strange man, and his daughter had left, along with his confidence that he was doing the right thing.

"SCIENCE HAS PROVEN that the very principles that govern the smallest particles of matter also control the movement of the stars and planets in the heavens. If there is an absolute, it is that students of quantum physics, who chart the movement of those celestial bodies, and investigate the properties of those smallest of minute particles, require an open mind. Many of the things I'll speak of today will defy common sense. Remember that at one time it was believed that the world was flat and monsters and dragons lived at the world's edge. Even as Galileo proved the Earth was round, he was labeled a heretic and not to be believed because he challenged the common sense of his time. Ladies and gentlemen, as you will see by the discoveries we will discuss this evening, common sense has no place in the quantum world."

The professor's voice projected more than any theatrical player Madeline had seen perform upon a stage. The clarity of his speech followed her even as she and the others stepped into a corridor outside of the auditorium.

He spoke of defying common sense, maintaining an open mind. Truly he would be the perfect person to explain what had happened. Then, with his knowledge, he would return her to her proper time.

"I don't think this little one will sit still in the auditorium," Doc said, with a quick glance at Kimberly. "Is there somewhere we can go until the professor is finished," he asked Jennifer.

"Daddy's office," Kim shouted before running down the hall.

"I guess we'll go to Daddy's office." Doc smiled then trotted after her. Madeline increased her pace, but refrained from running. Well-bred women did not run, though it would have made catching Kimberly much easier. The Jennifer woman kept even with her.

"I can't believe you are making me miss Grant's speech," she muttered.

"I am not making you miss anything," Madeline objected. "Antoine and I are capable of entertaining a small child." She glanced sideways, but couldn't hide her curiosity. "You truly wished to hear a lecture on string?"

"String *theory*," The woman corrected her with a roll of her eyes. She scowled at Madeline a moment before her face softened. "I'm not as much interested in the lecture as in the man giving it. I wanted him to see me intent and involved with his work. Now he won't see me at all."

Madeline considered this Jennifer woman. Kimberly had not called her "mother" and the professor's demeanor to her was not one of a husband to a wife. She hadn't the overt carnality of a clandestine lover…at least not like the many paramours at Queen Isabella's court. This Jennifer had more of a man's mannerisms than seductive sensuality. She walked with a broad stride in her crisp trousers. In her time, a woman's hair was a prized asset, yet this one had chopped hers off in a surprisingly pleasing style. Did men prefer such short locks now? She lifted her hand to her own braided and coiled tresses.

Still, by her own admission, the woman was obviously obsessed with Professor Stewart. Madeline's face twisted in puzzlement. "Are you engaged to the professor?"

"Not yet," Jennifer acknowledged with a tight smile. "But if all goes according to plan, we'll be filing a joint return in the near future." She turned toward Madeline. "I'm sorry. We weren't introduced. Kimberly called you Maddie?"

"Mademoiselle Madeline Rosette Allegra Charlebois," Madeline said with a smile, pleased that she remembered to offer her hand as she had witnessed Doc do. Jennifer, however, did not clasp it the way the Professor had done. She just stared at the extended hand until Madeline let it fall to her side.

"Well, *Mademoiselle*." Jennifer sneered. "Whatever ideas you have about laying claim to Grant, you'd best forget them now. I mean to win even if it means playing nice with his bratty little daughter."

Bratty, little daughter? She couldn't mean Kimberly. The professor must have two daughters.

The woman marched down the hallway, her heels tapping loudly on the linoleum floor.

Claim? It was a strange use of the word as she understood it. She called out in reassurance, "I have no declarations of ownership about the professor."

"Keep it that way," Jennifer said without bothering to turn around.

MADELINE FOUND THE professor's office by the sound of Kimberly's voice. When she entered, Kimberly sat at a low table rummaging through a box of supplies, reciting the names of colors.

"Color with me," she requested. She used what appeared to be a fat pencil that left a trail of color like paint with a glossy sheen.

As Maddie joined Kimberly at the table, Doc offered to take a note backstage so the professor would know where to find them. Jennifer wrote some words on a paper using some sort of writing stick from the professor's desk. Apparently, she needed no bottle of ink. It just flowed from the stick. Incredible.

"What do you call these waxy chalks?" Madeline asked Kim.

"Crayons," she said. "I have lots of colors. You make them pointy by putting them in that hole."

After completing the note, Jennifer retrieved a metal vial from her bag. A push of her finger and a spicy fragrant mist filled the air. Perfume! That practice hadn't changed since Madeline's time.

Unimpressed, Doc merely rolled his eyes then left to deliver the freshly scented message.

Once the door closed, Jennifer settled into a position of authority with a comfort that suggested familiarity. Her gaze narrowed across the desk at Madeline. "So why are you really here?" she accused more than asked. "Grant said he didn't know you."

Madeline shifted uncomfortably. The perfumed air could not mask her precarious position. Doc had warned her not to share her time leap with anyone, not even the professor. At least, not yet. *Sugah, they'll have you in a strait-jacket, they hear you talk like that.* How incredible that with all the many fantastical and imaginative innovations she'd witnessed this week, the strait-jacket restraint remained from her era.

"I met Kimberly when I visited the hospital." She smiled at the child's bent head. The hand of destiny had brought her to Kimberly, and Kimberly had brought her to the professor, but she doubted Jennifer would accept such an explanation. "I failed to make the professor's acquaintance at that time. When I learned of his speech this evening, I sought to rectify my oversight." She focused on the crayons, hoping Jennifer wouldn't recognize her partial truth.

Jennifer wasn't convinced. "Grant said he met a crazy woman when he hurt his head. Your friend seemed to think that crazy woman was you."

Madeline shrugged, keeping her distaste secret. "Antoine has many friends that others might call crazy." She glanced at Jennifer. Two could play this game. "How did the professor meet you?"

"I'm his accountant," she replied with a smug smile. "I do his tax returns."

"You're his man of accounts?" Amazing the opportunities afforded women now. It was one of the more appealing aspects of this time. "I've not heard of a woman assuming that responsibility but there's no reason they could not."

Jennifer seemed insulted. "What do you do?" she asked.

"Do?"

"What do you do for a living?" When Madeline didn't answer, she added, "Your work? Your day job?"

The woman reminded her of Queen Isabella. Her innocent questions hid a search for vulnerabilities to use later for exploitation. Madeline had survived the queen, and she would survive this woman of accounts. How dare she, a mere clerk, challenge a counselor to Royalty!

However, she wasn't a counselor now, was she? Certainly not to the queen, Isabella would be dead by now, as would her family. An intense wave of homesickness and desire to return to the time she knew so well rocked her to her soul. The professor had to help her return. She had to convince him. But first she had to get close enough to earn his confidence.

"Well?" Jennifer pressed. "Are you working or not?"

The question startled her from her thoughts on the past. Of what significance was this preoccupation with work? Madeline simply repeated something she'd heard last night. "I'm between jobs at the moment."

Jennifer sneered. "I thought that might be the case."

THE PROFESSOR RETURNED two hours later. Kimberly squealed the moment he arrived, then jumped into his arms. Doc woke with a start. Jennifer, who had been in the hall, wrapped her hand around the crook of the professor's arm as if claiming ownership. Madeline recalled the gesture from Isabella's court. Some things never changed.

"Thank you for entertaining Kimberly," he managed over Kim's explanations of her drawings. He reached in his jacket and removed a leather pouch with currency.

"Yes, thank you so much." Jennifer smiled graciously as if the undertaking was on her account.

Madeline shook her head. A lady would never seek payment for performing such a small favor for another. Especially when the favor involved such an adorable child. She smiled at Kimmy. "It was my pleasure."

Doc, however, quickly extended his palm. "Thank you, professor." The green papers disappeared into his pocket. "We had hoped to speak to you this evening about a matter of some importance." He glanced at Jennifer. "Perhaps this isn't the best time. May we come back to meet with you tomorrow? Say about five?"

"You can't meet tomorrow night," Jennifer interrupted. "We're to have dinner with partners from my firm, remember?"

"I remember," Professor Stewart said. "But I can't leave Kimmy without a sitter. We'll have to cancel and reschedule."

Doc brightened. "Madeline can watch Kimberly." He glanced her way. "Everyone contributes."

The professor briefly smiled. "I'm certain you're very capable, but I don't know you well enough to trust my most precious possession—"

"That would be wonderful," Jennifer said, exasperated. She turned toward the professor. "You need a sitter. She's unemployed. Let her babysit while you're home tomorrow. That way you'll have the

opportunity, just as I have had this evening, to see that she's reliable."
She preened a bit. "You'll be comfortable and we'll still be able to attend
that dinner."

Jennifer stroked the side of his face while extending her lip in what
Madeline suspected was a practiced pout. "Please Grant. This dinner is
very important to my career. I plan to make partner."

He was trapped, Maddie noticed, and not pleased about the offered
solution. His eyes narrowed on her. Heat rose in her cheeks imagining
that he still thought of her as unbalanced.

"You'll be right there in case of difficulty," Jennifer continued.
"There's no harm in having her spend the day." When the professor
didn't immediately respond, she added, "I'll even pay for her services."

"That won't be necessary," the professor said. "I'll pay for her to
watch Kim."

Maddie thought she could easily get lost in those stormy blue eyes,
especially if they ever looked at her with a little less suspicion.

"Oui," she said, holding his gaze. "C'est bien."

"Wonderful," Jennifer exclaimed. She grabbed one of Kimberly's
pictures from Grant's hand and, over Kim's protests, scribbled a few
lines on the back. "Here's Professor Stewart's address. He'll expect you
at what?" She turned toward him. "Eight? Nine in the morning?"

"Nine will be fine." He stared at Madeline as if he expected her to
erupt in madness at any moment.

"If this works out, perhaps you two can discuss a longer term
arrangement," Jennifer said, pleased with her solution. "I'm certain this
won't be my last business dinner."

Doc glanced at the address. "She'll be there first thing in the
morning. Come along Miss Maddie. The professor needs to take his
family home."

"Tomorrow then." The professor's lips tightened in a thin smile.

"Yay!" Kimberly whooped.

Madeline stood still, holding his gaze until Doc tugged her arm,
leading her toward the door. Once they were in the hallway, he pulled an
inscribed stone from his pocket and kissed it. "Let's just hope this gig
doesn't involve cooking."

Chapter Six

THE WORKED IRON fence circling the professor's property on Magazine Street gave Madeline pause. She wasn't certain of the circumstances that caused her initial entrapment in the gates, but she wasn't going to risk repeating the experience by touching anything iron. Fortunately, Doc reached around her to unlatch the gate. Familiar with the city in the way she was not, he'd come along to help her find the proper address.

They climbed the steps to a porch that ran the width of the small house. "Take this," he said, placing a tiny red bag in her hand. "For luck."

"What is it?" she asked. The filling was hard, solidly packed. She sniffed it and was rewarded with a rose scent.

"It's gris-gris, herbs, oils, charms…. you might need it with him." He tilted his head toward the house

She dropped the small packet in her corset. "I'm certain I'll be fine."

"You never know about these science types." He knocked on the door. "Remember what we talked about. Don't say anything about where you're really from, or when. He may be the key, but he wasn't receptive last night. He called you a crazy lady. He needs to believe before he can be of help."

"She's here! She's here!" The lovely home couldn't contain Kimberly's enthusiasm.

"Sounds like we found the right place," Doc said with a tight smile.

The professor opened the door. While surprised to see Antoine, his smile lingered on Madeline. She felt overly exposed in the long skirt and something called a tee shirt that she'd borrowed from Cici.

On the previous two occasions that she had seen him, he'd worn something resembling a matched ensemble with a colorful long cravat knotted at his neck. Today, however, his green shirt hugged his powerful shoulders with sleeves short enough to display his well-muscled arms. The back of her neck tingled as if a warm breath had swept across. Simultaneously, he raised his hand to the back of his neck as if he'd felt the same.

"Miss Madeline is new to the city," Doc explained. "I wanted to make sure she could find her way. You'll see her safely home?"

"She didn't drive?" He peered around them to the curb.

Before she could respond with a reference to Louis and his carriage, Doc silenced her with his hand. "She doesn't have a car." He hesitated a moment. "May we come in?"

"Yes. Of course."

They entered a parlor, with high ceilings and long windows that faced the street. While spacious inside, virtually every surface in the room was cluttered and disorganized.

"This is lovely," Madeline said. Though smaller than her apartment at the Royal Palace of Madrid, and much, much smaller than her family's estate, the furnishings made the residence warm and intimate, different from the professor's office. Beneath the hodgepodge surface, she sensed a woman's presence, a tasteful grace and elegance that existed in spite of the chaotic covering. The professor picked up a box of colorful wax sticks—crayons, Kimberly had called them--and large thin books from the wooden floor. He placed them on a low table.

"I'm not staying," Doc advised. "I just wanted to see Miss Madeline settled."

"That's reassuring," the professor murmured. Madeline doubted Doc heard him, but she had. There was mistrust there, but she wasn't sure why.

Kim waved from the foot of a stairway then bolted up the stairs shouting something about her dolly. Her feet boomed on the wooden tread, disproportionate to her small frame.

"The bedrooms are upstairs," Grant said, gesturing toward Kim's path. "I've converted one into an office, so I'll be nearby."

"That's...comforting," she said, though she knew her words were a lie. His presence was disconcerting. The man with deep blue eyes was anything but comforting.

"This is the dining room. We don't entertain so we use the dining room for other things."

Stacks of books covered the large table in the middle of the room. A portrait gazed over it all from the wall. A beautiful young woman with a mask of brilliant peacock plumage with eyeholes surrounded by sparkling gems smiled serenely from her high perch.

"That's Carolyn, my wife," the professor said from behind her, just over her shoulder, a note of longing evident in his voice. "She died a number of years ago. Drunk driver."

One of Maddie's childhood friends had died in a carriage overturn due to a similar problem. She nodded her head while she studied the portrait. "An intoxicated man has no business anywhere near a horse."

An unnerving silence ensued. Had she said something wrong? Heat rose to her cheeks. Where were her manners? She should have offered some sort of comfort to the man, not talk of her own experiences. "I'm so sorry for your loss," she said, adding a sweet smile. "At least you have the comfort that she's with a loving God in a better place."

His gaze hardened. "If God were so loving, he wouldn't have allowed her to be in that spot at that time."

Cold chilled her spine. The professor turned abruptly and walked toward the back of the house. She followed stunned. Had society abandoned God in this new age? She'd seen the grand churches and cathedrals, but now that she considered them, they were mostly empty.

"The kitchen," he announced, his voice without humor.

Sunlight shone through a wall of French windows and doors that opened to a lovely brick patio and gardens beyond.

"C'est magnifique!" she said with awe. "You know the French were the first to make doors like this. Have you visited the Hall of Mirrors in le Château de Versailles? It is very similar to—"

"Do you smell that?" The professor interrupted. "Is something burning?"

They both hurried back to the front parlor to see Doc waving a smoldering bundle of dried leaves in the front parlor.

"White sage," he explained while following the perimeter of the room. "I'm cleansing the room of negative spirits and energies."

"Negative what?" The professor's eyes shifted from surprise to anger as comprehension settled. "Out!" He pointed toward the front door. "The both of you. I won't have any of that voodoo-hoodoo mumbo-jumbo in my house. Get out!"

No! He was the key! She had to stay! While she didn't believe in voodoo, she did believe the professor was connected to her existence in this time. If she couldn't gain his cooperation, she might never be able to return home.

"He didn't mean harm," she pleaded. "He is trying to protect me."

"Protect you from what?" His eyes bored into her.

"You." Doc stepped forward. "And all negative energy. White sage smoke removes lingering evil spirits so a new venture starts fresh."

He wasn't helping. The two men faced each other as if to do battle.

"Antoine will leave," she said suddenly, hoping to ease the rising tension. She glanced at the professor's continued scowl. "Or both of us, if you insist. But I hope you'll reconsider."

She tried to disarm him with a smile. It had always been effective in the queen's court. But she needed something more, something that might cause him to overlook Antoine's antics. "There is still that matter for which I require your assistance," she said hopefully.

The professor crossed his arms across his chest. Her plea hadn't so much as dented his armor.

Kimberly raced from the bottom of the steps, her arms filled with her doll, a book and something fat and droopy. "Where is she going?" she shouted. She came to a sudden stop in front of Madeline. "You said you'd stay. I want you to stay and read a story. You can't go!"

Madeline's gaze lifted to the professor, a stern implacable force. He couldn't have been clearer in his demands that they leave. Madeline sunk to her knees in front of Kimberly. "I would like to stay, mon petit, but I fear I cannot at this time."

Madeline's throat constricted. Kim needed someone to listen and pay attention to her, that much was apparent at the hospital. Madeline needed to stay close to the professor to learn how to return. The white sage had severed both of their desires with one frail plume of smoke.

She heard Antoine's steps on the front porch. He was waiting for her.

Kimberly lifted tear-filled eyes to her father. "Tell her to stay, Daddy. I promise I'll be good. I don't want her to go."

Madeline stood, her own eyes burning. She paused as she passed the professor. "I'm sorry I did not suit you." She raised a watery gaze to meet his. "Adieu, monsieur. I wish you success on your project. Perhaps…sometime…our paths may yet cross again."

She continued toward the door, sensing that she had let down not only Kimberly and the professor, but the faint residing essence of the woman whose portrait hung on the wall.

"Wait!" The masculine command stopped her in her tracks.

She squeezed the small cross at her neck, issuing a silent prayer.

"You can stay today —"

Madeline turned just in time to catch Kimmy as she hurled her small body at her legs.

"—but know that I'll be upstairs. If I hear anything out of the ordinary, anything at all, I will be down here in a hurry. Do you understand?"

"Oui." Madeline managed before she kissed Kimmy's head. "Thank you. Thank you. I promise there will be no more ...upsets."

"No. No more upsets," he agreed before trudging up the stairs to his office.

Kimmy sniffed the air. "It smells funny in here."

"I know, mon petit," Madeline said, hugging her tight. "Let's open the windows and let the bad smell out."

Maddie walked to the front window and lifted the sash. Doc stood just out of sight on the porch.

"Don't forget what I told you," he whispered, his eyes seeking hers in understanding. She nodded.

"And for Ezulie's sake, stay out of the kitchen."

WHAT WAS HE thinking?

Inviting some crazy voodoo princess into his house to stay with his daughter? Intoxication and horses? Smudging the room for evil spirits? Now that she was out of her crazy period costume, she appeared sane...Who was he kidding? She still looked beautiful, but he'd known from the beginning that something wasn't quite right. Yet he'd invited her into his home. What an idiot!

He never suspected she practiced voodoo. Had he'd been fooled by the simple cross she wore about her neck? Although, to be fair, her boyfriend with the unsuccessfully concealed voodoo snake tattoo had smudged the house, not Madeline. Did it matter? He doubted Madeline would harm his daughter. The obvious mutual affection between Madeline and Kim had been the reason he'd considered her as a babysitter in the first place. It was more...something wasn't exactly right.

Shaking his head, Grant settled back at his desk. At first he listened for something, anything out of the ordinary, and periodically crept down the steps to spy on them. That lasted until he heard his daughter quietly note while they were coloring together, "he's back."

"He'll leave again soon," Madeline said. "He doesn't trust me."

He tried to concentrate on his theories, all the while knowing the delectable but different French woman was downstairs. Soon, however, he became lost in the world of quarks, hadrons, and baryons. That is, until he smelled smoke. What the hell? The smoke detector began to scream.

51

He flew out of his chair and sprinted down the stairs. Smoke billowed from the kitchen. Had she set the house on fire? Was Kimmy safe?

Once he entered the kitchen, he saw Kimmy sitting calmly at the counter while Madeline attempted to wrestle a pan of black squares from the oven without the benefit of oven mitts. Smoke hovered inches below the ceiling, swirling in curly wisps before escaping to the rest of the house.

"What's going on!" he shouted as he flipped on the fan above the stove to vent the smoke. "What are you doing?"

"I told her to use the toaster," Kimmy said nonchalantly playing with the peanut butter jar. "But she doesn't know how." Her tiny arms raised in bewilderment. "Who doesn't know how to use a toaster?"

Grant grabbed some oven mitts from a drawer and pulled the sheet of charcoal from the oven.

"Was this meant to be toast?" he asked, dumping the blackened pan into the sink. He glared at Madeline who stood with one palm awkwardly stacked on the other. Tears ran down her cheeks while she quietly bit her lower lip. His gaze slipped to her hands. Blisters had already formed on her reddened finger pads.

"Jesus, Mary and Joseph," he said. "You didn't try to remove the pan without potholders, did you?"

"I didn't know," she said softly.

"Kimmy. Go get the band aids." He turned the faucet on cold. Steam hissed and rose from the hot baking sheet. "Let me see." He reached for her fingers. A brief flash sparked between them the moment his fingers touched hers. Static electricity. Had to be.

"I know how to use an oven," Madeline said. "Cici taught me. I forgot about those." She nodded to the oven mitts on the counter.

He studied her two hands, then placed them both under the streaming cold water. "This will stop the burning. Just hold your fingers under the water."

Kimmy dumped a variety of band aids on the counter, some had smiley faces, others had zebra stripes or lipstick kisses.

"Thanks." He tossed her a towel. "Take that and chase the smoke out the window."

Kimmy took off with a whoop, jumping and swinging the cloth at the gray tendrils. She wasn't tall enough to be very effective but it kept her occupied. Grant pushed a button to turn off the annoying alert.

"So," he said softly, dropping his gaze to her hands so as to not upset her further. "Why *didn't* you use the toaster?"

"I...I thought I could do it in the oven," she said. "It's how I remember. This bread is so thin and...and...limp." She lifted her hand out of the water to swipe at her face, before putting it back in the stream. "It is not really bread, this bread."

He frowned, perplexed. It was not the answer he was expecting. As Kimmy had said, who doesn't know how to use a toaster? And what did she mean about the bread not being bread? He reached for a small bowl so she could continue to soak her hands and a clean kitchen towel to gently dry her palms. "I'll finish lunch. You sit at the counter and soak your fingers. The band-aides will protect the blisters. You'll be fine."

She did as he instructed, watching everything as if committing it to memory. When he smoothed a layer of peanut butter across the surface of toasted bread, made in a toaster, she finally broke into a smile.

"That's not butter with peanuts," she said. "I wondered about that."

The smoke had thinned and Kimmy returned to the counter. Grant sliced the bread in half for her small hands, then pushed the paper plate toward his daughter. Kimmy picked up a half, but Madeline stopped her.

"Not without serviettes," she said. "A proper lady never eats without a serviette."

Kimmy frowned toward her father.

"She means napkins," he said. "You know where they are." Kim scooted off her seat to retrieve the napkins. "I'm going to make myself a lunchmeat sandwich," he informed Madeline. "Would you like that or peanut butter and jelly."

She looked at him shyly. "Can I try both? I'd like to see what they taste like."

She was becoming more odd by the minute. She'd never had a peanut butter and jelly sandwich? Where did this woman come from? Yet his daughter had formed a bond with her. This could be problematic.

He bandaged her fingers so she could eat. Kimmy picked out the colorful band-aides, each one different, and Grant carefully wrapped them around her fingers. Madeline laughed at the plastic strips then tentatively ate her lunch. Her delight was infectious. Grant found himself laughing and teasing the two girls. It felt good, like old times. It felt as if—he caught himself—as if Carolyn were still alive. The pain of losing Carolyn slammed into his chest. He sat back in his chair. He would never love another so whole-heartedly again. The pain of loss was simply too great. Guilt weighed on him for even enjoying the lunch.

"Could you excuse me for a moment?" Madeline said. "I must attend to some amenities." She smiled, then headed toward the bathroom.

Kimberly watched her leave. "I want to be a princess like Maddie when I grow up."

Madeline a princess?

"What do you mean?" Grant asked.

Kim's face filled with wonder. "She lives in a castle with the queen and has lots of servants."

Grant started to laugh, but caught himself at Kimmy's frown.

"I don't think Madeline is a princess, Kimmy. You have to be the daughter of a queen to be a princess," he explained. Though, in truth, her royal status might explain why she didn't know how to do the simplest things.

"Then how come she gets to live in a castle?" Kim's eyes narrowed in challenge, a look he recalled from her mother. Love for his daughter tempered his earlier resurgence of loss.

"She doesn't," Grant said patiently. "There are no castles in New Orleans."

"But she has servants, cause she doesn't know about microwaves and toasters and peanut butter."

He couldn't reply. Fortunately, he didn't have to. Madeline returned chatting about the wonders of modern plumbing. Plumbing? He was sure that her enthusiasm was playacting, but ... odd and strangely believable.

He made himself a sandwich so he could join Madeline and Kim with their lunch. He watched Madeline carefully, looking for signs of something that would sway his judgment. But by the end of the lunch, he was still uncertain whether he could safely leave her alone with his daughter tonight. While he could easily pass on the dinner, the affair seemed especially important to Jennifer.

He wished he knew her better, or at a minimum knew someone he trusted to stay at the house just in case. Madeline reached for the carton of milk, her golden bracelet softly jingling with her movements. A blue gem attached to the bracelet flashed in the sunlight, and just like that, he had his answer.

He knew the perfect person to give him an objective opinion. It might be late notice but the lure of spending the evening with a beautiful woman might be just the incentive to cancel whatever plans his best friend might have made. Grant excused himself to make a call.

"HOW COME YOU don't know anything?"

The professor had returned upstairs, leaving Madeline and Kimmy alone in the kitchen.

"I know lots of things," Madeline replied, insulted. "I was the counselor to royalty. I know languages, etiquette,"—she caught the child's bored expression—"but I suppose that doesn't matter so much here and now," she admitted.

"You didn't know how to work the toaster or how to make hot water come out of the faucet."

"You're right." Madeline glanced about the kitchen. "So many of the things you take for granted terrify me." Her gaze settled back on the confused child. "Let me tell you a story. This is a story my father once told me when I was your age." She put her arm around Kim, tucking her into her side. "Once there lived a man called Rip Van Winkle. He was an ordinary young man who one day —"

"I know this story," Kimmy announced triumphantly. "Rip Van Winkle fell asleep and woke up old."

"You know that story?" Madeline drew back surprised that a modern child would be familiar with the old tale.

"Yeah. He woke up with a long grey beard and he didn't know anyone. He slept a long, long time." Kim laughed.

"But to Monsieur Van Winkle, he only slept overnight. Time sped up while he slept." Madeline held her finger to her mouth, looked toward the opening to the rest of the house, and lowered her voice. "May I tell you a secret?" she asked. "You have to promise not to tell anyone, not even your father."

Kim squinted. "I promise."

"Then go check to make sure he's not listening."

Madeline didn't want to encourage Kimmy to keep secrets from her father, but fear of his reaction when he learned the truth made the request necessary, at least until she could prove to him that she wasn't unbalanced. The child required an answer for Madeline's difficulties. Kimberly could be an immense help in teaching her about everyday wonders, but would she understand the significance of her dilemma? She turned their chairs so they could face each other without a table in-between. Kimmy returned and shook her head. They huddled with their heads close together.

"I'm like Monsieur Van Winkle. I was born a long, long time ago, even before your grandmother. In another country far away."

"But you're not old."

She smiled. "*Mais oui*. I am not. I am the same age I was when I fell asleep." Kimmy would understand falling asleep far better than the truth, which she, quite honestly, didn't understand herself.

"If you go to sleep again, will you go back?" Kimmy looked at her with wide concerned eyes.

Madeline shook her head. "I don't know how to go back. I may be trapped in this time and there's so much I don't understand." Madeline looked deep into Kimberly's eyes. "Please don't mention this to your father."

"Why?" Kim twisted awkwardly in her chair. "Will he be mad?"

Madeline thought of his earlier reaction to Doc and his white sage. "He may decide that I shouldn't spend time with you."

"I don't want you to go." Urgency underscored the child's concern. "You're not like the others."

With her bandaged fingers spread wide, Madeline pulled the young child onto her lap and kissed the top of her head. "And I don't want to leave. So may I trust you to keep our secret? Do you promise?"

Kim nodded her head.

"Good." Madeline squeezed her tight, then set her on her feet. "If I'm to stay, I'm going to need your help. Just as you showed me how to use the toaster and the refrigerator, I need you to show me how everything works."

"Everything?" Her eyes widened.

"Only those things that you can," Madeline said. "And tell me their names. I've a lot to learn."

Chapter Seven

HE CHECKED HIS watch, an extraordinary Rolex that featured the current time in different time zones. Jennifer had given it to him for Christmas. While he protested its extravagance, he did admire the time zone function. However, no matter which time zone he checked, Richard was late. Which meant Grant would be late collecting Jennifer, and Jennifer would be pissed.

The doorbell rang. Finally. Grant jaunted down the steps in his suit and tie.

Richard waited on the porch, a pizza box in his hands, topped with a six-pack of beer.

"It's about time." Grant urged Richard inside. "I was afraid you'd gotten lost."

"No, just had to pick up some —"

"Pizza!!!!"

Kimmy bolted from the kitchen to the front room. "Are we having pizza for dinner?"

"We sure are, sport." Richard rumpled her hair. When he lifted his gaze, his eyes widened and his face slackened, dazed. "Hello. I don't think we've met."

Grant's lips tightened. "Madeline, this is Professor Gaston, a colleague of mine." Grant gestured toward Richard. "Richard, Mademoiselle Madeline Charlebois."

Richard juggled the awkward box to extend his hand. "Pleased to meet you. Grant didn't tell me that he had found such a beautiful babysitter. I'm frankly surprised he plans to leave the house."

Madeline accepted his hand with a modest curtsy. "*Enchanté professeur.*"

"Ouch!" He glanced at her bandaged fingers, turning her hand from side to side. "What happened here?"

"She burned them on the stove," Kim said, reaching for the pizza box.

And just like that, Grant felt excluded from the threesome, which is what he wanted, wasn't it? He had to pick up Jennifer but hesitated, not anxious to leave. "I asked Richard to keep you company as this is your first time in this neighborhood."

"He is not going with you?" Her brows raised a moment, then settled as comprehension dawned. "You believe Kimmy to be insufficient company?"

"She's not an adult," Grant said quickly. "Once she's asleep you'll be here all alone."

She held his gaze a moment then turned toward Richard, instantly transforming into a gracious host. "Are you also a professor of time, monsieur?"

"Not exactly," Richard said, mesmerized. "I'm in the Art History department with a specialty in historic gemstones and jewelry." He pointed to her wrist. "I noticed your bracelet. Brilliant craftsmanship. Is that a family heirloom?"

She smiled, drawing her hand behind her back. "I'm jealous of your wife, monsieur. She must enjoy the fruits of such a specialty."

"I'm not married," Richard replied with a devilish glint in his eyes.

"Mais certainement!" She turned to Grant, annoyance in the set of her lips. "You invited a bachelor to stay with me, alone, after Kimmy has gone to bed?"

Crap! He hadn't thought about proprieties. But they were two adults. Who worried about such things?

Kim had successfully wrestled the box from Richard's hands and retreated to the kitchen. Madeline's lips tilted in a smirk before she turned to follow. "Decorum may change," she said. "But some things remain the same."

Grant waited until Madeline and Kimmy took the pizza to the kitchen then he turned to Richard. "See what I mean? She's not quite right."

"You think she's a serial killer?" Richard asked, his gaze following her path. "Because I can think of worse ways to go."

"Well…no…"

"A child abuser?"

"Don't be ridiculous," Grant said. "It's clear she loves children, but something's not right. She showed up this morning with her voodoo boyfriend, but it's not the voodoo—"

"Voodoo!" Richard interrupted. "Wait a minute. You never said anything about voodoo."

"The boyfriend's into voodoo, not Madeline," Grant explained.

"Once he left, she didn't do anything out of the ordinary. But still…"

"Let me get this straight. Madeline is off but not into voodoo and does nothing out of the ordinary." With his gaze firmly settled on the kitchen, Richard ran his hand around his waist cinching his shirt beneath his belt. "You go on with your dinner party. I'm happy to babysit the babysitter when she looks like that."

"No funny business," Grant warned. "Just watch her and let me know what you discover."

"Oh, I'll be watching all right." Richard's grin deepened.

Shoot. He hadn't considered Richard's obvious attraction toward Madeline, but what could he do? He needed a second opinion and Richard was as good as any. Perhaps he *should have* arranged for a chaperone after all.

"When will you be back?" Richard asked.

"Just as soon as I can get this over with. If this wasn't so important to Jennifer, I would have stayed here to work."

"Tell the ice queen I owe her one." Richard followed Madeline's path. "Don't hurry back on my account."

Grant stared after him, almost hearing his Grandmother's voice in his ear. "Son, you just left the fox to guard the henhouse."

HOURS LATER, GRANT slipped his key into the lock. The house was still standing. No flashing lights were waiting for him in the street. No clouds of incense greeted him in the driveway.

The dinner took far longer than he'd hoped. Accountants, he'd noted, had no sense of humor. While this lack of distraction was a characteristic he appreciated in his business-first girlfriend, it made for a long boring dinner, especially when his mind was elsewhere. He supposed his frequent calls to check on the new sitter didn't help matters with Jennifer.

The door opened easily to a darkened front room. A welcoming candle or two burned in the dining room. Soft laughter emitted from the kitchen. Crystal clinked.

Damn that Richard! Grant wasn't ready to explain the birds and the bees to his little girl, to say nothing of a miffed voodoo-inclined boyfriend with an ax to grind on his doorstep.

He stormed into the kitchen but drew up short to find Richard and Madeline at the kitchen table amicably chatting over a bottle of wine.

His heart jumped. A stab of memory, a sense of home and hearth and of easy acceptance pinged in his chest.

"Professor! You're back!" Madeline's face lit like a super nova.

"Grant, old buddy," Richard's smile widened. "Madeline and I were just enjoying some of your wine. She's not a beer drinker so I left a six pack in your fridge."

"I can see that." Grant smothered a small flare of jealousy. Richard was enjoying the sort of life he'd once shared with Carolyn. A life he'd lost and had vowed not to repeat. "Listen, can you stay here a bit longer while I take Madeline home?"

"Why don't I do that for you?" Richard popped out of his chair like water displaced by a rock.. "It wouldn't be any trouble and you can get back to your research."

Grant was sorely tempted. The quiet uneventful evening would make for a natural transition into his work. He longed to slip into the logical and pure world, free of French accents and distracting green eyes. The comforting company of black holes and dark matter would help him escape worries about his daughter's needs and Jennifer's demands. It would save him, as well, from deciding if the alluring Madeline Charlebois would ease some of his burdens, or simply add to them.

"No." He said. "I promised Antoine that I'd take her home. My promise, my obligation."

Was that gratitude he saw flash in her eyes? While Richard fancied himself a ladies man, he was fairly astute at judging character. It was the main reason Grant had sought his opinion. Still he hoped Richard hadn't imposed himself upon Madeline. She'd made her preference of a chaperone's presence clear.

"Do you mind staying to watch the news," Grant asked his friend. "This shouldn't take long."

Chapter Eight

COLD FOREBODING CREPT down her spine. "Is that iron?"

"Iron would make the car too heavy to be cost-effective." Grant rapped his knuckle on the door. "Reinforced aluminum. Titanium would be better but it's too expensive." He opened the car door for her.

Madeline slid into the seat, appreciating the leather upholstery. "I've seen people ride in these."

"I suppose you have."

He was laughing at her, she could hear it in his voice. He crossed to the opposite side and opened his door. "Don't forget your seat belt. It's the law in Louisiana."

"Seat belt?" They didn't have those in carriages.

"The clip? By your shoulder?"

"Oh!" She found the strange contraption and secured it just as the professor had done. Then she braced herself for the expected lurch forward with one hand on the side window and one on the strange padded form in front of her.

"Relax," he said. "I'm a safe driver."

"Without doubt," she replied sweetly, then gnawed on her lip. She'd seen these cars racing at death defying speeds. Forcing her hands to return to her lap, she closed her eyes and offered a prayer to Saint Christopher, the patron saint of travel. If she must die, please don't let it happen in this strange and confusing century.

"This should give us some time to talk," the professor said. "I wanted to apologize about this morning. I lost my temper when your boyfriend —"

"Why do you call him my boyfriend?" She rounded on him, surprised to see they were, in fact, moving. The conveyance proved far superior to a carriage. "Antoine is my friend but he is far from being a boy."

"I thought you two were dating," he said, confusion in his voice.

Boyfriend, dating...she'd not heard of these terms, but she suspected he might be referring to some sort of intimacy. Dealings with men always resulted in some sort of intimacy. Queen Isabella's court had taught her that much. So far, however, nothing of that nature had occurred. "He meant no harm."

"I don't want my daughter exposed to voodoo," Grant grumbled. "It's superstition and witchcraft, not scientific principle."

They rode in silence while she considered the best way to charm the professor into revealing his knowledge of time crossing. Suddenly she recalled that what worked for the daughter might work as well for the father.

"Have you ever heard of the story of Rip Van Winkle?" She asked.

"He falls asleep while drinking moonshine and wakes up later as an old man?"

"Oui! That is the one," she exclaimed. He was probably the one that told Kimmy the tale. "I told Kimmy that very story earlier. I wonder … could something like that happen?"

"It's just a children's story," he said. "A piece of fiction." His eyes crinkled and the car warmed with his soft laughter. "If drinking magical moonshine could cause time travel into the future, New Orleans would be riddled with people from past centuries, and not just on Mardi Gras."

Fat Tuesday. She smiled, recalling the tourists on those carriage rides asking if she was dressed for that period of celebration that they'd so recently missed.

"Then again, maybe people from the past wander the streets, " Grant continued. "This city has more than its share of ghost sightings."

He laughed a bit louder. Clearly he did not believe such "time travel" as he called it was credible. Maddie stared out the side window to hide her disappointment. Doc was right. The professor had dismissed the idea as fiction.

"Every year," he said. "My quantum students talk about building a H. G. Well's time machine. Just climb aboard and select your year."

"A time machine?" Her disappointment lifted. "Where might I find this Mr. Wells?" Perhaps that gentleman could return her home.

"In a library." Grant frowned. "It was fiction, Madeline. Don't you remember H. G. Wells and the Time Machine? Or The Island of Doctor Moreau, or The War of the Worlds?" He shook his head, returning his gaze to the road ahead. "So many people confuse actual science with science fiction."

Frustration extinguished her brief flare of hope. Now what was she to do? She'd been so certain that escaping from the iron gates into the company of a time professor was not just coincidence. Even Doc and his voodoo saints thought Professor Stewart held the answer. At least Doc and Cici believed that she had somehow stumbled into this period from the past. Professor Stewart clearly would not.

"Right now there's an experiment with entangled particles that holds promise," he said. "A transporter may result from that discovery. Of course, a transportation device like the one on Star Trek is still decades away. It wouldn't connect the strings of time, but a transporter...that would be a step into the future."

"Strings of time?" She dismissed the confusing combination of otherwise ordinary words, like entangled and particles, stars and trek. "What are strings of time?"

"That's right. You missed my lecture last night." He glanced quickly her way. "Thank you for coming, by the way, you were a life saver. Sometimes Kimmy can be a handful, and if you hadn't come when you did..."

"Professor," she urged softly. "Strings of time?"

"Yes. There's a theory that our existence occurs on a specific string of time, simultaneously with other strings that hold alternate existences. Thus, our medieval past might be occurring in real time on one string and our distant future on another string. Some scientists believe these strings to be an infinite number of bubbles on a plane in space called a brane, but the entire concept is still called string theory."

"That is astounding." She felt her jaw might have unhinged at the discovery and dangled unattractively. She quickly composed herself. "This is what you spoke of yesterday?" she asked. "I would have liked to have heard your speech."

Perhaps his speech was the very reason fate had led her to this professor. She needed to hear his speech. And yet once again she'd managed to miss the opportunity. Still, she couldn't dwell on her disappointment, not with a time professor with such valuable information seated next to her.

"What happens if two strings were to touch," she asked. "Say a string from the medieval past and our string of the present?"

"Then it might be possible for an armor-clad knight to chase a dragon down Canal Street." He laughed. "But the fact that such an occurrence only happens as playacting proves that such time collisions are not possible."

A time collision...could that have been what happened? She'd survived the colliding of strings? But if that were the case, why did the others touring the foundry not follow her in this collision? Why was she alone in this dilemma? She shook her head. None of that mattered now. What mattered was finding the way back.

"Suppose a person from the past *did* manage to journey to this time," she asked. "How would they return? In theory, of course."

"In theory, there is something called the arrow of time. Time only goes forward, never back. So while I don't believe a person from the past could ever conceivably show up in our time, if they did there's a strong likelihood that they could never go back."

She was trapped here. The reality swirled in her stomach in a dizzying bout of nausea.

"Of course, as long as we're talking theory and infinite possibilities," he continued, obviously unaware of her distress. "If such a person were to have discovered a time portal that connected the two strings, I suppose they'd have to return the same way they'd arrived. However, as I mentioned earlier, science has found the existence of time portals highly unlikely."

Of course! She could return by simply reversing the process. Why hadn't she thought of that herself? Granted, she'd been thrust into a different society, a different country, and a different time. She hadn't been thinking logically due to her confusion. But now she had a clear direction home. Laughter bubbled past her lips.

In the light of the passing streetlights, she noticed his eyebrow raise in question. He must think she was a candidate for the lunatic asylum. Not that she could blame him. He'd truly been the key to her return. He'd provided her with an answer. And now she'd most likely never see him or his sweet daughter again.

The car slowed then stopped in front of Doc's apartment. "Is this the place?" He looked past her with a frown toward the building.

She nodded. It was shabby compared to the professor's residence, but Doc had offered shelter when she had no other place to go. The professor reached in his jacket to withdraw his wallet. He counted out a number of bills and handed them to her. "I hope that's sufficient."

How would she know?

"Thank you for all you've done for me," she said, accepting the offered currency. "Please thank Kimmy as well. She was asleep when we left so I could not bid her *adieu*. Tell her. It's important."

"Adieu? Doesn't that mean goodbye?" He looked confused, puzzled. "Look, I've already apologized for my earlier outburst. And I meant that. I still need someone to watch over Kimmy and she takes to you like…entangled particles." He laughed briefly at his joke before he quickly sobered. Taking her hand in his, he gazed into her eyes. "I hope I didn't scare you off."

She felt that gaze clean to her womb, unsettling her in a distinctively pleasant way. Her hand warmed beneath his touch, as honey warmed by a pleasant sun. She savored the brief moment. Her one regret upon her return to her world would be leaving the professor and his daughter behind. Kimmy was a true delight and had showed her the miraculous inventions of the future. The professor…well, he stirred dreams of a different sort.

He left the car and walked to her side to open the door. Holding out his hand to assist her, he smiled in a tilted sort of way. She slipped out, and upon impulse, pressed her lips to his. A moment bloomed, a magic. His lips softened generating a vibration deep in her ribcage, which hummed and pulsed through her limbs. His arms pulled her close, which she deeply appreciated as her knees seemed to have lost the ability to keep her upright.

Much, much too soon, he broke the kiss. She stepped back, her body trembling, just as she had trembled when she left the gates. This time, however, her body surged with heat and desire, not the ice of iron. Surprised by her reaction, she gazed up through her lashes at the professor. The famed Seducer of Seville could not have stirred her more.

"I shall miss you," she said, tempted to slide her finger along his lower lip. She fought the urge and stepped back.

"You don't have to," Grant said, his raised brow in opposition to his upturned lips. "I'll be waiting for you on Monday morning."

She slowly backed away then hurried to the safety of the apartment building's front door. She glanced back. The professor still waited, scowling at the ground as if lost in thought with the open car door still in his hands. She offered a smile, though she doubted he saw it. He would be waiting a long…long…time.

RED LIGHT! HE slammed on the brakes throwing his car into a short slide. The horn of the car passing in front of him blared. Damn! He needed to take his thoughts off that brain-numbing kiss before he got himself killed.

It was a good night kiss, he told himself. She just confused her words. She'd done that before. It was a good night kiss. It *had* to be a good night kiss, he mentally repeated, hoping that his repetition would make it so. He was loath to admit, her good night kiss had stirred his senses more than any other kiss before.

I will miss you. Did she just mean over the weekend? She would be back on Monday, right?

Richard's car waited at the curb in front of his house. The far more experienced Richard could tell him how to interpret that kiss.

"So?" Grant asked the moment he entered the house. He hid his perplexing emotions beneath a somber exterior. "What did you think?"

"Where did you find her? She's fantastic!" Richard toasted him with over-bright eyes and a raised glass. He'd moved from the kitchen table to a barstool at the breakfast counter and raided the liquor cabinet along the way. "Did you know she's been to the Prado? She called it something else but her descriptions matched the real thing to a T. She's seen the Rubens there and the Raphael. El Greco, Goya…she was even familiar with Vincent Lopez. It's as if she'd read my book on the Spanish renaissance."

"Maybe she did." It occurred to Grant that he didn't know anything about Madeline's past. Perhaps she was one of those stalkers that had researched his past in order to be the perfect babysitter. He scrapped that idea as soon as it entered his mind. She was knowledgeable about Richard's specialty, not his, and no stalker could have orchestrated that lightning strike at the restaurant.

Richard shook his head. "I asked her and she said no, but I wouldn't have expected some of her observations from a normal babysitter." His speech held a slight slur. "Where on earth did you find her?"

"Actually, she found me," Grant grumbled, pouring himself a finger of scotch. He explained how they met at his speech, but neglected mention of that first encounter at the Court of Two Sisters. He was still trying to sort that one out. "Kimberly was really taken with her so I asked her to babysit."

"Smart move." Richard's lecherous grin struck a discordant nerve. "Gotta say, I understand now why you're working from home. I wouldn't mind having a fine piece of ass like that greeting me at the end of a day."

Without thinking, Grant punched him in the jaw knocking Richard clean off the barstool.

"Shit," He mumbled to himself while he helped Richard to his feet.

"What the hell, man." Richard's hand covered the spot of impact. "What was that for?"

"Sorry." Grant assisted him into a chair. "I don't know what came over me. It's just - she's not that kind of girl."

"You just met her," Richard protested, working his jaw from side to side. "You don't know what kind of girl she is." He scowled at Grant. "Isn't that what you wanted me to find out?"

"Yes, but that was before." Grant walked to the refrigerator to fix an ice pack.

"Before what?"

"Before she kissed me."

"She kissed you?" Richard's eyebrows lifted. "You dog! What does the ice queen say about that?"

Crap. Jennifer. Richard's derisive inference aside, Grant had forgotten about Jennifer. He handed Richard the ice pack with a scowl.

"Look," Richard said. "You asked for my opinion and this is it. Maddie is fine. So fine, that I'm thinking of asking her out. In fact, I asked for her phone number and she said she didn't have a box. Ha! She called my phone a box." He tried to laugh, but quickly applied the ice pack to his jaw instead. "Hell, I suppose it does look like a box. But you are a real jerk. *You* asked *me* here, remember? It's a good thing we go way back, my friend, or I'd beat you to a pulp."

"Again, I'm sorry," Grant apologized. "I don't know what came over me."

"I suppose I shouldn't have mixed wine with scotch. Maybe I said something, I don't remember. But I'm leaving now before I say it again." He wobbled a bit gaining his feet.

"Thanks for the pizza and the company for Madeline and everything. I really appreciate you coming over."

"You have a funny way of showing it."

"I do." He agreed. "I owe you one. But I think you might want to stay here tonight. We've got an extra bed upstairs. You can head home in the morning."

Richard started to protest, but then grabbed the breakfast bar for balance. "Maybe I'll take you up on that offer."

Grant helped him up the stairs then directed him to the spare bedroom. Closing the door behind Richard, Grant remembered that he forgot to ask about that kiss. There was always the morning, he reminded himself, heading downstairs to straighten and lock up.

It was a good night kiss. It had to be.

Chapter Nine

THE NEXT MORNING Cici helped Madeline dress in her tiered gown. She'd cleaned it the best she could but some of the rips and tears proved beyond mending. Her corset and multiple petticoats pinched and restrained in ways her loose borrowed attire and something called a "sports bra" hadn't. She straightened her spine and set her shoulders back to ease the tightness. Had it always been this way?

She brushed her hair and twisted it into a chignon—not as elegant as her maid might have done—but serviceable. She recovered her ear bobs, two bracelets, and the jeweled tortoise shell comb she wore to raise her mantilla fashionably high. Once done, she checked her image in the mirror. All in all, she looked serviceably correct for returning to nineteenth-century Madrid.

She said her goodbyes in Jackson Square after assisting Doc with his table and umbrella. She encouraged him to bid adieu to Louis on her behalf.

"Are you sure about this?" he asked.

"The professor said the gates may be a portal to take me back," she replied.

"What if you get trapped again?"

It was the very fear she'd tried hard to conceal. The tips of her fingers numbed at the memory of her time in the gates. She suppressed a shiver of foreboding. "Then I'll pray to St. Christopher that I'll find someone like you when I'm again released."

Doc smiled, his even white teeth gleaming against his bronzed face. "And I'll beseech Ogun to keep you safe in your iron journey."

She hugged him close, squeezing her eyes closed to hold back the impending tears. When they parted, she hurried away before she lost her composure. She headed for her destiny at The Court of Two Sisters.

SHE REMEMBERED RUNNING this route in reverse on the day she'd arrived, frightened by what she understood now to be routine occurrences. The restaurant hallway stood just ahead on Rue Royale, the shutters open to encourage entrance.

Her heartbeat quickened, a sheen of perspiration blossomed on her face and arms, her throat dried to dust. She wasn't certain she could do this…but then a woman she suspected was a tourist pointed from across the street.

"Look! Quick! Take a picture!"

What better reminder that she didn't belong here. Madeline passed into the hallway and walked toward the iron gates and their identifying sign. *Touch them*—the sign implored—*and receive their charm.*

Goosebumps raised on her arms. Had Isabella known she would be trapped in these gates? After all, she'd been called "the charm teacher." She hadn't considered that possibility. The thought made her dizzy. What would the queen do once she returned?

She positioned herself in front of the gate. She'd worry about Isabella once she was secure in her own time. Perhaps she could return home to Paris and see her brothers and father again. Reaching with her left hand, she stopped just short of actually touching the metal. Would it matter that she wore a glove? Just in case, she pulled the glove off so her skin would touch the metal.

She closed her eyes and tried to disassociate from the impending chill. Think of good thoughts, happy thoughts, she instructed herself. Otherwise she worried she wouldn't be able to face the bone-numbing cold.

She thought of the professor, remembering his deep midnight eyes. He truly had been the key to direct her home, though he didn't know it.

"Adieu," she whispered a moment before her extended fingers touched the gate. She grabbed the iron frame and…

Nothing.

Not a sound. Not an explosion. Not even the anticipated freeze.

She opened her eyes. The sign naming the worked iron gates, the Charm Gates, that invited passers-by to touch them, remained on her right. She was still standing in the tiny hallway in hot, modern New Orleans.

She pulled off her other glove and stuffed both of them in the reticule tied to her wrist. Perhaps she needed more contact. She took a breath, steadied herself, then grabbed the iron bars with both hands. "Let me in," she pleaded.

Nothing. She continued to be trapped in the current time. Her portal seemed only to function in forward mode, not in reverse.

Tears burned her eyes. She rested her forehead against cool metal, hoping to gain some sense of her former home in the gates. How perverse that the very thing that had held her captive for well more than a century would be her only connection, her symbol of her former life.

She was stuck here. How could such a thing happen to her, an elevated diplomacy expert in the queen's court - *the Queen's Court!* She drew a deep breath to stop the sob in her throat, but it was to no avail. Her body shook while tears rolled down her cheeks. *What was she to do? What could she possibly do?*

A family of four stepped into the hallway but stopped at the sight of a grown woman dressed in period finery sobbing at the Charm Gates. How ridiculous she must appear. Maddie stepped back from the gates, slipped her hands into her gloves, then swabbed the tears from her cheeks.

"Are you okay, dear?" the woman asked.

"I'll be fine," she lied with a sad attempt at a charming smile. "Thank you for your concern."

With that, she lifted her chin and held her head high. She was a member of the queen's court, after all, a position of importance and responsibility, even if the queen, her family, and everything she'd ever known were buried an ocean away and over a century ago.

ST. JUDE THADDEUS, the patron saint of lost causes.

Madeline bowed her head and offered a prayer. If ever there existed a saint that could intercede in her unique situation, it would be St. Jude, for no one could be as lost as she.

After she'd left the restaurant, she'd wandered in search of a place to go. Admitting her failure to Doc in Jackson Square while surrounded by tourists held no appeal. She needed someplace quiet, someplace where she could think. A passing carriage, full of gawking tourists provided the answer. Louis had pointed out Our Lady of Guadalupe church with its international shrine to St. Jude when she'd ridden with him on that first day. They made that circuit so many times, she knew exactly how to find it. Walk toward that old crumbling cemetery, the one where the voodoo queen was buried. The church would be right by it. Perhaps at some level, she recognized even then that she'd eventually need Saint Jude's intervention.

In a small alcove to the left of the altar in the empty, softly lit chapel, she discovered the shrine. She used one of the provided sticks to transfer the flame from one candle to another placed around the statute of the namesake saint. The action caused her to think of Doc lighting candles to his loa, asking for their assistance. Perhaps their faiths were not so far apart, after all.

She offered the provided novena but paused when she came to the section to make her personal appeal.

"Help me find my way home," she said, knowing in her soul that this would be the all-encompassing request. Reliable shelter, nourishing food, acceptance of who she once was and perhaps remained, all this was embraced in that one word, *home*. She could deal with Queen Isabella once she returned. She understood now how trivial that disruption truly was. She would leave Madrid behind and move someplace where her skills were desired. "Show me the way," she whispered.

She finished the prayer, then added a few Hail Marys believing that they were appropriate for all circumstances.

"Excuse me, miss," a man's voice said to her right. "Do you have any change or anything so a veteran can get something to eat?"

Maddie looked up to see a man in dirty clothes who appeared to be in far more dire circumstances than herself. Life could be worse, she supposed. Searching the bottom of her reticule, her fingers located a few céntimose de reales coins from Spain.

"I have these." She placed the coins in his extended palm.

The man's face furrowed as he studied the copper pieces. "Are these real?"

"Oui." Maddie sighed. "I haven't much use for them in this time."

He squinted down at her. "In this time, miss? We don't have no other." His face brightened. "I bet these will be worth something to an antiques store. Might be enough for a meal. Thank you, miss." He shuffled off.

We don't have no other. The words resonated. Could it be true? Was she foolish wishing for return when there was the distinct possibility that return was impossible? Hadn't she learned that lesson already?

While it was true she was ill-equipped for this modern age she wasn't without resources. If her Spanish coins truly had worth as the man had indicated, perhaps her gown and accouterments had value as well? They certainly didn't serve any real purpose in this century. She was tired of being an object of amusement whenever she wore them.

And if her clothes were valuable, surely her mind would hold her in good stead as well. She was not uneducated. She was an intelligent diplomat, knowledgeable in multiple languages and, albeit outdated in the twenty-first century, many cultures. She'd been told that she had a way with people. Certainly that talent would prove useful no matter the year. She wasn't lost without means to survive. She had some assets and some new friends and—a vision of midnight blue eyes flashed in her mind—a position that provided compensation.

She rose from the kneeling pad with determination and a plan. She'd been placed in this century for purposes beyond her understanding, but not beyond her ability to thrive. She would learn. She would acclimate.

"Thank you," she said to the depiction of St. Jude. Someone had listened to her after all.

Chapter Ten

"WHY WON'T SHE come?"

"I don't know," Grant repeated for the tenth time.

Monday morning, and still no Madeline. Apparently, her kiss had been to say goodbye after all. He tried not to think of why. He picked up the knapsack his sister-in-law had purchased for Kimmy, the one with pastel ponies galloping across a pink background, and searched the toy-strewn room. "Did you pack your coloring books?"

"I don't want to go to your office. I want Maddie." Kim stood in the doorway of the bedroom, arms crossed defiantly. She'd draped sheets across furniture creating a child's labyrinth of fabric tunnels that she could duck into with no notice, making leaving more difficult. He didn't have time for this.

"Well, I want Maddie too," he grumbled. "But I guess she doesn't want us."

Kimmy's face collapsed and he immediately regretted his outburst.

"She said if you found out, you'd send her away," Kim shouted. "I hate you. I hate you."

"Found out?" He paused. "Found out what?" But his questions went unanswered as Kimmy ran from the room. A moment later he heard the lock click on the bathroom door. He hung his head and let out an impatient breath. What else could go wrong today?

He stood outside the bathroom. "It's okay Kimmy-bear. I miss her too. But if you can pack up your things, we can go to daddy's office, and I can have one of the secretaries sit with you while I teach my class. Afterward, we'll do something fun, okay?"

"You never do anything fun any more." Her sullen voice slipped under the door.

He froze, feeling as if a laser had carved out his heart with determined precision. In that instant he saw Kimmy as Beth had described, hurting and desperate for a friend. He wanted to hold her in his arms and reassure her that he was trying to make things better. Once he married Jennifer, they'd be a family again. She'd have a mother figure and he'd have someone who respected his work. But this conversation was for another time when he wasn't already late. They had to go.

The doorbell rang. Maddie! Thank God, she'd returned. He dashed down the steps, then paused at the closed front door just long enough to wipe the ridiculous smile from his face. It was a goodnight kiss. He knew it. He grabbed the door handle and jerked the door open to discover…

Jennifer in her self-proclaimed power suit. "This is not the best time for me, Grant."

"I'm sorry," Grant said. His nose registered her spicy cologne as she brushed by without waiting for an invitation. "I wouldn't have called if it hadn't been an emergency. When you didn't answer, I assumed you weren't coming."

"I have a client coming in this afternoon for some preliminary tax planning. I'm already behind, and" — she glanced about the room — "what happened to Madonna?"

"Do you mean Madeline?" An image of Madeline in the pop star's bustier sprang unbidden to his mind. Appreciation woke up the non-thinking sections of his anatomy.

"Where's Maddie?" Kimmy demanded, her head pressed against the spokes on the banister.

"I don't think she's coming, sweetheart," Grant yelled.

"I'm not your emergency babysitter, Grant," Jennifer lectured, one hand on her hip. "I don't have time to play nursemaid. You should really consider a boarding school for your daughter. That way we could both get on with our careers and—"

A knock on the doorframe interrupted. Both Grant and Jennifer turned to see Madeline standing on the porch, a bright red tote bag on her shoulder. Grant stared for a moment. She looked different, brighter somehow. He couldn't put his finger on the exact change, but something was definitely different.

"Thank God," Jennifer said before directing an irate glance toward Grant. "It's good that you brought her back for the day, but think about what I said. Boarding school would solve a host of problems. We'll talk later." She pressed a kiss to his cheek, then stormed off.

"Maddie! Maddie! Maddie!" Kimmy flew down the steps to hug her jean-clad leg. "I made a fort. Come see."

Grant gently pried his daughter loose. "Why don't you go upstairs and Maddie will be there in a minute. Daddy needs to talk to her before he goes to work."

"You'll stay, won't you, Maddie?" Kimmy pleaded. "You won't leave again without saying good-bye?"

She stooped to Kimmy's level. "I promise, mon petit. When that moment comes, I will find you."

They exchanged a hug, Kimmy's short arms reaching around Maddie's shoulders. The two obviously cared for each other, Grant observed. Kim had never showed this level of devotion to the earlier sitters. Then Kim broke away and raced upstairs laughing. "Bet you can't find me," she challenged from the top of the stairs.

Grant offered his hand to help Madeline stand. She placed her hand, so soft and fragile, in his. A scent of warm, fresh-baked bread reached his nose, causing his stomach to grumble in anticipation. She smelled like home, delectable comfort. She watched Kim's antics on the stairs while Grant absorbed everything about her like the parched earth would absorb a spring rain.

"Her mother's death came too quickly," Madeline said, her eyes on the stairs. "She never had a chance to say good-bye. Now Kimmy worries whenever someone close to her leaves without saying farewell."

She was asleep when we left so I could not bid her adieu. Tell her. It's important. Madeline's words slammed him with a broadside. He'd forgotten her request from Friday night and tried to ignore his daughter's resulting despondency. "I didn't know," he said.

And yet this woman had, this French enigma that had crashed into his life from God-knows-where. This stranger…she knew. His brow furrowed. "How did you…?"

"It's in her eyes," she replied, turning toward him. "A wariness. An uncertainty, then a flash of panic." She softly smiled. "We talked quite a bit last Friday. I got to know her better." She brushed the knees of her form-fitting jeans. He hadn't recalled seeing her wear those before, and he definitely would have remembered. "You wished to speak to me?"

He had so much to say. He wanted to tell her how that kiss had scrambled his thoughts all weekend. How Kimmy had talked of her non-stop, and how he anticipated her arrival this morning with tremendous expectation. Then when she didn't show…

But his voice dropped low in a husky demand, and he uttered the only words he could find. "You came back."

"You said you expected me on Monday morning." Her lashes lowered.

He couldn't see her eyes. He wanted to see her eyes. His gaze drifted to her lips, wishing to taste them again.

75

"I've returned," she said.

"I see." His fists clenched by his sides as he fought the strange desire to pull her close. Good grief, what was wrong with him? He'd been rendered incapable of saying the things he needed to say. He grasped her by the elbow and guided her back to the front porch. What he wanted to say, he didn't want Kim to overhear in case Madeline's answer wasn't what he hoped. "I need someone I can count on for this week and beyond. I have classes to teach and I need to work on my research, so I have to know, and I have to know now…will I be able to count on you?"

"As long as you need me, I shall be at your complete disposal," she said, glancing up at him through those long eyelashes.

His awakened non-thinking parts could have danced a jig, so powerful was her gaze. One disturbing issue still nagged at him.

"What about Richard?" he grumbled. "Will you be at his complete disposal as well?"

"Richard?" Her face scrunched as if confused.

"Richard Gaston, Professor of Art History." Her feigned confusion irritated him, though he wasn't sure why. "You and he had a lengthy conversation about art and wine Friday night. You seemed very engrossed."

"Oh yes. Professor Gaston." She brightened. "He's doing research on the Spanish Renaissance."

"You kissed me goodbye." Even to his ears, it sounded like an accusation. That was not what he originally intended to say.

"Is that not done?" Her smile dissolved. "I apologize if I offended you."

"No. You didn't offend me." Crap! He sounded like a crotchety old man, not at all how he had thought this conversation might go in the hundred times he'd mentally practiced it. "Employees don't normally kiss their employers." There, that should set the record straight.

"It won't happen again, I assure you." She worried her lower lip. "Do you want me to stay?"

"Yes. Yes." *Good Lord, yes!* He ushered her inside, then added in case she'd misinterpreted his enthusiasm, "Kimmy would be upset if you weren't here."

Her kilowatt smile returned. "As I would be if I didn't spend more time with her…and you."

"Me?" He couldn't help himself, he was drawn to those lips.

"You two go together like … peanut butter and jelly." She grinned.

"Hmm…" He already regretted his comment about employers and employees not kissing.

"It's a beautiful day," she said with a glance over her shoulder. "Kimberly and I might have a picnic. I brought real bread, not that card paper kind." She gestured toward the red tote bag on her arm. "Would you like to join us?"

He glanced at his watch. Damn, he needed to get going.

"I wish I could but I have a class to teach, then office hours…Mondays are not the best." He smiled softly. "You look different."

"Do you like it?" She smiled. "I bought modern clothes with your currency." She spun in a little pirouette in front of him. "I've spent the weekend trying to get used to wearing them."

And he would spend the entire morning trying to get her pert little backside out of his head. Damn! She looked good.

"I've got to go." He felt for his keys and his phone. "I almost forgot. Do you have a mobile?"

"A mobile?"

"A cell." He held up his own. "I'll need to put your number in my cell in case I have to call you, or if you need to get hold of me…say in an emergency?"

"No." Her smile dimmed. "I haven't … one of those."

Richard was right. She hadn't a cell phone.

"Not a problem," Grant said. "I'll pick one up on my way home. I'd feel better knowing you could call me at any time." He smiled to himself, thinking that now she'd have no excuse not to call and let him know if she would be late. He wouldn't panic if he knew she was merely detained. "Goodbye." He paused, wishing he had an excuse not to leave. "I'll be back this afternoon."

"Goodbye." She smiled. "And I promise I won't kiss you this time."

Crap.

Chapter Eleven

AS SOON AS the professor left, Madeline set her tote bag on the table and sought Kimberly.

"I'm hiding." Kimmy cried out the moment Maddie reached the bedroom. "You can't find me."

The child's hiding place was obvious, of course. A sheet draped over the back of a chair and the bed made a long narrow tent. Maddie played along, looking in the closet, the drawers, behind a crate of stuffed animals, all to the accompaniment of childish giggles. After she'd exhausted all possibilities except the tent, she sat on the bed. "Oh dear, I can't find Kimmy anywhere. Guess I'll have to go have a picnic all by myself."

Kimmy popped up like bread from the toaster. "Take me! Take me!"

"So I shall." Maddie crouched down. "Where shall we go?" Before Kim could answer, the doorbell rang. "Now who could that be?"

Maddie went downstairs with Kimmy on her heels. A strange woman waited on the porch.

"Aunt Beth!" Kim yelled with a whoop. She scuttled around Madeline's legs and raced for the door beating Maddie by several steps. She threw open the front door and hugged the attractive woman.

"Hello," she said, her hand outstretched. "You must be Jennifer, Grant's girlfriend."

Kimmy howled with laughter. "It's Maddie, not Jennifer."

"I'm Mameoiselle Madeline Charlebois," Maddie said. The stranger had a familiar appearance, though she didn't know why. "I watch Kimberly for Professor Stewart. And you are?"

"Beth Kincaid," she replied. "Kimberly's aunt. Grant sent a text earlier that he needed someone to watch Kimmy for the day. I couldn't reply at the time, but I thought I'd stop by and see if the need still existed."

"Would you like to come in?" Madeline asked, smiling. "Perhaps you'd care for something to drink?" Say no, she thought, hoping the aunt would go away much as Jennifer had. Madeline was still learning her way around modern appliances. She didn't need a stranger judging her, asking for explanations.

"Thank you," the aunt said, brightly. "I'd love to."

Merde!

Madeline led the way to the kitchen, though the woman was obviously familiar with the house. A tea kettle sat on the stove, the one beverage she knew she could handle…assuming she could locate the tea.

"How about a cup of coffee?" Aunt Beth asked. Perhaps Madeline hadn't concealed her panicked expression as much as she had hoped. The woman added, "Sit down. I'll take care of everything. This kitchen is as familiar as my own."

Merci, Mother Mary, she prayed.

"How long have you been watching Kim?" the aunt asked, fishing two mugs from a cabinet.

Kimmy answered before Madeline could.

"She read me a story in the hospital," Kimmy said with great enthusiasm.

"The hospital?" Though Aunt Beth's back was turned, Madeline heard her surprise.

"I met Kimmy by accident," Maddie explained. "Though I believe it was Kimmy who read me a book." She poked Kim in the ribs and earned a giggle in response. "When I went to Professor Stewart's speech last Thursday, he explained his need of someone to watch over her while he worked on his research."

The aunt fiddled with one of the machines on the counter and flipped a switch. She sat at the table while the smell of fresh coffee filled the kitchen.

"So you haven't been here long. That would explain your lack of familiarity with the house." She smiled.

Thank Heavens! Maddie nodded enthusiastically.

"So tell me. Have you met this Jennifer person?" A manicured brow arched.

"She's mean," Kimmy answered with a pout. "I don't like her. She told daddy to send me away."

"I'm sure she's not mean, mon petit," Madeline lightly scolded, though she personally thought *mean* was the least of Jennifer's attributes. "Perhaps you misunderstood her intentions."

Kim crossed her arms and slipped low in her chair. Aunt Beth rose and returned with a glass of milk and a plate of cookies for Kim. She set a mug of steaming black coffee in front of Madeline and took one for herself. Madeline tasted the dark brew, then reached for the sugar and cream.

"May I ask you a question," the aunt asked Madeline. "Do you speak Spanish?"

An odd question. "Si," she answered. "I speak many languages. Why do you ask?"

"You're the one," she said softly, with an assessing glance.

"I'm sorry," Madeline said, confused. "I'm the one what?"

The aunt smiled brightly. "I cleared my day thinking that Grant needed a sitter. I thought Kimberly and I could have a girl's day out…get our hair cut, our nails done. How about you join us? It'll be my treat. Your long hair is beautiful but it must be uncomfortable in New Orleans's heat. How about we all get a new look. What do you say?"

Madeline hesitated, uncertain about leaving the safety of the house. Beth was correct in her assessment. Indeed, Maddie's hair was thick and heavy in the humidity of New Orleans and the style outdated by at least a century. Kimberly trusted the woman…and she seemed kind. Having relied on her instincts for years as they related to strangers, she made her decision.

"Thank you, Beth Kincaid. I would love to join you in this."

THE NEXT DAY, Grant slipped his arms around the padded weights of the chest fly machine. Normally, he could count on Richard joining him at the Student Recreation Center for their twice-weekly workout, but he had his doubts that Richard would be up to it this morning. Grant had managed three repetitions on the machine when Richard walked toward him with a black and purple bruise squarely on his jaw.

"Man, I'm really sorry about that." Grant winced. "I don't know what got into me, I know I said it before but I'm really sorry."

Richard flopped on the bench of the lat pulldown next to him. "I don't know what got into you either. You asked me to come." He tenderly touched the bruised area. "Heck of a way to say thank you."

Grant reached into the pocket of his shorts and removed a folded piece of paper. "Maybe this will help." He tossed it over to Richard.

"What's this?" he asked, unfolding the square.

"Maddie's phone number." Grant continued his reps. "I bought her a phone so she could call me if she needed anything. I figured giving you her phone number is the least I could do." He hated the thought of

Richard actually using it. The man had a reputation, after all, and Maddie…Maddie had a vulnerable quality, perhaps she was a bit too trusting of strangers. As if to underscore his concern, a young co-ed passed by, wiggling her fingers at Richard. Grant frowned. "Mind you, I'm not saying you should use it."

Richard attempted to grin at the co-ed, but his leer turned into a wince, the result, no doubt, of that punch.

"Thanks." His hand covered the sensitive area. "This is almost worth the sock in the jaw…almost." The paper disappeared in his shorts pocket. "So I take it everything is working out with your new babysitter. Any more on the kissing front?"

"That….won't be repeated." Though Grant wondered yesterday evening when she left to catch the trolley if she might try again. Much to his dismay, his censure about inappropriate behavior must have made a difference. Richard should hit him in the jaw for his sheer stupidity. "She cut her hair."

"Why?" Richard scowled. "That long hair was a total turn on. I kept imagining running my hands through it."

Grant's fist clenched behind the weight. He'd imagined the same thing, especially after that kiss Friday night. "My sister-in-law took her to one of the salons at the mall yesterday. I guess when they let it all down, her hair reached past her waist."

Richard whistled through his teeth.

While Grant didn't admit it, he would have loved to have seen it. All that hair tumbling from her head like a waterfall. His groin stirred and he cleared his throat.

"She donated the excess to Locks of Love. It's still below her shoulders." And he still longed to wrap his hands in those silky strands. He paused to take a swig from his water bottle. Thinking of Madeline always turned his mouth to dust. "It's shorter around her face. Wispy, she calls it, and insists that now she looks thoroughly modern."

"Thoroughly modern." Richard let the weights settle with a clang. He leaned forward looking pensive. "That's the one thing that seemed out of place. She was so knowledgeable about artists from the masters to the nineteenth century, but she drew a complete blank on modern art."

"She draws a blank on a lot of modern developments," Grant admitted. "You would have thought I was handing her a death sentence when I suggested she get in the car so I could drive her home."

"Maybe she's seen you drive before," Richard teased.

"Ha - ha," Grant panned. "You ready to switch?"

At Richard's nod, they traded places.

"I know what you mean, though." Richard slid his arms behind the weights. "It's like she's been living on an island frozen in time and was just now released."

Grant snorted. "Frozen in time. You realize there's no such thing?"

"I know that science mentality of yours would never accept it, but the issue of being out-of-time fits. Have you asked her where she's from? You met her where? The Court of Two Sisters? What was she doing there? She's certainly not native to these parts."

"I've been working. You know how it is," Grant frowned, embarrassed that he hadn't raised any of those issues. He'd been mostly focused on finding someone to watch his daughter so he could write. "I haven't had a lot of time to ask a lot of questions."

"Understand that," Richard answered, facing a similar deadline in the Art History department. "I've been pushing it as well. I wish I had something in my research that would make a big splash. You know? Something that would really seal the deal." He settled back and pressed the weights. "Did I ever tell you about my notorious jewel thief of a relative?"

Grant shook his head.

"Ever since I was little, I've heard stories about this guy on my father's side. He operated in Europe stealing necklaces and bracelets. I sometimes wonder if those stories were part of the reason I declared my specialty in historical gems and jewelry."

Having heard similar stories in his own family, Grant nodded. "It's surprising the impact a story like that can have when you're young. Was he ever caught?"

"Not that I heard of. I thought I could do some research and publish a book on him. He would have been my big splash. But I couldn't find anything, not a word to verify his existence. My paper would have been all rumor and innuendo, and that wouldn't fly. So I changed my subject. Don't get me wrong. My compendium on Spanish art is good, but it's no home run for a named professorship."

"I know what you mean," Grant commiserated. "At least, you're working with factual history while my work is all theory. If I could prove just one theory in a big way, I'd be set."

Richard let his weights settle, then lifted a water bottle in a toast. "To finding our big splash."

Grant touched his plastic bottle to Richard's. "A big splash."

They both gulped the water.

"Are you and the ice queen going to the faculty dance?" Richard asked with a grin.

Crap! He'd forgotten about that dinner dance affair. He'd asked Jennifer weeks ago and she'd been anxious to go. For his part, he'd be content to stay home and work, but Jennifer had convinced him that it would be good politics to attend. He nodded. "You know she hates it when you call her that."

"That's the whole point." Richard smiled.

"How about you?" Grant asked. "Have you invited someone?" Given Richard's reputation, he imagined the man had a bevy of women waiting for the beckoning of his little finger.

Richard patted his shorts pocket where he'd placed Madeline's new phone number. His smile deepened. "I will shortly."

Chapter Twelve

"THE STORY LADY is at the library today. Can we go? Can we?"

Kimberly met Maddie at the door the moment she arrived at the professor's house.

"The library?" Maddie thought of the Biblioteca Nacional in Madrid, a huge structure that would never allow children access to the valuable works.

"We sit on the floor and the story lady reads to us," Kim explained. "Please?"

"We can't go far," Maddie said, though the thought of someone else reading the stories sounded attractive. "We'd have to walk."

"I've walked there lots and lots and lots of times." Kimmy jumped around her in a circle. "The other sitters took me all the time."

"Then it's decided," Maddie announced. "Why don't you gather rabbit for company, while I let your father know what we're about."

TICK...TICK...TICK...

Passing seconds audibly passed by on Grant's office clock, reminding him that he was losing his race against time. He glanced at his computer. Gravity's relationship to time theories and their corresponding component in the time tesseract failed to lure him into the deep focused zone of theory and exploration.

Instead, he considered the immediate zone of the kitchen and the French enigma downstairs. Why hadn't he asked any of those questions Richard had mentioned? Where did Madeline come from? Why was she in that hallway at The Court of Two Sisters? He'd only been unconscious for a moment or two. And why had she stepped into his life now to disrupt his thoughts when he had so many important things demanding his time?

A soft knock preceded the opening of his office door.

"Excusez-moi, professor," Madeline said. "I stopped at the bakery on my way. I thought you might enjoy one of the éclairs that I bought." She slipped a plate covered by a napkin on his desk. "Also Kimmy and I are leaving for the library. We may be a little late returning for lunch. Do not worry. We shall return. Au revoir."

"Wait," he interjected before she could close the door. "There's no need to rush off." He took her hand and pulled her back inside. "I was just thinking about you."

Damn, she looked good. Fresh, with a child-like curiosity to rival that of Kimmy. Perhaps that's the explanation for Kimmy's recent change from the young hellion she once was. The two were always thick as thieves, but he could see Maddie was winning her over. "I was just thinking that I don't really know much about you. I don't even know where you're from."

"But of course you do," she said, her eyes twinkling. "I'm from Paris."

"Yet, you spoke Spanish when we first met."

"Oui, I speak many languages. My father was a diplomat so I've lived in several countries with my family." She looked about his office momentarily then pointed toward the words on his computer screen. "Is that the book you are writing?"

"Yes. I've encountered a bit of writer's block, I'm afraid."

"But where is the paper? A book requires paper like this." She held her forefinger and thumb about an inch apart.

"I've probably cut at least that amount." He kicked the near empty can under his desk. "But all the pages are saved in the computer."

"I see," she said, staring at his computer configuration. Then she turned toward him, her eyes soft while a gentle smile played about her lips. "I'm certain that your book shall be wonderful. You are a very kind and brilliant man, one destined to great things. I, however, am destined to deliver Kimmy to the story lady at the library. She is most insistent. We shall see you later in the afternoon."

Just like that she was gone, and he was no further along in solving the Madeline enigma than he was his physics conundrum. How did she do that? One moment she was here and the next, gone. Yet she managed to leave him feeling lighter and more relaxed than before she arrived. And hungry, he thought, peeking under the napkin. He might not know enough about her to be able to answer Richard's questions, but he knew he liked having her around. Whatever the reason, her smile, her delight in small things, even her belief that his paper would be great, which it was far from becoming, was beginning to rub off on him. She brought in the sun and lightened his outlook.

He took a bite of the éclair, tasting the yummy custard. He ran his tongue around his lips to capture the sweet chocolate, and his gaze caught the framed picture of Jennifer in the back corner of his desk. Somehow, he didn't think she'd approve of Maddie's habit of bringing him something sweet in the morning. Without giving it much thought, he turned the picture to the wall and continued to enjoy the éclair.

WHILE NOT AS visually impressive as the Biblioteca Nacional, the Milton H. Latter Memorial Public Library held treasures all its own. At first, Maddie thought the building was a private residence, but Kimmy raced up the steps of the wide front porch with the familiarity of one well acquainted with the facility. She burst inside, then quietly joined the other children of a similar age where they sat on the floor.

While tempted to join Kimmy on the floor, Maddie noted that the other women sat on chairs around the outside edge of the circle like guardians. She joined what she suspected were the nurses and governesses. Interesting that they didn't wear the drab colors of their profession. However, given all the changes she'd noted in this society, uniforms barely rated a ripple.

An older woman with several books in her hand assumed the chair facing the children. Maddie lasted through the introductions, but as the first book was the familiar Velveteen Rabbit, a book she'd read to Kimmy a number of times, she thought to explore the library instead. Books of all descriptions were stacked on the shelves. Maddie removed several books about cooking, setting them on a table to read later. Now that she had Kimmy's assistance in how appliances worked, she could tackle something more advanced than peanut butter and jelly on toast.

In a different area of the library, she found small paper-covered books with the most interesting covers of men and women dressed in the sort of gowns with which she was most familiar. In fact, if she squinted her eyes, she could easily imagine herself on the cover of one book, with a man who looked remarkably like...the professor! She almost dropped the book to the floor. Her mind was playing tricks on her as the man on the cover looked nothing like Professor Stewart.

The book promised the reader a titillating love story. She sighed, realizing the possibilities in that area were limited. Who could love a discarded charm teacher who had no frame of reference for the modern world? Still a woman could live vicariously through a good work of fiction. She looked right and left, then added the book to her stack.

In yet another section she discovered a volume on history - history as it had occurred after 1853. Her hand shook as she removed the heavy tome. Like a gypsy's crystal ball, the book spoke of the past, which was actually the future of the world as she once knew it. Now she could discover what happened to Queen Isabella after she left. What happened to her brothers, to her father?

"Is there something I might assist you with?"

The stranger's voice so startled her that the book slipped from her hands and, this time, thumped to the wooden floor. Maddie stooped to recover it. "Pardonnez-moi," she said embarrassed. "I thought the books were available to read. I'll put this back."

"No need," the strange woman put a restraining hand on Maddie's arm. "You're welcome to peruse any book here. I thought you might be better served by a computer, unless of course, you want to manually search that history book."

"A computer?" The professor had used that term earlier. She'd asked Kimmy for an explanation of that and of the "block" the professor said he had. She had noted no visible cube of any sort in his office.

While Kimmy couldn't explain the block, she could describe the computer in terms of games to be played and movies to be watched, but Madeline suspected it was much more. She doubted the professor would have such a device in his office otherwise.

"We have several computers available. Let me show you."

The woman walked her to a small area of partitions. Each partition held a raised black screen with a black rectangular box in front. Raised buttons with letters haphazardly assigned sat on the rectangle. She touched the flat box. "And this is called…"

"A keyboard," the lady replied as she sat down. "You sign in with your library card."

"I don't have a library card," Maddie said, contemplating the use of "sign in." She could see no paper or signing implement in the vicinity. But then neither had she seen such implements on the professor's desk when he was "writing" his book. "Is it necessary?"

"I'll sign in with my name then we'll get you a library card before you leave." The woman pushed various letter boxes that left a series of spots on the screen. "What would you like to know?"

Maddie thought for a minute, skeptical that this box could provide the information she sought, but then she was discovering that boxes in this century often contained miracles. "I would like to know what happened to Queen Isabella II of Spain."

The woman tapped letters on the rectangle and a page full of references to the queen suddenly appeared.

"Let's check Wikipedia," she said. "It generally has a nice summary. You just move the mouse."

The woman had obviously never seen a rodent if she thought that oblong apparatus resembled one. However, she noted that moving the apparatus moved a pointer with remarkable qualities. An article with a picture of a much older Queen Isabella than the one she recalled appeared.

"There you go," the library woman said, vacating the seat. "Let me know if you have any questions."

Thus Madeline learned of the coup that had chased Isabella from the throne and forced her into exile just fifteen years after Madeline's departure. Hah! Wouldn't that be valuable information when she returned? But then, hadn't she learned a return was not possible? She supposed she hadn't completely accepted that she was trapped in this age.

The box provided amazing information and in a burst of curiosity, Maddie carefully tapped out her father's name. One would have thought that the keys would be placed in an alphabetical order, but that would be incorrect. Her progress was slow, but she managed.

She knew her father had occupied a very distinguished place in political affairs, thus she was not surprised to read the long list of his accomplishments and honors with pride. She read about his background, his life as a child, his marriage and his offspring…but there was no mention of her name. A chill rose gooseflesh on her arms. She stared at the screen, her two brothers were noted with a list of their accomplishments. The article mentioned her younger sister who died in childbirth. But there was no reference to Madeline.

She waved to the helpful woman for assistance. "This cannot be right," she said. "I don't see mention about …about the person I'm looking for."

"Did you search directly on that person's name?" the woman asked.

"No. I —" she slowly tapped each letter in her own name. A page of references appeared but none matched her name exactly. "What does this mean?" She asked, fighting to keep the panic out of her voice. "What does it mean when nothing matches."

"It just means that the individual hasn't accomplished anything of note yet." The librarian smiled. "Most people only get a mention if their obituary is in the paper. I'm sure your friend has time to develop an internet presence. Eventually, most do."

Madeline just stared. She had already *had* accomplishments. She'd been a counselor to the queen. The woman's reasoning did not explain why she wasn't mentioned in her father's article while her stillborn sister was. No. There was another explanation. There had to be another explanation.

Kimmy appeared with three books under her arm. "I want these, Maddie."

"Kimmy." She dropped her voice to a whisper. " I haven't any money to pay for books."

"It doesn't cost anything to check out the books." The helpful woman laughed. "They're free. That is, as long as you return them on time."

"Free?" Maddie smiled. Such a strange and wonderful concept!

"I can sign you up for a library card right here." The woman sat at the computer next to her and rapidly clicked the buttons.

Maddie tried to follow but the woman moved so fast. It was as if her fingers knew exactly where to go. "How do you do that?" Maddie asked.

The woman raised a brow in question.

"You move your fingers so fast."

"Oh," she laughed. "That's typing. I've been doing this so long, I don't even think about what my fingers are doing."

"Typing," Maddie repeated, committing the new word to memory, along with mouse, computer, screen, monitor and Wikipedia. Who knew a trip to the library for a storybook reading would prove so educational without even opening a book?

"Do you have some proof of identification," the lady asked. "A driver's license perhaps?"

"I don't drive." Maddie said. "Is that a problem?"

"I just wanted to use it for your address. You can give it to me and I'll type it in."

Maddie gave her the professor's address as that felt more like home than the apartment in which she slept. Within a few minutes she had her very own library card.

"You can check out any of the books in the library, the DVDs, or books on tape," the helpful woman said.

While Maddie wanted to ask what those things were, that could wait for another day. She quickly retrieved the history book, one of the intriguing fictional stories and a book on cooking. Adding Kimmy's books to hers, she returned to the counter to "check out" their choices with her new library card. She smiled down at Kimmy while they waited.

"I believe we'll be visiting the storybook lady much more frequently in the future."

FOR THE FIRST time, with the help of her library cookbook, Madeline made a truly edible dinner for Antoine and Cici. Even better, she felt in control of the outcome. As a reward that night, she opened the intriguing historical romance novel instead of the rather boring history tome. She had planned to read just a few pages, but before she realized how much time had passed, she'd read three-quarters of the romance of Edwina and Ashton.

Placing herself in Edwina's position, she felt Ashton's kiss with a stirring deep inside, almost as if she were experiencing Grant's kiss again. That memory made her sigh. If only he didn't belong to another woman.

"You shouldn't be reading that," Cici said, from the opposite bed.

The tips of Maddie's ears heated. "I was curious," she explained. "I realize the actions of the man and woman are scandalous, but —"

"That's not what I meant." Cici leaned over and opened a drawer in the bureau that stood between the beds. She removed a slim volume. "You shouldn't be reading about how things used to be. You should be reading about how things are." She tossed the book over to Maddie's bed.

The cover of a naked man and a naked woman clenched in a kiss suggested a high degree of carnality within. Maddie felt her entire face flame.

"Times have changed, girl. You need to be ready."

Doc walked in the bedroom. Madeline quickly hid the scandalous book under a blanket.

"So how're things with the professor?" he asked.

She wasn't sure what "things" he referred to, but she understood the expected response. "Things are fine."

"Has he kissed you yet?"

"That is a private matter." She hadn't mentioned that she'd initiated a kiss a week earlier.

"Ezulie said he was the key." His eyes twinkled.

"I realize that," she answered. But she was beginning to have her doubts.

"Which means you've got to be with him."

Why was he saying all this? She was trying her best. "Which is why

I'm watching his daughter," she replied, confused.

"I think Ezulie wants you to be closer than that." He nodded to Cici, who immediately left the room. Doc sat on the bed and took her hands in his. "You can't live here indefinitely, Maddie."

Shocked, she pulled her hands away. "You want me to leave?" Where would she go? Doc and his sister were the only ones who understood her difficulties with her abrupt arrival in this time. Who else would offer the support she needed?

"You've been with us for two weeks and we like having you here, but it's time to stand on your own two feet. You've found the professor and he will guide you home. Ezulie has promised. Legba says it's time to give another the assistance they need."

"You're casting me aside?" The reality made her panic. She wasn't ready to be on her own. Not yet.

"I'm saying you need to keep your eyes open for better opportunities." He smiled. "And I'm thinking I can help with this. Do you have your gris-gris bag?"

She removed the satchel of herbs from her bra. Was he doing this because she never fully accepted his voodoo philosophy?

He accepted her scarlet bag and pulled a small vial of liquid from his pocket. He allowed two drops of the liquid to fall on the gris-gris bag. "This will mark you as the benefactor."

Benefactor of what?

Reattaching the cap to the bottle, he handed that to her as well. "Put this in the professor's coffee in the morning. Perhaps he will be inspired to move in the proper direction."

"What is this?" She held up the bottle and peered at the contents. The liquid had a very faint green tint.

"Nothing that will harm him," Doc reassured her, then stood. "It will just open his mind to possibilities that he might otherwise ignore. Just see that he drinks it all."

The proper direction? What direction was he talking about? Flummoxed, she sniffed the gris-gris bag, but noting nothing out of the ordinary, slipped it back into her bra. When she looked up, Doc was gone.

Cici returned with her magazine in hand. She looked at the bottle in Maddie's hand and laughed. "You better read that book I gave you, Maddie-girl. The sooner the better. You should keep some of these with you as well."

She opened the drawer and tossed Maddie some foil packets.

"Why? What are these?"

"Read the book," Cici said. "Then you'll know."

Confused, Maddie glanced up at her. "Why are you doing this?"

"That bottle you're holding?" Cici nodded with her chin. "It's a love portion. It'll open your professor to Ezulie-Freda's charm, and you to his."

Chapter Thirteen

SHE HAD NO intention of putting anything in the professor's coffee.

Prayer, she understood. Beseeching the help of a deity was fine, but charms and potions were no more real than the threats of *le croque-mitaine*, the monster that stole naughty children from their beds. Those stories terrified her as a child. But they weren't real. It just wasn't *scientific*.

That thought caught her off-guard. When had she begun to concern herself with science? She smiled, knowing the answer. The professor was rubbing off on her.

She stopped at the bakery on her way to the catch the trolley. Both Kimmy and the professor seemed to relish the simple gift of a sweet cake or a hearty piece of good bread in the morning. Today, she'd purchased beignets, small bits of fried dough sprinkled heavily with powdered sugar. She slipped the pastry box into her tote bag where she'd placed Doc's love potion.

It wasn't that she didn't appreciate all that Doc Antoine had done for her. She honestly wouldn't have known where to begin if he hadn't allowed her to stay at his apartment and watch the speaking television box. He'd helped her find the professor. And while she did not necessarily believe in his voodoo religion, she still believed the professor would be the one to show her how to get home. Though, home seemed farther and farther away with each passing day. Two weeks had passed since she ran into the church on Jackson Square, yet she was no further along in finding her way back in time.

She arrived at the professor's house and, as the door was unlocked in anticipation of her arrival, she walked to the kitchen at the back of the house. Kimberly had arranged her rabbit and dolly around the breakfast table on pillows placed on top of the chairs. Five tiny place settings of a tea service had been set around the table.

"We're having a tea party!" Kimmy said. "Today is Rabbit's birthday."

"It's a good thing I stopped and picked up these treats for just such an auspicious occasion." She held up her tote bag then set it on an empty chair to unpack. Immediately, her bag sang loud musical notes.

She looked to Kim in a panic. "What did I do?"

"Answer your phone," the child replied with a giggle.

"My phone!" Maddie removed the pastry box and Doc's potion from the bag, so as to find the loud "cell" underneath.

"You push this button when someone calls you," Kimmy said, pointing of a button with an odd image inscribed. "And that one to call somebody." She handed the musical box to Maddie.

She pushed the answer button and put the box to her ear.

"Hello, Maddie?"

Her eyes widened when a voice spoke to her through the box. Miraculous! "This is Dr. Richard Gaston. Remember we met a little over a week ago when you watched Grant's daughter while he went out with Jennifer?"

"Yes, yes, I remember." Maddie walked toward the sliding door that led to the outside patio. Something about speaking to a disembodied male voice required privacy. "You were the one interested in the Spanish paintings at the Prado."

"Yes. That was me." His soft laughter felt particularly sensuous so close to her ear. "I know this is short notice but I was hoping you could accompany me to a faculty dance in a little over a week."

"A dance?" Her heart beat a little faster. "They still do that?"

"At Tulane, they do." He laughed again. "We could go with Grant and Jennifer, a sort of double date, if you will."

A dance! Finally, something she knew about!

"Yes. I believe I would enjoy that," she replied.

"Great. I'll make all the arrangements with Grant, and I'll see you a week from Friday. Hey, that's tomorrow!"

"I shall look forward to seeing you at that time," she said. She continued to listen but didn't hear anything else.

A dance! Could there be anything more magical? And while she would be accompanied by Professor Gaston, she would likely dance with Professor Stewart as well. She knew just where to look for a dress. Cici had taken her to a used clothing store where her limited currency could purchase more. Surely they would have a gown suitable for dancing. She might still need help with the accessories, as she wasn't certain what was expected in modern times. Cici wouldn't be interested in such things, but Beth…Beth was the perfect person to call.

Maddie studied the phone and pushed buttons until she found the one with people's names. Beth had put her phone number in Maddie's phone just in case. She pushed the button and in moments she was making plans with the professor's sister-in-law.

CHARMING THE PROFESSOR

GRANT'S STOMACH GROWLED. He checked the corner of his computer screen for the time. Maddie should be downstairs by now. Instantly, he envisioned her lively eyes and lovely smile, and a body that would whet any man's appetite. She'd be holding a plate with a cloth napkin neatly folded over the top …

Damn! There was no reason he had to stay and wait for her to climb the stairs. He grabbed his backpack filled with the day's lesson plans and headed downstairs.

"Daddy!" Kim enthusiastically greeted him. "Maddie brought beignets for my tea party!"

Her favorite animals were around the table, an open box of powdered sugar goodness sat in the middle. He reached in the box for a beignet and Kimmy hit him playfully on the leg.

"You can't do that." She giggled. "You have to use a napkin. Maddie says it's bad manners to stand and eat. I poured tea. Sit down. It's Rabbit's birthday."

Why not? He hadn't heard his daughter laugh so much since Carolyn had died. He could spare a few more minutes. He pulled out the chair, scored a beignet and sat down. "Happy Birthday, Rabbit. How old are you now?"

"He's three," Kimmy said, holding out the proper number of fingers.

Grant sucked the sugar from his fingers as he checked the kitchen for Maddie. She should be here enjoying this. "Where did Maddie go?"

"Her phone rang and she went outside. Have some tea, Daddy."

He lifted the tiny cup, draining the contents. Crap! It most likely was Richard. He said he'd call but Grant had hoped he'd forgotten. He hated to see Maddie become one of his conquests.

From where he sat he could see the patio and Maddie's blonde hair gleaming in the sunlight. She was prettier than any of the spring flowers. He took a bite of another beignet, but the sugar caught in his throat. His teacup was empty so he drank the one next to him.

"Daddy!" Kim frowned. "You drank Maddie's tea."

"What kind of tea is this?" he asked, suddenly realizing the taste was a little different.

"It was with the box." She shrugged.

"Must be some kind of vitamin water," he said, glancing at his watch. "Gotta go, Kimmy. Give your Dad a hug." As he squeezed his daughter tight, he reminded her about her swimming lesson that afternoon. "Don't forget to tell Maddie. I'll see you later. Love you."

"I love you too, Daddy."

He stopped and smiled. It had been a long time since he heard Kimmy say those words. Beth was right. He needed to be more involved in her life.

"A BALL? ARE you sure?"

"Yes," Maddie said. "There's to be a dinner and dancing." Her eyes closed in bliss. "I haven't danced in ages." More than a hundred years, in fact, but she couldn't say that.

Maddie interpreted silence from the box to mean that Beth doubted her abilities. "I'm an excellent dancer," she assured her.

"But do you care about him?" Beth asked.

This conversing through a box had its difficulties. Beth's voice had assumed a morose quality as if she were disappointed. But as Maddie couldn't actually see Beth's expression, she wasn't certain.

"Professor Gaston behaved as a gentleman even though we were alone in this residence," she said. "I was comfortable in his presence. He was entertaining and a scholar." Enumerating her feelings helped her realize she didn't feel the same way about Professor Gaston as she did about Professor. Stewart. But Professor Gaston had one important quality in his favor. Maddie hesitated, then added, "and he's not seeing another."

The phone box was quiet, but she felt it to be an accepting sort of quiet.

"I see," Beth said. "Grant asked me to babysit Kimmy tomorrow night while he went out with Jennifer. Why don't the three of us go shopping?"

"He asked you to babysit?"

"He thought you deserved the time off as you've been there all week."

"Oh," she said. "He was considerate." In truth, she would have stayed in a heartbeat. But now, she wouldn't have to.

The two finished discussing their plans. By the time Maddie returned to the kitchen, Kimmy had already found the beignets. Powdered sugar covered the counter. Maddie sat at the table and pretended to sip her tea.

"It's empty," Kim said. "Daddy drank it all."

"Your Daddy was here?" *Merde.* She'd missed him. "Never mind, I'll make more tea." Maddie took the small play teakettle to the sink to fill it with water. That's when she noticed the empty vial on the counter, the bottle Doc had given her last night.

"Kimmy, what happened to the contents of this bottle?" She held it up so Kimmy could see.

"That's the tea." Kim rolled her eyes. "Daddy drank it all."

HOURS LATER, MADELINE stared horrified at her reflection.

"I can't be seen like this," She exclaimed. "It's vulgar!"

"Vulgar? What's that?" Kimmy asked. "Everybody wears them at the pool. Let me see." She knocked on the closed door. "Let me in. Let me in."

Maddie opened the bathroom door. "Where did you find this?"

"It was in a box of old clothes in the attic. It's pretty."

"It's not decent." Maddie studied the mirror. The navy bath suit garment fit like a second skin and left nothing to the imagination. She'd tried to wear the modern bra under the suit, but that didn't work. The suit was cut low in the front exposing some of her cleavage, but worse than that, one could view the outline of the nipples of her breasts!

A ruffle at the bottom of the suit suggested a skirt, but no skirt would allow that much leg for public purview. She was practically naked!

"Why must I wear this?"

"Everyone wears one. Even me. See?" Kim spun around showing her even skimpier outfit that was little more than legless pants and a tiny top that might indicate where her breasts would eventually be when she grew them. "You have to wear a bathing suit. You'd look stupid if you didn't."

Stupid. She froze. That one word lodged dead center in the middle of her chest. An image of her father came unbidden to her mind. *You're a stupid little girl,* he'd lectured. *You'll never amount to anything. Not like your brothers. Stupid.* All because her tutor had given her father an unfavorable report about her grasp of Latin. For the rest of her life, she'd strived to prove that she wasn't stupid. But now, according to the library, he'd never know.

"Do I wear something over this?" She asked, praying the answer was yes.

"This was in the box, too." The little girl with wide eyes held up a long white shapeless jacket. "I think it belonged to my mother."

Her mother! The woman in the portrait downstairs. Surely the wife of the professor would not wear clothing that wasn't suitable for public display.

"In that case, I will be honored to wear these." She slipped the jacket overtop the bathing attire. While she appreciated the covering, her legs were still on display, much as they would be had she consented to wearing those short pants she'd seen on others. She steeled her spine and swallowed, hard. "As the proverb says, when a man goes to Rome…" she mumbled.

Kim held out a small pair of tinted glasses shaped like stars. "You should wear these too. Just like me." She held up a second pair with two hearts surrounded by frogs. Both woman slid the glasses over their noses and looked in the mirror.

"Now," Kimmy said. "We're all set!"

WHILE MADDIE EXPECTED they would walk toward the large river that bordered the city, Kimmy led her instead to a building bound by a tall fence only a few blocks away. Much like the roman bath she recalled from their stay in England, bright blue bodies of water had been created out of cement. Bare-chested men and boys, as well as sparsely attired women, some even more than herself, gathered around the water. Kimmy skipped off to a section where other children her own age waited. After her initial shock of seeing so many people wearing so little, Madeline located a chair near the young swimmers. No one seemed to notice her as she stretched a towel over her legs and ankles. Some of the women wore shorts in lieu of a bathing garment, while no one wore her uniquely styled eyewear. On the whole, however, she blended in with the crowd.

Kimmy frolicked in the water with other children. She ducked her head underwater and blew bubbles. All under the watchful gaze of another woman wearing a red colored second skin. Seeing the woman's garment made Maddie feel better about her own outfit. Still, she suspected Kimmy had an expectation that she wouldn't be able to fill. They would discuss that on their return to the house. In the meantime, she reached into her tote for Cici's book recommendation then opened to a dog-eared page with great anticipation.

"I'M HOME!"

Silence. Grant headed toward the kitchen which had become the nerve central for the family. *Family.* That word surprised him. After the loss of his wife, he never thought he'd feel part of a family again. Yet, that was precisely what they'd become.

"Anyone here?"

The unanswered question left a hollow, empty sensation. Just a few weeks ago, that same unfeeling emptiness would have been welcome. He'd have wrapped solitude around him like a blanket to close out the world and all its painful memories. Yet now he felt a loss in the silence. No joy. No sorrow. Just a sense that life should contain more.

Grant had begun to climb the steps when the front door opened allowing his two favorite females wrapped in gaily-colored towels entrance. Kimmy's swimming lesson, of course! He changed his direction to intercept the welcomed commotion. The house instantly felt right, full of laugher, chatter and ... legs!

"You've got legs!" he exclaimed.

And shapely legs they were, going straight up and up until they disappeared beneath her thin white cover-up. In spite of his efforts, his lips turned in a wolfish grin.

A deep pink rose on Maddie's face to the roots of her hair. "Of course, I have legs. But you were not to see them." She wrapped her towel around her waist like a bulky skirt.

"Why not?" Grant asked, disappointed. Now that she'd mentioned it, she always wore long skirts or jeans. Her legs had always been covered.

"Maddie can't swim," Kimmy moped. "The other moms got into the water with their kids but Maddie couldn't."

He glanced at Maddie's face and saw her soften. She'd heard it too. *The other moms.*

"I never learned," she said, by way of an apology.

"We could learn together." Kim sounded hopeful.

"They teach adults as well as children at the pool," Grant said. "It's never to late to learn."

"We'll see," she said. "I need to change."

Just as she walked toward the steps, Grant remembered that Maddie wouldn't have known about the swimming lesson when she arrived this morning. "Where did you find that bathing suit?" he asked, then squinted. "Is that my wife's?"

Madeline wouldn't meet his gaze. A cold awareness rippled down his back. "Have you been going through her things?" he accused.

"I found it in a box in the attic," Kimmy said, grasping his leg. "Don't be mad at Maddie. I told her she had to wear it."

He looked down at his daughter. He hadn't realized Kim knew where he'd stored Carolyn's clothes. "You went through that box?"

"Oui," Kimmy said. Her sad tone cut a swath into his heart.

"May I change, s'il vous plaît?" Maddie angled past him, walking toward the stairs. Before she stepped on the riser, she paused. "I'm sorry. I thought that these"— she ran her hand down the white jacket —

"might be your wife's, but I hadn't the necessary bathing garment. As I wore it for Kim, I didn't think she'd mind."

Kim followed her slowly up the stairs. His daughter's disapproving glare stabbed at his heart.

What a heel, he'd been. One minute he's enjoying the sound and the sight of Madeline then the next he's accusing her of snooping in the attic. He glanced at the lofty portrait of Carolyn that oversaw his moment of poor judgment. Would she have minded?

The portrait gave no answers. It was, after all, a lifeless portrait, not a real live breathing woman. A lonely heaviness settled about his shoulders, then slipped to his heart.

Chapter Fourteen

MADELINE RETURNED A few minutes later, dressed in her jeans and looking as she had this morning. In fact, now that Grant thought of it, her wardrobe had been very repetitive all week. Her clothes were always clean, but they hadn't varied to a great degree.

"I apologize," he said as she collected her things to leave for the day. "I shouldn't have accused you like that. I was just surprised, that's all."

"Professor." She turned toward him. "May I please be paid for the days I've worked this week."

She wanted to be paid? Now? Not Friday?

"If I pay you now, how will I know you'll be back tomorrow morning?"

Her brows lowered. "I promised I would be here. Is that not enough?"

He waited and eventually she softened.

"Professor Gaston invited me to a dance and I need to purchase a proper gown."

Crap. That *was* Richard on the phone this morning. He should have known. "In that case, I'll write a check."

"A check?"

Feeling proud of himself for helping her out this way, he removed the checkbook from a drawer and hastily scribbled numbers. He added extra to atone for his brutishness. "Deposit this in your checking account."

He ripped the paper from the pad. "Don't tell Jennifer but I didn't withhold anything for taxes. I may have to do that later, but I didn't have the time to figure all that out right now."

He smiled and extended what he felt was a generous sum for the week.

Madeline just stared. "What bank account? How am I to go to a bank?" She put her hands defiantly on her hips. "I need currency, professor, not a slip of paper. Antoine expects me to pay for my lodging and food and clothing and…."

Her face had turned a deep shade of red. She closed her eyes and took a breath. "I sold some of my belongings last week for currency, but I have nothing more to sell." Her eyes, shiny with unshed tears, gazed up at him. "I thought you'd pay me with those green bills. I can spend those, not this paper."

What the hell? He hadn't expected this! He foolishly thought she'd be grateful for his generosity, not awash in tears.

"Calm down," he said. "We'll fix this. If you can stay a little longer, I'll run to the bank and get cash. I just don't keep that kind of cash in the house." Hell, he'd go anywhere, do anything if he could return her to the joyful woman she'd been when she first walked into the house, before he screwed everything up.

"I can wait an hour longer." She bit her lower lip, her embarrassment evident in the pink of her cheeks.

"Antoine takes a portion of your pay?" He asked cautiously.

"I sleep in a room with his sister. They provided food and shelter when I arrived in this city and had neither. He takes half of everything I earn. Everyone contributes."

She wasn't proud of the arrangement, he could see that from the way she avoided looking at him. But more than that, she'd confirmed that she was not involved with the voodoo scam artist. *I sleep in a room with his sister.* Those words made him inexplicably happy.

"That's ridiculous," Grant said, barely able to contain his smile. "Why don't you stay here? We have a spare room. Stay here and keep the money you earn."

"I can stay?" Those luscious lips fell open.

"Of course." He grinned. "Actually, that would be far more convenient for me as well."

"Thank you!" Her body slammed into his in an unexpected but much appreciated hug.

His nerve endings sizzled every place her body pressed against him. His hands slowly drifted up and down her back, exploring the delicious curve of her spine. The perfume of her slipped into his bloodstream like a drug, he just couldn't get enough of the old-fashioned scent that whispered of moonlit nights and rose blossoms. His body ached and sopped up the sensation like a sponge. He hadn't held another like this for far too long.

But a niggling thought tapped against his foggy brain like a puzzle piece that just wouldn't fit. Something that Richard had observed. Something she had mentioned. Something that wasn't as it seemed.

MADDIE SLIPPED HER arms around his back, feeling the strength in his shoulders. She longed to tilt her head back and capture his lips, but she couldn't. He was taken. Someone else had claimed him.

As if he could read her mind, he set her back a step.

"I have to ask," he said, questions clouding his eyes. "Why don't you have a bank account? It just requires your social security number."

"Social security?" What was he talking about? "What is this social security?"

"Maddie." He drew back, his face troubled. "Are you illegal?"

Illegal! Even in her time, that word had serious connotations. "I've done nothing wrong," she said, panic building. "I abide by the law." At least, those laws with which she was familiar.

"You came into this country without permission, didn't you?" He nodded as if he'd already arrived at some conclusion.

Permission from whom? She hadn't any choice in her arrival to this place, to this time. "I have a job," she said, rebellious. "I take care of Kimberly."

"But how did you come here?" he asked, then quickly changed his demeanor. "Wait, I don't want to know. You probably just overstayed your visa. We've had students at Tulane who do that. They come for an education but stay for the Big Easy."

She didn't know what he was talking about, but his questions regarding her arrival were becoming increasingly difficult to avoid. She wanted to tell him the truth, that she wasn't from this time, but she knew him well enough that she could see Doc had been correct. Without definite proof, the professor would assume she was demented and ban her from the house. Now that Doc was planning to withdraw his offer of shelter, she needed the professor's assistance more than ever. But what if he was acting under the influence of the love potion? Would she be wrong to just accept his offer without telling him of the possible spell?

Fortunately, the professor resolved the issue without further explanation. He pulled his car keys from his pocket then paused at the door. "I'll pay you in cash from here out, but don't say anything about this to Jennifer. She'd call the authorities in a minute."

"But I—"

"Stop." He held up his hand. "Don't say another word. I'll get the cash. Once I'm back you can get your clothes or whatever else you have at Antoine's and we won't speak of it again."

She followed him out on the porch. "Professor Stewart. Wait!"

He turned at the bottom of the steps. "Was there something else?"

She didn't want to say anything. She gnawed at her lower lip. But maintaining silence was as good as lying, and she felt buried by lies already. She owed him honesty. So she told him about the "tea."

"YOU GAVE ME a what?" He stared at her while he processed what she'd just told him. "A love potion? Voodoo?" In a moment, he was back up the steps and in her face.

"I didn't really give it to you," she said. "You drank it by accident." She backed away from him, her eyes wide.

He wasn't going to let her off that easily. He advanced on her retreat. "How can I drink a love potion by accident?"

"It was in your teacup this morning. I didn't realize Kimmy had poured it."

"Kimmy!" He could feel his face heat with anger. "You're telling me you involved my daughter in your schemes. Was that what this is? Some sort of scam?"

"Scam? I don't even know what that means." Her eyebrows lifted, then her gaze narrowed slightly. He knew that look. Her sharp mind was analyzing something he'd said. He had to admit, she had that innocent act down pat.

"The potion was in a bottle in my bag," she said. "Kimmy found it when she got the box of beignets for Rabbit's birthday."

"Why did you have a love potion in your bag in the first place?" he asked. "If you weren't planning to use it on me, who was your intended target?"

Instantly, he knew. He remembered how she and Richard had been laughing and drinking wine, so companionable, so bewitched by each other. His eyes narrowed in accusation. "Richard Gaston."

"Professor Gaston?" Her face twisted as if repulsed. She pushed on his chest. "Non! Antoine gave me the potion to use on you. He says you need to open up to Ezulie-Freda."

"Ezulie-Freda?" He asked exasperated. "Who the hell is Ezulie-Freda?"

"One of the loa." She brushed off further explanation as if it wasn't important. "I had the bottle in my bag to appease Antoine. He wants me to find another place to stay, and he thought if I gave you the potion, you might provide accommodation." Her face softened. "And you did. That's why I thought you should know. I had planned to pour the potion down the sink, but Professor Gaston called on that cell box and I went outside to talk. You know the rest."

Her explanation was plausible. She was outside using the cell phone when he came down this morning. This morning...Damn! He'd been under the influence of that love potion all day. "How long does this potion last?"

"I don't know," she admitted. "Perhaps twenty-four hours, perhaps longer, perhaps it doesn't work at all." She tilted her head a little. "Do you feel differently?"

He looked down on her pert upturned nose and those sweet lips. Was it the love potion that made him want to kiss her? *No!* His scientific mind argued. There's no such thing as a love potion. Yet he couldn't deny the urge to slip his arms around her right here on the porch and taste those lips.

"Perhaps," he admitted. "When you hugged me a moment ago. I definitely felt something. I wanted to kiss you."

"You did?" Her voice practically squeaked. "I wished to kiss you, aussi."

She did? Her lips parted in invitation while her words drew him forward. He took a step. This time, she didn't back away.

"Then we should do it...for scientific purposes." He knew he was using a flimsy excuse to kiss her again, but he just couldn't help himself.

"Scientific?"

He nodded, and put his hands on her tiny waist. "Then we could compare this kiss to the one before and know if the love potion made a difference."

"Then we mus—"

He didn't let her finish. He captured her luscious French lips, sucking lightly on them, asking through his actions for her to let him inside. The moment she did, he was lost. He pulled her close and deepened the kiss. The more he took, the more he wanted. His body sprang to attention, recognizing his carnal interests. Before he realized what he was doing, he'd moved to her ear, then he kissed a path down her neck. His palm found the turgid nipple of her breast, a sign that she was not unaffected.

If it wasn't for the blast of a car horn, he wasn't certain what he would have done right there on the porch in open display. But the sound brought him back to reality and he slowly backed away.

"Was it different?" She asked, her chest rising and falling rapidly.

How could he tell her that this kiss was every bit as incredible and seductive as the last? Just as before, he wanted to feel her beneath him, straining to reach that pinnacle, that loss of control. He wanted to tell her of his desire, but he had other obligations. Another woman to whom he'd promised to be faithful.

"I...I have to get to the bank before it closes," he said, turning awkwardly. "We'll talk when I get back."

BUT THEY DIDN'T.

Shortly after he returned, Jennifer called. He retreated to his office and Maddie went to retrieve her few belongings from Doc's apartment. Doc praised Ezulie-Freda and Maddie for her progress. Cici watched her, then pulled her aside as she gathered her few possessions.

"Be careful, Maddie," she warned. "Sometimes a man chases the challenge and not the prize. Once they get what they want, they move on to something else."

"The professor isn't like that," Maddie said. "He still loves his wife even if she no longer walks this earth. He's not the type of man to toy with a woman like a cat and a mouse.

Cici looked at her skeptically. "Have you been reading that book I gave you?"

Maddie nodded. She'd read it twice in fact. She found the wild amorous adventures fascinating. Could such pleasures be found in the carnal acts described? Were couples truly that free in current times? Her cheeks heated with the thought.

The flush seemed to please Cici. She nodded. "Good. Then you know a woman needs to be self-sufficient, because the only person you can depend upon is yourself. The professor may be the key, but he's still a man."

SHE RETURNED TO the professor's residence that night. Kimmy was beyond pleased and helped her move into the extra bedroom.

Professor Stewart stayed behind his closed office door. They hadn't talked about that shared kiss. They both had much to consider as a result of Antoine's potion.

"What's this?" Kimmy asked, holding up a dried rooster foot.

Merde! Doc or Cici must have slipped that into her suitcase. "It's for good luck," Madeline improvised. "Some people keep a rabbit's foot but I have a rooster's foot."

Kimmy's face paled. She clutched her rabbit close to her chest. "People keep a rabbit's foot for good luck?"

"Not your rabbit, Kimmy." Madeline hugged her. "No one would ever take your rabbit's foot."

She slipped the rooster charm out of sight in a drawer. The love potion was bad enough. After the burning sage incident, she certainly didn't want the professor to see a dried up old rooster leg and slip into another rampage. The next time she saw Doc, she'd ask him what the foot meant. Till then she'd keep it hidden.

ON FRIDAY, MADDIE, Beth and Kimmy went shopping for the perfect dress for the Tulane dance. Finally, an activity with which Maddie was familiar, or so she thought. Certainly choosing a design or material was ageless, but she'd learned even the most fundamental of occurrences were different in this modern world. Lights illuminated with the flip of a switch, tiny squares played music without the benefit of an orchestra and, of course, the most miraculous box of all – the one no thicker than a crêpe that told stories and carried conversations without the benefit of actual people inside.

Professor Gaston had assured her real musicians, with their full range of instruments, would be present to play music for dancing. And dancing, Maddie knew, was eternal. Absolutely nothing could compare to gliding across a dance floor on the arms of a handsomely attired man, particularly a man with the broad shoulders and the titillating touch of Professor Stewart. Her heart sank a bit that he would be accompanying that woman of accounts, but she hoped Professor Stewart would offer her a turn about the floor. At least she'd have that memory to take with her once he discovered how to send her back home.

In her first days in this new age, Cici had recommended a store with gently used clothes. Cici had assured her the prices would be reasonable, though at the time, this meant little to Madeline who had no resources. Her shock came in viewing clothes hung on bars already assembled in various shapes and sizes. She recalled that the store also carried gowns. It was to this store that Madeline directed Beth with the hope of finding a gown for the dance that she, herself, could afford. Fortunately, she found a beautiful construction that only required a slight adjustment to the hem.

The dark lavender bodice fit tightly to the chest, allowing her shoulders to be bare. In her time, fashion dictated that puffy sleeves should be off the shoulder, creating the illusion of a gown about to fall off entirely. Of course they never did. A band of fabric on this gown had a similar effect, providing a low neckline with a hint of cleavage.

The skirt of a bolder color flared due to the stiff netting beneath pretty beaded lavender material. Yet the draping of the bodice swept in a diagonal below the hips, thus restraining the fullness of the skirt. The skirt was not nearly as wide as her old petticoat-buoyed skirts, but the long tight-fitting bodice created a silhouette that both Beth and Kimmy said was quite striking.

The storeowner had wearied of ever selling the gown and gave her a good price. The color, he explained, was from a past season. Madeline smiled. In 1853, purple dyes were so expensive, only royalty could afford them. Obviously, such matters were not a concern in the current century, but she almost wished Isabella could see her now.

The following week passed in a blur of library visits, cooking experiments, etiquette discussions and swimming lessons. When not teaching on campus, the professor closeted himself in his study to work on his research. She only saw him when she brought him a sweet that she'd made with Kim's help, and at meal times. In the evenings when he would quit work for the day, she would help Kimberly get ready for slumber, so the professor could read or tell stories to his daughter until her bedtime. Kimberly loved this special time with her father. The professor appeared relaxed and more patient. Madeline stood witness as the bond between father and daughter grew.

After Kimmy was settled in bed, she and Professor Stewart would go downstairs and share some wine. Sometimes they would talk about incidental things, sometimes they'd watch television together.

"Have you always wanted to be a scientist?" She asked one evening.

"I think so. Yes," he said after a moment. "I was always good at science in school. Continuing on in college just seemed natural."

"Was your father a scientist?" It seemed logical. Her father was a diplomat and thus steered her into a vocation he loved.

"No. My dad was a farmer from Ohio." He smiled. "I was more influenced by comic books...and there was this painting my Gram picked up that intrigued me. But that was a long time ago."

A long time ago... Her life in Madrid seemed like it was a long time ago, yet she could remember that last day with great clarity. Why was that?

She'd adapted quite well to this modern age. Her father, who had also lectured her on the need for self-sufficiency would be pleased. She was fluent with the language and understood the currency. She'd attempted the culinary staples of this time, the hot dog and the hamburger and something called french fries, which did not resemble anything she could recall in France. She'd cut her hair and exposed her legs to fit in with current fashion. She'd learned how to flip a switch to turn on lights, machines and even a computer, which she could use albeit awkwardly. She could push a lever to flush the most amazing invention, the toilet. She'd even ridden in a car without suffering a fiery death.

She still visited Doc and Louis on occasion. At Doc's request, she'd attended one of his gatherings, but she didn't tell the professor as she feared he wouldn't approve. She learned the rooster foot was a charm for protection. Doc couldn't be with her so he provided the next best thing. While she continued to seek comfort and advice from the Catholic saints of her upbringing, she could understand Doc's assertion that the voodoo loa were similar. Hadn't he beseeched Legba for assistance, while she did the same thing with St. Jude and the Virgin Mary? Hadn't both the loa and the saints responded?

A woman transplanted to an alien time was in no position to upset a powerful deity in either religion, so she went to Doc's gatherings and continued to wear the gris-gris sachet.

But it bothered her to no end that she could not find mention of any contribution by herself in history. She'd been raised to leave a mark, to make a difference. Her two brothers had done exactly that, but as far as the history records were concerned, she'd never been born. That thought kept her up at night.

Chapter Fifteen

THE TULANE DINNER-dance had always been a black tie affair. Grant had the tuxedo that he'd purchased years ago just for functions such as this dry cleaned. He'd eschewed the dinner-dance for years after Carolyn's untimely death, but Jennifer felt his appearance at these functions were important and necessary for his advancement in the Science department. He hadn't wanted to argue, so tonight he found his gold bowtie and suspenders that he only wore with the tux. For a moment, he imagined Carolyn tightening his tie, but the image morphed to a sweet blonde with a decided tilt to her nose. He took a deep breath, reminding himself Maddie was Richard's date, not his. He had career-driven, focused Jennifer.

Due to their close proximity, Richard had agreed to pick Jennifer up at her condominium and bring her to Grant's house. The four of them would then depart for the dance together. The double-date aspect hadn't pleased Jennifer, but she had agreed it was both simpler and more efficient this way. Jennifer and Richard, however, arrived before Maddie had finished her preparations for the evening.

Beth, the babysitter for the evening, arrived early to let Grant know that she approved of Maddie. Given her earlier ultimatum, Grant wasn't particularly concerned about Beth's blessing, but it was good to know that she liked Maddie as much as Kimberly. That meant two people important to him approved of Maddie.

"She's genuinely charming," Beth said. Then she addressed Richard. "You're one lucky guy."

"Don't I know it," he replied, much to Grant's annoyance. Make that three people.

Crap. Richard bought flowers for Maddie. Grant hadn't gotten anything for Jennifer, this being just another faculty dance, but he could see her disappointment. Next time, he told himself. Next time he'd spring for the flowers.

Beth served glasses of wine to Jennifer and Richard while they waited. Richard's bruise had faded to nothing. Grant was just about to ask Beth to see if Maddie was ready when she appeared at the top of the stairs.

He forgot to breathe.

He hadn't seen anyone so beautiful since Carolyn walked down the aisle in her wedding dress. Maddie wore a floor-length gown, a vision in lavender with a top that fit her through her impossibly tiny waist before draping off to one side over the full skirt. Her bare shoulders glistened, set off by the long white gloves he'd seen in old movies. Her blonde hair had been pulled back and tucked in some sort of bun, with long feminine coils down one side. A fancy comb was placed in front of the arrangement, almost as if she wore a crown.

"I told you she was a princess," Kimmy said by Maddie's side. Grant was speechless. He couldn't argue with that.

She started down the stairs.

"Quit gawking at my date," Richard said, bumping into him. "You look absolutely beautiful, Madeline. I'll be the envy of all the men present."

"Thank you, Richard," she smiled.

Grant's chest tightened. She'd never called him Grant, but she called his best friend by his first name. With him standing so close, Grant could see Richard's resulting grin.

As if Maddie read his thoughts, she turned those beautiful emerald green eyes Grant's way. "With so many professors present, I thought I'd best be less formal. Otherwise no one would know whom I was addressing. N'cest pas?"

Richard laughed. "I like the way my name sounds on your lips. You can call me Richard anytime."

"And Grant," He rushed to add. "You can call me Grant."

An awkward silence settled in the room as Maddie reached the bottom of the stairs. Neither he nor Richard thought to move out of her way. She was beautiful, stunning, arresting...

"Now that we've settled the issue of names, perhaps we should get going," Jennifer said, interrupting the moment.

"Right," Richard said, handing Maddie the flowers. "I bought these for you but they dull in comparison to your beauty."

"Merci," she murmured. "Perhaps Beth can put them in water?" She handed the flowers to Beth who observed the whole party from the kitchen-side of the landing.

"We should take Grant's car. My little roadster won't fit us all,"

Richard said.

"And that dress," Jennifer added with a snort.

Maddie turned toward Jennifer who stood in a simple black dress that ended at her knees. He noted concern cloud her eyes, dimming their earlier brightness. She glanced up at him, her voice hushed. "Is this gown not appropriate?"

"Don't listen to her," Grant said close to her ear, so Jennifer couldn't hear. A sensuous fragrance of roses and something exotic lifted from her neck and played havoc with his senses. Tempted to linger there, he closed his eyes to savor the scent, then gushed on his exhale, "My God, you are beautiful."

He drew back. The impish light returned to her eyes. "I'll save a waltz for you on my dance card if you'll favor me with a request."

"I'd be honored," he replied, before she took Richard's arm as escort.

He stood and watched, imaging her in his arms, until he thought about their recent exchange.

A dance card? What? Wait--

THE MOMENT SHE stepped through the door to the faculty dining room, she realized her mistake. The dinner-dance was not the festive ball she'd imagined. Instead of a string ensemble, five people played unusual instruments near a small empty dance floor. Where were the lilting violins? Or the rich deep notes of a cello? In her time, furniture would be removed from a ballroom to allow room for dancing and socializing, while dinner would be served in a separate room. Here, large tables with chairs filled the room as if to encourage people to be observers and not participants in the festivities. But worst of all, she quickly realized she had indeed dressed inappropriately.

While some woman wore long dresses, and a few wore dresses without sleeves, none of them wore a gown as elaborate as hers. She could feel heads turning her way and saw the whispering behind shielding hands. She was again the target of ridicule and imagined if they had those little flashing boxes that she'd encountered on her arrival in this time, they'd be firing in unison.

Stupid. She heard her father's mocking voice in their tittering. *Don't be stupid.*

There was nothing for her to do but shift back her shoulders and smile. Kimmy said she looked like a princess, which Kim insisted was better than a queen. Grant had said she looked beautiful. She would let their encouragement bolster her spirits as she faced the room of strangers.

Seating was assigned by department, so she and Richard separated from Grant and Jennifer. Richard escorted her around the room, introducing her to the various learned professors of one subject or another. In between those introductions, she'd search the room for Grant's tall, broad stature. It comforted her to know that he was in the room.

She particularly enjoyed meeting the language professors, the ones who taught French, Spanish and Italian. She could converse in their languages with ease which they found endearing. She met history professors and longed to prod them on their knowledge of the role of Queen Isabella's court in Napoleon III's Second Empire. But this was neither the time nor place. She made a mental note of their names and moved on.

"I've been admiring that comb in your hair," Richard said, in a quiet moment. "Is it an heirloom? Such an intricate pattern."

"It was a gift." She caught herself before she added *from the queen*. "It was to acknowledge my services."

"You must babysit for some impressive people," Richard observed. "Champagne?"

"Yes, please."

He wandered toward a crowded corner of the room. Maddie searched the room for Grant and found him alone at a table on the other side of the room. She made a path toward him.

His face brightened. "Hi there." He stood as she approached. "Are you enjoying the evening?"

"It is not as I expected," she admitted.

"No?" His eyebrows lifted. "What did you expect?"

"I thought there would be dancing," she said, trying to keep the whine from her voice. She had so looked forward to this evening, primarily for the opportunity to dance. Now that was not to be.

"There's dancing. Look." He pointed to a couple on the edge of the dance floor. "They're dancing."

The two people stood opposite each other clearly twelve inches between them. They both swayed but she would hardly call it dancing. She sighed, hating to think that this one timeless pastime was not so timeless after all.

"I remember when two people would hold each other in their arms and glide in tandem across a dance floor," she said. "There was music and magic and"—she caught his grin. Was he laughing at her? She frowned back—"great enjoyment."

"As in a waltz?" he teased.

"Yes, in a waltz." She smiled, remembering she'd invited him to dance one with her. The dance was apparently unknown in this time as no suitable music had been played. It was indeed a cultural loss. She glanced up. "Why aren't you dancing with Jennifer?"

His chin pointed across the room where Jennifer spoke to an older man in a dinner jacket without a swallowtail. It was another cultural loss, the lack of tails on a man's jacket.

"Dancing with me doesn't have the appeal of a stimulating discussion of the business climate in New Orleans." He pulled a peacock feather from the centerpiece and handed it to her. "It's just as well. I haven't danced since…" He stopped, took a sip of his drink, then looked at her with eyes that tried to hide the pain. "In a really long time."

"I'm sorry," she said softly, remembering how happy he'd looked with his wife in the life-like picture Kimmy kept next to her bed. She reached over and squeezed his hand, then pulled her hand back, wondering if the gesture was appropriate.

She looked to the tiny dance floor and remembered another ballroom bright with candlelight. "I've always thought of dancing as a celebration. The music would fill you and sweep you along as if on a cloud. The room would be full of people, but you're only aware of your partner, his scent, his eyes, his touch. If he didn't hold your hand, you might slip away with your gown swirling with the lilting phrasing of violins." She sighed with her memory.

Grant stood. "Come with me." He took her gloved hand in his and pulled her across the room toward the group of musicians. He left her to speak to the leader for a moment. She thought she saw something pass discreetly between Grant and the leader. A few minutes later, the strange instruments played a melody that had the rhythm of a waltz. The couple that had swayed together left the tiny wood floor, but she saw other older couples make their way toward the small space.

"Shall we?" Grant asked, slipping his hand lightly about her waist. The press of his fingers sparked her ribcage as if he'd flipped one of those magical switches. She glanced up into his lowered eyes and wondered if he had felt that tantalizing connection as well. She placed her gloved hand on his upper arm and together they moved with the music. The tiny band of musicians produced an amazing rendition. She felt as light as feather and, if not firmly tethered by Grant's strong arms, she was certain she'd be soaring among the chandeliers. Dancing in the manner to which she'd been born, she felt at home, only in a modern century with an extremely handsome and eloquent man.

The waltz ended too soon, and as the other couples clapped their hands in tribute, Grant just stood there watching her as if reluctant to let her go. She was content to stand in the circle of his arms forever.

"Thank you," she said. "You are a marvelous dancer."

"Carolyn and I took lessons before we were married." He smiled, but his mention of his deceased wife penetrated the magical aura that had embraced them. "I thought I'd be rusty—"

She stepped back, putting distance between them. "Such a lovely waltz. I don't recall hearing that melody before."

"You've not heard of the Blue Danube waltz?" His face crunched up in concern.

"That was the Blue Danube?" She improvised. "It's played a little differently in Europe, you know." She avoided his eyes by glancing to the side of the dance floor. Richard waited with two champagne flutes. Jennifer stepped forward saving Maddie from embarrassing herself further.

"I think you promised this dance to me," Jennifer smiled brightly. Her eyes narrowed as she glanced toward Maddie. "And all the rest."

Grant laughed. "You may not say that once I've trounced your toes. As I explained to Miss Charlebois, I'm a bit rusty." He winked at Maddie and raised her gloved fingers to his lips. "Thank you for the lovely waltz."

She curtsied by instinct, too late realizing that this was no longer the custom. Jennifer's glare was sharp enough to draw blood, and for a moment Maddie wished she had that rooster foot. As a slow song began, Madeline turned her back toward Jennifer then, in an act of faith, walked off the dance floor toward Richard.

He handed her the bubbling wine. "I think we'll sit this one out. The dance floor is no place for bloodshed. Come on." He took her hand. "There's someone else I'd like you to meet.

Chapter Sixteen

AFTER THE DANCE, Richard walked her to the front door while Jennifer and Grant lingered by the car.

"Thank you for inviting me," Maddie said as they stood on the porch. "I had a lovely time." She could see Jennifer and Grant over Richard's shoulder. While she couldn't hear what was said, Jennifer was clearly agitated.

"Thank you for agreeing to come," Richard said. "You made what would have been a boring evening far more enjoyable." He had a carnal smile, the sort Maddie had seen often on men seeking Queen Isabella's favor. "In fact," he said, "Perhaps we can do lunch later this week?"

"I cannot," Maddie quickly replied. Perhaps too quickly judging from the look in Richard's eyes. "My first priority is to watch Kimmy," she explained. "I couldn't leave her alone."

"Then bring her along," Richard said. "I have a book on Spanish art that you might enjoy. Bring her to my office and then the three of us will go out for lunch."

"Alright," she agreed hesitantly. Surely Richard would not make advances if a small child was present. "Where are your offices?"

Richard retrieved a small calling card from the inside pocket of his jacket. "How about Wednesday? About eleven-thirty?"

She nodded. Richard leaned forward and kissed her on the cheek. "Till Wednesday."

MADDIE WENT INSIDE. Beth handed her a glass of ice water then listened while Maddie told her about the evening, the peacock table decorations, and the people she'd met. Grant walked in before she'd finished.

"You lied to me," she told him.

His eyebrows shot straight up. "I did?"

"You said that my dress was appropriate and it clearly was not. Those other women were not similarly attired." He obviously had no sense of the importance of being appropriate for each occasion.

"I bet those other women will be dressed in similar gowns at the next Tulane faculty dinner-dance but none of them will look as lovely as you did this evening," he said.

She melted a bit inside.

"You should have seen the men watching you on Richard's arm as he made the rounds." His smile showed his appreciation in a way his words could not. Her pulse quickened under his gaze.

"And did you make the rounds with Jennifer?" Her words carried an accusatory tone. Immediately, her cheeks warmed.

He stared at her a moment, then retrieved a bottle of wine from the refrigerator. He poured himself a small glass.

"I'm sorry. I shouldn't have said that," she apologized, mentally blaming Cici's novel. Maddie had imagined Grant so often as the hero of that book she'd developed a certain jealousy where he was concerned.

"Jennifer spent time with the business department provost. She may have even secured a small teaching position." He glanced to Beth, "Did everything go okay here, tonight?"

"Of course, Kimmy was a dream," she replied. "Did you know that she's learning French? Where do you suppose that came from?"

Maddie blushed again at Grant's glance.

"Where indeed," he said. "Normally, I'd invite you to spend the night, but Maddie has moved into the spare room."

"That's okay. I'm anxious to get home." Beth said goodnight to them both, accepting a kiss of gratitude from her brother-in-law. She left the two of them alone in an awkward silence.

"You made a big impression on Richard. I think he likes you," Grant said.

"He wishes to have lunch next week."

"Oh?" He sipped his wine.

"He invited me to bring Kimmy so we wouldn't inconvenience you," she hurried to add.

"That's considerate." His lips tilted in a half smile, a smile that somehow wasn't. "Do you like him?"

"I...I don't think I know him very well." She didn't want to have this conversation. Not here. Not now. The professor might discover her vulnerabilities where he was concerned. That could only lead to trouble, yet she felt powerless to leave the room and this conversation behind. "He seems like a fine friend," she managed.

Grant considered this a moment, neither pleased nor displeased.

117

Just pensive. Then he looked down abruptly. "I'm going off to bed. You know where everything is. We can sort out the rest tomorrow. Good Night."

"Wait," Maddie called. He stopped then turned toward her. "Is everything all right? I thought Jennifer was...not happy."

"Jennifer and I had a disagreement, a spat."

"I'm so sorry," Maddie said. "She so wanted to file a joint return."

He looked at her strangely, a smile teasing the edge of his lips. "A joint return?"

"It's something she mentioned the night of your speech," she explained. "I'm not sure I understood what she meant, but she sounded so passionate about it."

Grant stared at her a moment, then shook his head, laughter in his eyes.

"I'll see you in the morning when we go to church." Maddie said, returning her glass to the sink. "What time is Mass?"

"Church?" His eyes widened.

"Tomorrow is Sunday," she said, surprised at his reaction. "I thought I'd go to church with you and Kimmy, if you will allow me to join you."

"But you believe in Voodoo. Why would you want to go to church?"

"I believe in the power of prayer and belief," Maddie said. "Antoine believes the same, just a deity with a different name." She cocked her head. "What do you believe?"

"I believe in the power of science," he stated with a tightening of his lips. "But a little prayer and belief never hurt. Tomorrow, the three of us will go to church. But I warn you it's another of those things at which I'm rusty." He smiled. "I'll see you about eight in the morning. Good night." He trudged up the steps.

"Good night," Maddie called quietly listening to the reassuring sound of his footsteps while wishing in her heart that it had been this professor that had been her escort.

GRANT WENT INTO his room and loosened his bow tie. She'd called it a cravat. Wasn't that some old word for those floppy ties men wore a hundred years ago? He shook his head. Maddie was nothing if not a lot of contradictions, sweetly packaged in that ball gown. Yeah, he knew it was overdone for the faculty dance, but Good Lord, the woman was delectable. And every blasted man in that room was ready to eat her up, even Dean Chen had an appreciative look in his eye. He could still remember the way her waist felt beneath his hand in that waltz. His groin remembered as well as it stirred to attention.

Calm down, he told himself. Maddie was off the table in terms of a relationship. He had Jennifer, after all. Wasn't she the type of woman he wanted? Practical, dedicated to work, no time for laughing for absolutely no reason. He could stay focused to his project with someone like that waiting for him at home. The burgeoning bulge in his pajamas disappeared.

But that waltz, that was another of those contradictions. How could she have not heard of the Blue Danube waltz? Even carousels played that music. Didn't they have carousels in France, or Spain, or wherever she came from? Damn. He remembered Richard scolding him for not asking her that very question. There was something else he said that resonated. It was as if she was from an island frozen in time. Was such a thing possible?

Well, now that she was staying at the house he'd have more time to ask questions. Questions of a personal nature.

The bathroom door closed with a click and water ran in the sink. Maddie was preparing for bed. He remembered Carolyn's routine when she...Stop! He couldn't think of Carolyn. She was gone.

But Maddie wasn't. It couldn't hurt to think about her. Just a little... No one would know if she slipped into his dreams. It wasn't cheating if he dreamt of the woman. Was it?

THE NEXT MORNING the three of them dutifully dressed, although Kimmy made her protest known, then drove the short distance to St. Mary's Assumption church. While Maddie made certain that she'd covered her head with the lace mantilla she'd purchased weeks earlier, she had to pin a lace doily to Kimmy's hair. The child apparently didn't own a hat. Maddie protested to the professor. How could any young girl grow to be an appropriately attired woman without the proper accessories?

Once they'd arrived at the church, she'd discovered her concerns were needless. Few women in these times bothered to cover their heads. She supposed the lack of covering did not affect the quality of the prayers. Kimberly quickly swiped the doily from her head, annoyance sprinkled across her face like freckles.

The service in the beautifully ornate church continued without incident...or Latin. Maddie bowed her head and prayed. She thanked the

119

Father for the professor and Kimmy. They had eased her transition into this world causing her to imagine life if she couldn't return...

Stop that! she scolded herself. She couldn't abandon her efforts to return to 1853, though in truth, the images of her family were less sharp in her mind. Why hadn't she thought to carry a remembrance of them with her? A miniature or a lock of hair, perhaps. The guilt associated with leaving them behind created an invisible immense burden, but lessened every day.

After the service, Grant took them out to lunch to the oddest place, a Chinese restaurant. Kimmy made a great show of placing her napkin on her lap before she and the professor attacked their meal with sticks. Maddie sat in shock at the uncivilized and primitive methods, yet others in the restaurant did the same. Tentatively, she tried to copy Kimmy's technique to snare a particularly slippery piece of chicken. Grant and Kimmy laughed openly at her failed attempts. She eventually had to request proper silverware else she'd never get a bite to eat, but was delighted with the flavorful food once a fork arrived.

"You've never had Chinese food before?" Grant asked.

"No," she blushed. "Obviously, this is a new experience."

He chewed his food and watched her carefully. "Where do you come from that they don't have Chinese?"

"Well," she stabbed a small piece of chicken and chewed it thoughtfully before answering. "I was born in Paris, but we traveled a great deal due to my father's profession. I've lived in London, Lisbon, and Madrid."

"And they didn't have Chinese?" Kimmy asked aghast.

"Perhaps they do now," Maddie smiled. "Many things have changed since I lived there." A true enough statement, that, but it hardly indicated the extent of the changes.

"What did your father do that caused you to travel?" Grant asked.

"My father was always involved in politics. I was raised to do the same, to leave a mark, make a difference." She thought of her position in Queen Isabella's court and wondered what her father would think of her now as a companion and housekeeper for a small child. All of her training in the culture of other nations and not a bit of it mattered, except...perhaps...

"Interesting." Grant nodded. "I wouldn't have thought you had a political bent. And yet here you are in New Orleans eating Chinese."

"I've been meaning to speak with you about an opportunity that has presented itself," she said hesitantly, not sure how he would react to her request.

"I'm listening."

"Some of the mothers at the library and at the swimming pool." Her cheeks heated just at the memory of that embarrassing presentation of flesh, "have asked that I teach their daughters some basic languages and etiquette."

"Etiquette?"

"They've noticed Kimmy's improved manners as those befitting a young lady." She beamed across the table at the child.

"Where do you propose to hold these classes?"

She saw the fleeting scowl and the rumble of irritation in his voice. He certainly wasn't overjoyed with her proposal. However, she'd faced similar circumstances before. She turned toward him.

"I thought we might utilize the house on those afternoons when you teach at the university. The children and I would never disturb your work. That is of the utmost importance."

He looked at her as if to speak, but said nothing. She knew she'd removed most of his objections.

"May I be excused?" Kimmy asked. "I'd like to feed the fish."

The pool of Koi near the entrance had attracted a small audience. Maddie heard children laughing there.

"No talking to strangers," Grant instructed. "And you'll come straight back when you're done."

Kimmy nodded. "Yes sir."

It was the "sir" that did it, Maddie thought with pride. Grant nodded and Kimmy bounded from her chair.

Grant watched her cross to the entrance. "I must admit she's a better behaved child now than she was before. I can see why those mothers took notice." He leaned toward her. "You are charging a fee for your services, correct?"

She concentrated on her food, uncertain how to express her misgivings at charging a fee. Her services had been offered to the queen for the prestige and for lodgings at the Palace. While the professor gave her paper currency at the end of every week, accepting that payment felt beneath her. Doc had taught her the necessity of money, but neglected to teach her how to handle the demeaning aspect of it all. "They have offered to pay, of course, but I'm not certain…"

"Jesus, Madeline. Jennifer would tell you that you should charge a fee that would include a provisions for taxes and retirement."

"Taxes? But I'm not paying…"

"Ssh," Grant interrupted. "Keep your voice down." He looked from side to side. "I'll help you set a payment schedule provided you don't hold the classes while I'm working." He looked at her sternly. "The distraction would be detrimental to my work."

"Yes, of course."

"I suppose having such a program would benefit Kimmy," he murmured. "Make her feel less alone with other children her age."

"I don't think she's been particularly lonely," Maddie said, hoping to alleviate the concern in his face.

"Not since you came." He smiled tightly. "But I remember before." He hesitated. "Do you have any brothers or sisters?"

"I have two brothers." She sipped her water. *Had* two brothers. She would never see them again. Not as long as she stayed here. "One holds a position in the armée de terre, and the other in the légion étrangère."

Both were gone now, dead and buried, with honors as her father would have wished, though medals seemed of little consequence now.

"How about you?" she asked, wishing to change the subject. "Do you have any brothers or sisters?"

"No." He grimaced, a quick affair. "My parents died when I was young," he continued. "They were shot. In the wrong place at the wrong time, the police said. My mother was pregnant, but they couldn't save the baby. So there's just me…and my grandmother."

Kimmy squirmed back into her chair.

"She's the one that raised me," Grant finished, then smiled in approval at Kimmy.

"Granny Stewart," Kimmy said enthusiastically. "Can we go see Granny Stewart? Pretty, pretty please?"

Grant reached over and rubbed her hair affectionately. The creases at the corners of his eyes deepened while his lips pulled into a wide smile of reawakening. Maddie smiled in response. Can one do that, she wondered, categorize smiles? Yet this one, she thought, was a long time coming.

"It's been a while," he said, pensively. "My wife used to make sure we visited her regularly, but I've been so wrapped up with this paper… Tell you what, Kimmy-bear. If you're really good this week and listen to Maddie so I can get my work done, then perhaps we'll go over for the weekend."

Kim cheered and Grant suggested that they should leave. He had plans for a new chapter this afternoon and it wouldn't get written in a restaurant. So they left for a blissful day of reading, playing quiet games and watching the moving-picture box. The day felt peaceful and normal. She could become accustomed to this.

Two days later, she managed to disrupt that easy sense of contentment.

Chapter Seventeen

"A DOG!" GRANT thundered, causing the small bundle of fur to cower behind Kimmy's legs. "You bought my daughter a dog!"

"I didn't buy her. She was free," Maddie said. "And she's only on loan. The puppy needn't be permanent."

Kimmy scooped the cocker spaniel puppy in her arms. "But we can keep her, can't we?" Her eyes shimmered as if on the verge of tears.

"Why don't you acquaint Praline with the backyard," Maddie urged, sending the child and canine out to the fenced enclosure. Once they had left, she turned toward Grant. "Mrs. Sibbritt's dog had puppies and she'd found a home for all of them except that little one. Mrs. Sibbritt is leaving to visit her grandchildren and she wanted the puppy to have a good home while she was gone."

"And how long is that to be?"

"Just a few weeks," Maddie replied. "If the puppy doesn't work out, she said she'd take her back and find another owner."

"Of course, taking the dog back will break my daughter's heart which is the last thing I want to do." He frowned. "Did you think of that?"

She looked into the yard. "Perhaps we won't have to take her back."

"But the distraction! How am I supposed to get anything done with a dog racing through the house?"

Madeline straightened. She was taking a stand. He'd come to know this stance of hers which spoke of a steel spine hidden beneath all that sweetness and charm.

"Kim and I will make certain that you are not inconvenienced or distracted by one little puppy. We will feed her, make certain she gets exercised, and clean up after her." She pointed out the window where Kim and the dog played. "Look at your daughter. She needs that little Spaniel more than that little puppy needs her. Perhaps you should be distracted if the distraction allows you to see your daughter's need for someone or something to love."

"Kimmy has you," he replied. Hadn't she noticed how much Kim adored her?

"I might not always be here."

His stomach flipped in free fall, as if racing downhill on a rollercoaster.

"Why not?" He'd just assumed…

"You have your life," she said evasively. "I may not always be a part of it." She turned away quickly. Was she hiding tears? Why would she leave him?

"Maddie." He wrapped his arms around her waist from behind. "Don't leave me. You're right. I've been too distracted to see what is evident to everyone else." He kissed her neck and glanced out the window over her shoulder. "Look at them."

Kimmy chased the sandy colored puppy around the yard, giggling and laughing all the while. When the puppy stopped running, she'd crouch down, her tail wagging so hard it shook her entire body. He had to admit it was a good fit.

He turned Maddie to face him then wiped her tears with his thumbs. "If I'm not careful I might fall in love with you, you know."

She looked up, her heart in her eyes. "You are?"

"Can't you tell? Of course it might be that love potion working." He laughed. "But ever since we kissed on the porch, I've suspected. The argument with Jennifer on Saturday was the final straw. We broke up."

"Oh Grant." Her eyes searched his face. "I'm so sorry."

"I'm not." He kissed her. He meant it to be a light kiss but as soon as she reciprocated, he took it deeper. He wanted her. His body responded. "Come with me," he said, taking her hand and tugging her toward the stairs.

"But Kimmy is outside." She glanced out the window. "We can't just leave her."

"The yard is enclosed. She'll be safe." Though in truth, he did feel a bit guilty about putting his needs before his daughter. "The gate is latched. We'll hear her if she needs us." He followed Maddie's gaze to the frolicking outside the window. "Look at her. She's happy as a clam. They both are."

Grant laughed, realizing he felt the same. It all came back to Maddie, making him want her all the more. They had this one moment for themselves and he meant to make the most of it. He leaned close to her ear. "Perhaps the dog is a good idea after all."

HE LED HER to his bedroom, closed the door, then kissed her again.

Mother Mary, she thought she would melt from the sheer pleasure, but then she soon learned this was only the beginning.

He slipped his hand inside her shirt and found her breast. As a scientist, he obviously knew the secret way of using his fingers to make her gasp with delight. He massaged her breast, activating stimulations that went straight to her womb. Mother Mary in Heaven! With a low growl, he pulled off her shirt and pushed up the bra so he could see what his fingers recognized.

"My God, you're beautiful."

She unhooked her bra, before she undid his shirt buttons. One could be liberated from modern clothing so easily. Soon they were both naked. She had thought she'd be embarrassed, as she had been in that second skin, the bathing suit, but this was different. This was Grant.

She swallowed hard then slipped her hand down his gorgeous chest to lightly grasp his manhood. She wasn't surprised it was hard or that it stood straight, eager to implant his seed. She'd read about this masculine reaction in Cici's book. What surprised her was how much she wanted him inside her. Her womb demanded with an urgent throbbing.

He bent and lifted her in his arms, carrying her to the bed. His lips took their turn at her breasts, his tongue making short work of tightening her nipples. My God, the things he was doing to her and she wanted to experience it all.

His finger slipped inside the surprisingly moist area between her legs. She resisted her immediate reaction to close her legs. *Relax!* She commanded her muscles, eager for the enlightenment his finger promised.

"Good Lord, you're so tight," he said.

"I'm a virgin," she said in between gasps.

His exploring finger stilled. "You're a what?"

"A virgin. This is my first time." In at least a hundred and fifty years, she could have added, but didn't. An explanation was necessary in case she did something wrong. She was obviously less experienced than the typical modern woman in this promiscuous society. "It's all right. I've read books," she reassured him. "Please don't stop!"

But he did. He retracted his finger and brought it slowly to her side.

"Madeline, I don't want to do anything that you're not ready for. Perhaps we should take this slow."

"No! I want you deep inside," she pleaded. "I want to thrash about on the bed, and taste your...cock? Did I say that right?" At his surprised nod, she continued. "I want to feel used and sated and content." She used every word she could remember from the novel. "And I want it all with you."

"Do you?" he said with his wonderful soft voice and sweet gentle smile. "Do you truly?"

"Oui."

He raised himself up on an elbow. "In that case, Madeline Charlebois, prepare for some thrashing." He kissed his way down to curls, and then spread her legs wide enough that his body fit between them.

She was about to remind him of the foil packets that she had in her tote bag. The couple in her novel used them every time they embarked in this physical activity. But she wasn't prepared for the professor's tongue swirling about her private parts. My God, the things that magical tongue could do. Sensation rippled clear to her breasts, building and building. She grasped hold of the blankets on either side of her while her hips rose to offer him more. Jesus, Joseph and Mary!

The sensation suddenly exploded sending waves of calm and complete lack of control throughout. One minute she was lost in the awe of the sensation, the next her body wanted more.

"Was that good?" He asked, though she could tell by the light in his eyes he already knew the answer.

Before she could answer, they heard the door open from the back yard and the click of puppy feet on the floor. "Maddie," Kimmy called. "Where are you?"

"I'll take care of this," Grant said, already off the bed and getting dressed. "We can talk about this later. Come down when you're ready." He gave her a look that made her know that they weren't finished. In fact, they'd barely begun.

She stretched out on his bed, hesitant to pull clothes over her tingling, sensitive body. If he could do that with his tongue, she couldn't wait until he demonstrated his talents with his ...penis. She was a modern woman now. She needed to use modern vocabulary.

HE DEALT WITH Kimmy's needs easily, then sent her back out to play. He hadn't worked all day, but it was impossible to keep a smile off

127

his face. She wanted him, just as much as he wanted her. He could envision much thrashing in their future, but she was a virgin? How could a woman who looked like that be a virgin at this stage of her life?

He was sure to find out the reason in time, but first he had something he needed to do. Grant quietly went into the dining room and took Carolyn's portrait from the wall. It just didn't seem right to have one woman's portrait in this prominent position while another woman occupied a more intimate one in his bed.

He gazed in the cold, unresponsive eyes of his wife one last time. "I think you'll be happier in Kimmy's room," he whispered, before taking the portrait upstairs.

Chapter Eighteen

"MADDIE, LOOK!" KIMMY stopped and pulled on her arm.

"What is it?" Maddie asked, her mind focused on other things, such as when she and Grant would finally consummate their building relationship. He worked late last night to make up for time lost in their more enjoyable afternoon pleasures. But as long as she stayed at the house, she knew it wouldn't be long.

They were walking about the Tulane Campus on their way to meet Professor Gaston as she had promised after the dance. She didn't particularly want to have lunch with him, but she couldn't think of a suitable excuse to turn him down. This would be like the countless meetings with dignitaries that she'd entertained at Isabella's court. She'd smile and be pleasant while she inquired as to the true purpose of their request to meet the queen.

Kimmy pointed at her feet. "Look at the leaves!"

Impressions of tree leaves lay frozen in the pavement. Some were on their side, some showed the deep impressions of their ribs just as if they'd fallen from overhead. Maddie looked up. Yes, a tree with that same shape of leaf arched above. How could the leaves from one tree make such a lasting pattern? She stooped amid the passing students to feel the rough edges of a leaf.

"It's like my hand," Kimmy said, standing next to her. "Mommy had me push my hand in cold gray stuff when I was little." She giggled. "They're leaf prints."

Maddie remembered the cast of a tiny hand hanging in the professor's office. Kimmy's handprint was frozen forever, as were these leaves. Even leaves whose only contribution was providing shade for a lingering student had made an impression in time, whereas she had not.

The computer said she'd never been born. But that couldn't be right, she reassured herself. She was standing right here.

"I want to go to McDonald's," Kim tugged on her arm. "You promised Uncle Richard would take us to McDonald's."

"I said he might," she corrected. "I made no promises." Standing again, she searched the surrounding buildings, looking for the address that matched his carte d'visite. "His office must be...over there."

She pointed toward a stone building with many semi-circular windows. They found the building and the address. She knocked on the partially open door that led to a small office.

"Come in, come in," Richard rose from his desk. "I was expecting you." He smiled at Kimmy. "Hey, shrimp!"

Like Grant's campus office, the place was cluttered with photographs and open books. Unlike Grant's office, she saw none of the interesting structures hanging from the ceiling, or tucked into the corners. There was no basket filled with those waxy chalk sticks or picture books. She tightened her hold on Kimmy's hand, this was not a proper place for a child.

"Give me a minute," Richard said. "After we spoke the other evening I thought you'd enjoy seeing a catalogue from the Prado." He disappeared into a closet. She could hear him shuffling materials. "I apologize for the mess," he yelled. "I'm in the process of writing a book on jewelry through the ages."

Papers and books, did these men do nothing else? Mattie glanced at some of the pictures strewn across his table.

"Why is she wearing a snake?" Kimmy pointed to a glossy picture, a "photograph" Mattie had learned it was called, which showed a woman wearing a bracelet of small figurines.

"It's symbolic," Mattie explained, pointing to each of the figurines. "The serpent stands for eternity, the anchor for hope, the cross for faith, and the heart for charity."

"And love," Kimmy said with a smile.

"And love," Mattie reaffirmed, thinking of Grant. They weren't able to finish what they had started the day before. She dressed to explore the pounding in Kimmy's room, and then Kim came up the stairs as well. One thing led to another and she and Grant weren't able to rendezvous. But she wasn't concerned. They had plenty of time now that she lived in the professor's house.

"Is she a queen?" Kimmy asked, moving on to a picture of a lady in an extravagant tiara. "She's wearing a crown."

"N'est pas," Maddie answered. "That's a diadem. Many rich women wore them to show their wealth. That one is made of pearls." A corner of her mouth lifted. "No queen would wear a crown of pearls." She shifted some of the photographs. "Now this is a picture of a real queen. This is Queen Victoria."

"But she's not wearing a crown," Kimmy pouted.

"This is her wedding portrait," Maddie explained. "She's wearing a wreath of orange blossoms instead."

Maddie remembered when Victoria married her Prince. Isabella had been so jealous. Victoria, everyone knew, had married for love. While Isabella had been forced to marry the Duke of Cadiz, a man, it was rumored, with perverse appetites.

"Now this"—Maddie pointed to a book opened to a portrait of a familiar face —"this is Queen Isabella II. See, she's wearing a crown." Of course she would, she thought to herself. Queen Isabella always wanted people to remember that *she* was the queen.

Her gaze drifted to Isabella's necklace. Her lips lifted in a smile while her voice lowered to just above a murmur. "I remember when she sat for that portrait."

"You *remember* when she sat for that portrait?" Richard repeated from inside the closet. "That was over a hundred years ago."

Merde! She'd forgotten he was so close. She should have noticed that the closet had become suspiciously quiet.

"Does he know the secret?" Kim asked in a loud whisper.

"I meant to say —" Maddie raised a finger to her lips in the hope that Kimmy would remain quiet "—I've heard rumors about the necklace Queen Isabella wore in that painting," she improvised. Please, please let him accept the ruse.

"Rumors?" Richard asked emerging from the closet. "About a necklace?"

"Yes," Maddie responded brightly, hoping to mitigate her inadvertent slip. "I believe they said the ruby was called the Moor's Tear."

"The Moor's Tear." Richard stood with his arms crossed in front of his chest. "I've not heard of that stone."

But he had. Maddie could see it in his eyes. So she lied, hoping that her silly story would prove she didn't know all that she did.

"It's the shape of the gem." She leaned close as if sharing a secret. "Amour means love in French. They say one of the queen's paramours gave her the jewelry."

"Who said?" he challenged.

"Can we *pleeeasse* go to McDonald's! I'm starving!" Kimmy said, tugging on Maddie's arm.

Maddie could have kissed her. She smiled sweetly at Richard.

131

"Perhaps we should go. I can get the catalogue another time." She turned with Kimmy to leave.

"Wait." Richard grabbed his jacket off the coat rack. "I promised to take you ladies to lunch. I thought we might do better than McDonald's but if that's what the shrimp wants, that's what the shrimp gets."

SHE WOULD HAVE preferred to go alone with Kimmy so as to avoid Richard's watchful eyes. She would have preferred to go someplace other than McDonald's as the food left much to be desired. But this was not to be an enjoyable lunch, so she sat quietly and ate fries.

Kimberly dashed off to play in some gaily-painted combination of tubes and ladders in the playroom, leaving Maddie and Richard alone on the other side of a soundproof window.

Richard leaned across the table toward her. "Madeline, I am intrigued by your knowledge of nineteenth century, especially as it relates to jewelry. How did that happen?"

Maddie avoided his eyes. "I don't know what do you mean?"

He smiled, tightly. "Where did you hear rumors about the Moor's Tear? Most people wouldn't even know what that is?"

"My mother told me the story of the Moor's Tear when I was a little girl," she improvised. "Perhaps they don't tell such stories in America."

"Did your mother ever tell you what happened to the necklace?"

She looked sharply at Richard. "What do you mean?"

"After Queen Isabella was deposed and fled the palace, the Moor's Tear disappeared."

"Then you *have* heard of the Moor's Tear." Her suspicions were confirmed.

"Of course I have." His eyes narrowed. "Who hasn't heard of the stone the first Queen Isabella used to finance Christopher Columbus's journey. There is speculation as to its ownership before the presentation to the second Queen Isabella. But the real mystery is what happened to it when the queen fled the palace."

"Queen Isabella was deposed?" Maddie pretended to be shocked, just as she'd been actually shocked when she read the account in the library. "Who succeeded her?"

Richard smiled with his lips closed and pushed a french fry around in ketchup. "I told Grant that you must have lived on a distant island where history stopped in the mid-nineteenth century. You know more about the past than you do the present." He popped the fry in his mouth.

"I know the present," she objected. "Microwave, internet, automobiles, blender, toaster —"

"You know, of course, the name of the current president."

That she did, as she'd been watching the evening news with Grant in the evenings. She responded with a great deal of pride.

"Very good." He smiled, selecting a french fry. "And, of course, you know this restaurant was named in honor of the previous president."

She wasn't sure about that, but it was a popular restaurant and from the trolley rides she knew this was just one of many McDonald's in the area so it must be an honored name. She nodded her head.

His lips tightened in a secretive smile.

"Kimmy said you had a secret. What's the secret, Madeline?"

"Children." She laughed, though she wasn't sure she'd fooled Richard. "Who knows what they mean." She looked through the glass searching for Kimmy. They needed to leave. Now.

"Even that gives you away. A normal person would have used the term 'kids' instead of the more archaic 'children.' " He settled back in his plastic chair. "Why do I get the sense that you're not of this time?"

She rose. "We have to go back. Kimmy has afternoon obligations. Thank you for the lunch but I think it's time to go."

He stood as well. "I'm not going to let this drop. You might as well tell me."

She whipped her head up to meet his gaze. "Not until I tell Grant."

The response surprised her. She hadn't meant to say that and she regretted it immediately, because she had admitted a secret existed. That was good as a confession. She hung her head.

"When will that be?" He fidgeted in his pockets for his keys. "I ask because I think you might be very important for my book on period jewelry and gemstones. You, my dear, may be my 'big splash' so, you see, I have something of a vested interest."

He rapped his knuckles on the partition catching Kimmy's glance. Crooking a finger, he motioned her to come. "In fact," he said. "Grant will find you valuable for his research as well." He turned toward her. "So when will you tell him?"

"Tonight," she said glumly. "I'll tell him tonight."

"Fine. I'll respect your wishes for now, but I'll expect a phone call from either you or Grant tomorrow." He placed his hands on her shoulders. "Relax. I'm doing you a favor. You'll feel much better once your secret is out in the open."

She doubted that.

GRANT STOOD AND stretched. He'd accomplished quite a bit since his return from teaching earlier in the day. He took a brief respite to eat some of Maddie's roasted chicken. She'd made amazing progress in her cooking skills since she'd been here. Kimmy appeared more helper than hindrance in the kitchen as well. The two were inseparable.

You should send her to boarding school. Jennifer's voice sounded in his head. Sitting across from them at the table this evening, he knew that would have been impossible. He should have realized Jennifer was the wrong woman for him the moment she made that suggestion. So many clues and he'd missed them all.

After dinner he'd returned to his work for a few hours, but now he was ready for a break. He left his office and almost collided with Maddie who moved out of his way effortlessly, even with a thick book balanced on her head.

"Careful Kimmy," she said. "Keep your chin parallel to the floor, your back straight."

He looked down the stairs and saw his precious daughter balancing a much lighter book on her head as she managed to come up the steps. Praline watched mournfully from the restraint that kept her in the kitchen. "And this is to…?"

"Teach her proper posture and deportment," Maddie answered without so much as a glance in his direction. Her mouth twitched making him cautious. Something felt off, a bit wrong. In fact, ever since he'd come home, Maddie had been acting odd.

"Isn't she a bit young to worry about deportment?" he asked.

"One is never too young to learn the basics," she said. "In time, she won't even think about her carriage. It will come naturally." But the book slipped off Maddie's head and crashed to the floor. "It's time to get ready for bed, Kimberly," she said, stooping to recover the book.

"Nooooo. Let me practice longer. I don't want to go to bed yet."

"Listen to your charm teacher," Grant added, hoping to be supportive.

Instead, Maddie spun around, staring at him in horror.

"What? What's wrong?" he asked, doing a mental step back to review his words. "What did I say?"

She lowered her eyes to the book in her hands. "I need to speak with you."

A cold sense of foreboding settled over him. He was right,

something was definitely wrong. He recalled how she spoke earlier about the possibility of leaving, but that was before they'd landed in bed.

"Someone has offered to pay you more to watch their children," he said, remembering that mere days ago she was approached by some mothers inquiring about her services. He should have known that she'd be in high demand. "How much did they offer?" he pressed. "I'll match it."

"Maddie's going away?" Kimmy rushed up the stairs, holding her book. "You can't go. You can't leave." Praline barked at the sudden commotion.

"N'est pas!" she replied to Grant, her eyes narrowed in accusation. She got down on one knee to talk to Kimmy face-to-face. For the life of him, he couldn't recall Jennifer ever making a similar effort.

"I'm not leaving." She kissed the top of Kimmy's head. "But I do need to speak with your father... alone. Could you prepare yourself for slumber without my assistance? I'll be in soon."

"Oui, Mamoiselle," Kimmy replied with a smile. She hugged Maddie so fiercely, Grant imagined it bordered on painful. Then she dashed down the hallway. Maddie watched her the entire way.

Grant moved his lips close to her ear. "Shall we talk downstairs? I can open some wine?"

"Oh," she turned toward him as if awakened from a deep sleep, then glanced at her hands. "On second thought, I really should tuck Kimmy in first. I'll join you shortly."

Something was definitely wrong. He heard it in her voice, saw it in her fleeting glance as if afraid to meet his eyes. Still, he'd let things play out her way. He went downstairs and selected a Chardonnay. He glanced upstairs with a yearning, wondering what could be wrong and how could he fix it. His cell rang.

It was Jennifer. Though they'd decided it was best to separate, she insisted they remain friends. So, as a friend, he answered her call.

She'd attended some tax seminar and was all hyped up on the IRS code. At one time, this was one of the qualities he'd enjoyed most about her. She demanded very little mental engagement on his part. She just wanted an audience and in this he had been happy to serve. He could just mumble at appropriate intervals while she rattled on. She engaged neither his brain nor his heart, which is what he had thought he wanted.

But after last night, he knew exactly what he wanted...needed actually. He wanted Maddie.

He tried to imagine his household without Maddie bringing him something sweet in the mornings with that mischievous twinkle in her eye, without her delightful French accent and unique perspective of society, without the many changes in her expressions. The woman wore her heart on her sleeve. One look at her face and you knew her thoughts – except today. Today, she was secretive, troubled.

"Grant, are you listening to me?"

"Of course," he lied. It was what Jennifer wanted to hear. His reassurance was enough for her to continue on her discourse, and for him to continue his wondering.

A mental vision of Maddie's face smiled before him. Her eyes sparkled like emeralds in sunlight at the least provocation. Sometimes he teased her just to see that sparkle, or to hear her laugh. Her laugh was so musical and infectious, it made him want her to always stay there …with him. Loving him. Loving Kimmy.

Oh crap! He was falling in love with her.

But that can't be! He'd sworn never to go down that road again. Never to care so deeply so as to risk devastating pain when the other person was yanked from this life.

He would not love her, could not love her. He should be grateful that she planned to leave now before he fell even more deeply in love with her.

"Grant, I'm not comfortable with Madeline living in your house," Jennifer said. "You'll talk to her about finding other arrangements, won't you?"

"I think she may have found them on her own," he said and hoped that was true.

Best to end this relationship before he'd sunk too deep.

He heard Jennifer murmur goodnight in his ear. He thought he responded in kind, but to he honest, he wasn't sure. His phone said "call ended" so perhaps she beat him to the punch.

Which was exactly what he would do with Maddie. He would suggest that she move on…tomorrow. Let her have tonight. Everything would be easier tomorrow.

He hoped…

"WHY ARE YOU so upset, Sugah?"

Maddie slipped into her room and held the phone box to her ear. Kimmy was in bed, but Maddie just needed some assurances before she went down to confront Grant with the truth.

"He had to find out sooner or later. He's the key, but he can't be opening no doors he don't know about."

"But I've no proof," Maddie protested. "He won't believe what I'm saying."

"Did you have proof for this other professor?"

"He figured out that I'm from the past based on something I said and should have known." The sly connard tricked her with that McDonald's question. "He doesn't know how I got here, just that I'm here."

"If one professor believes you, you'll find a way to convince the other. Just stay close and work with him. Trust Ezulie," he sais. "He's the key."

Doc clicked his phone off leaving Maddie in a quandary.

Stay close, he'd said. Which meant she couldn't exercise her immediate inclination to run away. But where could she go? She believed, as did Doc, that Grant was the one who could send her home, but she didn't know how he could do that, or how to prove to him where her home was.

He was waiting for her downstairs. She steeled her spine, said a quick prayer and went downstairs. Doc was right. Grant was bound to find out sooner or later, but she sure wished it would be later. Darn Richard with his threats!

Their talk never occurred. Grant was on the phone with Jennifer when she came down and after waiting a little while in another room, she decided to go to bed. Tomorrow would come soon enough, and with it, most likely, a call from Richard. Maybe Grant would believe Richard. Perhaps that was the best way for him to learn. Yes, she decided. He'd more likely believe a peer than if she were to tell him the truth. Then they could talk. Tomorrow. All would be revealed...tomorrow.

Chapter Nineteen

"DID SHE TELL you?"

Grant looked at Richard, wondering to which "she" he referred. The man had a grin on his face as if he'd just discovered gravity. Perhaps this wasn't his first glass of bourbon that afternoon. "Tell me what?"

"Madeline. Did she tell you where she's from, or to be more precise, when she's from?"

They met at a quiet off campus bar at Richard's request. Someplace they could talk, he'd said.

Grant ordered a beer then turned back to Richard. "You sound like a mad man. What are you talking about?"

"Madeline! You lucky bastard," Richard exclaimed. "She's the one. She's the big splash."

"The big splash?" He shook his head. "Maybe I should just leave you to your musings. This conversation makes no sense."

"Didn't she tell you? I can't wait to hear all the details myself, but I figure she's from sometime in the nineteenth century. It only makes sense."

Grant thought of Madeline's expression when she said she had to talk to him. Was that somehow connected to Richard's lunatic ravings?

"Frankly, I'm surprised you didn't nab her yourself," Richard continued. "I bet time travel would shake things up in the Physics Department."

Time Travel!

"Are you saying you think Madeline is from the nineteenth century and twitched her nose or something and ended up here?" Grant shook his head. "Are you crazy? That's impossible. How many bourbons have you had?"

"I don't know how she did it, that's your department. But I know she did it." Richard leaned close and dropped his voice. "She knows things - things that a normal person wouldn't know. Hell, things that have escaped current textbooks."

"What sort of things?" Grant asked dubiously.

"Think about it, Grant. Didn't we just a month or so ago talk about how she knows a lot about nineteenth century history but nothing about current day affairs? That's because she lived in the nineteenth century. I'm guessing she lived in nineteenth century Madrid. She mentioned she'd seen the art collections in the Prado the first time I met her."

And she spoke Spanish the first time they met and kept asking about Queen Isabella...

Grant shook his head. "Just because she's seen an art collection doesn't make her a time traveler."

"Are you not listening?" Richard grew agitated. "She knows things. She knew that the ruby in Queen Isabella's necklace is the Moor's Tear. It's not commonly known that this was the stone sold by the first Queen Isabella to finance the journey by Christopher Columbus. Nobody but extreme academicians knows that."

"Time travel is not possible," Grant insisted. No way was he going to concede that Madeline might be from the nineteenth century. The whole idea was preposterous.

"It's possible if you don't have a closed mind." Richard moved closer. "Look, if you don't want to believe - that's fine. But I think Madeline might know what happened to the Moor's Tear after Queen Isabella left the throne. And if she does?" He settled back in his chair. "I'm going to ask her to travel back in time with me."

Grant choked on his beer. "Travel back in time! What makes you think you can travel back in time?"

"She traveled forward. There has to be a way to travel back. We'll find it and once we do, I intend to travel back with her to get the necklace."

Grant sat back in his chair. "You're insane. You know that."

"Insanely brilliant." Richard's eyes grew wide with excitement. "This is what I've been waiting for. This will make me legendary in the department. You'll talk to her, won't you?"

"Talk to her? Of course, I'll talk to her," he grumbled. Time travel nonsense. He wasn't sure what she'd said to Richard, but whatever it was, he'd find out and explain that she couldn't string Richard along on some ridiculous theory. Nineteenth century...

A sudden thought rocked him. What had she been saying to Kim? Could Madeline have convinced Kimberly that she was from the nineteenth century? Was that the reason for all the talk of queens and castles?

He glanced over to see Richard's silly grin. "What? Wait - what did you want me to talk to Madeline about?"

"About taking me with her when she goes back home."

"MADELINE!" HE ROARED once he returned. "I need to talk to you."

The house was strangely quiet. No chattering in different languages, no bent heads in the kitchen over a cooking project, no little girls parading down the hall with books on their heads, no puppies nipping at heels. "Madeline?"

Silence.

What if she'd gone? What if Richard was right and she'd traveled back to the nineteenth century because her secret had been discovered? He felt a blow to his gut the likes he hadn't experienced since Carolyn had died. What if he never saw her again?

A cold chill slipped into his bones. He rushed upstairs needing to confirm either her absence or presence. He opened the closed door of her room and tugged open the bureau drawer to ensure that she hadn't cleaned it out.

Relief flooded him at the sight of folded whites and pastels. She was still here! He picked up a pair of panties on the top of the stack. Not much more than a froth of lace. Instantly, he was hard just imagining her wearing the "almost not there" panties, spread out on his bed, begging him to make her thrash.

He'd make her thrash all right. Just after they settled this time travel nonsense.

He put the panties back and was about to close the drawer, when he saw some dried old thing sticking out from the pile of lace and silk.

"What the…"

The dried rooster leg dangled from his fingertips. Voodoo. It had to be.

Just then Kimberly's laughter slipped through the bedroom window. With the rooster leg firmly in hand, he looked out to see Madeline and Kimmy, with grocery bags in their hands, just a house down. Praline trotted alongside on a leash. Grant rushed downstairs and out the front.

"Is it true?" he asked when they approached the porch. "Is it true what Richard said?"

Maddie stopped and gazed up at him. God, she was beautiful. Her expression shifted from light-hearted to somber. In that moment, Grant knew the answer.

"What is it?" Kim asked, looking from Maddie to Grant. "What's wrong?"

"Here, take this to the kitchen." Madeline shifted, putting a small bag in the girl's arms. "And let Praline loose in the yard. I think your father wishes to speak with me."

"But he looks angry," Kimberly said in a near whisper. "Why is he so mad?" She hesitated a moment. "And why does he have the rooster leg?"

That too! His daughter knew about the rooster leg! His eyes narrowed in accusation.

"I think," Maddie replied never taking her eyes off him, "he knows about our secret."

"*OUR* SECRET?" PRESSURE pounded at his temples. Heat flamed up his face. "You've been encouraging my daughter to keep secrets from me?"

"Just this one," Maddie admitted. "If I'd told you I was from 1853, you would have had me locked up"—she borrowed a term she'd heard on the Saturday cartoons — "in the looney bin."

"The looney bin!" He waved the rooster leg in the air. "Don't count your rooster legs, or chicken wings, or whatever this is." He tossed the leg in the front yard. *Good Riddance*! He shook his head. "You may end up in the looney bin yet...or I will."

Mrs. Nettles, the next door neighbor, stepped out on her porch. She squinted into the yard. "Is that you, Madeline?"

Madeline's expression transformed from serious to something light and airy. "Yes, it's me." She walked close to the neighbor's porch. "How are your grandchildren? I was just admiring this vine? What do you call it?"

"Oh, that's my passion fruit vine," the older woman tittered. Then she leaned towards Maddie and said something too low for him to hear. Maddie shook her head in response.

She was charming his neighbor, just as she charmed everyone around her. The old woman was probably sharing her gardening tips not realizing that the woman she addressed was from 1853. Good Lord, he slapped his head. Had she done the same to him? Had she used her beauty and charm to cloud his judgment?

Maddie waved goodbye to the woman next door, then pushed past him into the house. "There's too many ears out here," she said tightly.

He followed her inside.

"The loud voices scared her. I convinced her not to call the police," Maddie said. "If we keep our voices down, I promise to answer any question that you may have."

"Okay," He drew himself up and crossed his arms over his chest. "What imperial evidence do you have that you come from the past."

"None. I have no proof," she said. "If I had, I would have presented it to you immediately." Her face twisted. "You're a scientist, the sort of man that would have reacted to evidence. But I have none."

He scowled. While he really hadn't expected her to produce verifiable evidence, he had hoped she'd offer some sort of proof. "How did you get here?"

"You were there," she retorted, mirroring his crossed arms. "You tell me."

"What do you mean?" But he feared he knew exactly what she meant. He still remembered that first encounter when she was dressed like a tour guide and babbled in French and Spanish about a queen.

"I remember I was at a foundry in Madrid on a tour with Queen Isabella and there was an explosion." Her voice sounded serious and grave. "I remember that as clearly as if it were yesterday. But then the next thing I knew I was huddling in a hallway with a bundle of rags that turned out to be." Her gaze caught his. "You."

"A bundle of rags?" He lifted his brow. "That was a new suit!"

"You were not dressed in the manner of a gentleman of 1853." A slight smile teased the corner of her mouth. "At the time I hadn't realized I'd traveled to the future. Your clothing looked like rags to me. Then you woke up."

"I thought you were an angel," he said, remembering the lyrical sound of her voice and her sparkling green eyes that shone like twin emeralds.

Her face softened. "You did?"

"But then you slapped me."

"You were mumbling--speaking nonsense." She drew back. "The slap was for your own good."

"We'll see about that," he challenged.

"I recall the iron gates at the end of the hallway and a sign announcing that they were the 'charm gates.' All who touched them would receive their charm. Queen Isabella often referred to me as the 'charm teacher,' so I thought somehow…"

"You think she knew?" The idea astounded him. "She somehow knew you were imprisoned in the gates?" The idea was laughable, but Madeline was so serious.

"At the time, I didn't know what to think," she said. "I hadn't realized what had actually happened. But now…" She nodded slowly.

"You truly believe Queen Isabella would do something like that?" He repeated slowly. "Because that would require extreme cruelty."

She nodded again. "I'm not a scientist. I don't know how she did what she did, but I believe she was responsible."

He snorted. "Well, I *am* a scientist, and I say number one." He extended one finger. "What you're describing is impossible, and number two…" He threw up his hands in frustration. "It's simply impossible."

She started to walk away.

"Wait…" An idea occurred to him, like a puzzle piece that suddenly fit in place. "Is that why you're here? Did you come to me thinking I could somehow use science to send you back to your time? Because I'm telling you, it can't be done."

"Then how do you explain why I'm here in this modern age?" She squinted up at him. "Why now?"

He softened his voice, falling back on the only explanation that made sense. "Just because you have no memories of the time before you woke up in that hallway—"

"I have memories," she interrupted. "I have lots of memories, but they are all from the nineteenth century."

"You might *think* you have memories, but they could be from some sort of dream inspired by a television show," he explained. "What you really have is amnesia of the time before you woke up."

"Amnesia?" She fairly shouted.

"It's a loss of memory," he expounded. "Sometimes it's permanent but often it's temporary, resulting from some sort of traumatic head injury." Yes, amnesia would explain everything.

"I know what amnesia is," she snapped. "The word is the same in Spanish. I know it means someone is a shell of the person they had been. Is that what you think of me?"

"I don't know," he said. "I don't know much about you before you appeared in that hallway."

"And my gown? My clothes?" She bristled with irritation. "How do you explain that?"

"I think you were a tour guide, maybe coming to the restaurant for lunch," he said very calmly. "That same lightning bolt that threw me across the room must have impacted you as well. You developed amnesia and just assumed when you came to in that hallway that you had somehow miraculously traveled from the nineteenth century."

It was so simple really. Even as the words left his mouth he appreciated their elegance. Yes. That's probably what happened. You'd think she'd be pleased to have an explanation for the phenomenon they both had experienced. Well, *he* didn't experience any amnesia, but she should be pleased nevertheless. But she didn't look pleased. She looked...pissed.

"Look. I'm sorry," he said, moving toward her to wrap his arms around her. "I know that's not what you want to hear. We'll figure this out." He kissed the top of her head and squeezed her tight, hoping to lessen that steel rod that had taken residence in her spine.

"One thing I still don't understand," he said, lowering his gaze to shield his hurt. "Why did you trust Richard enough to share your secret with him? Why couldn't you just trust me?"

Chapter Twenty

HIS EYES SAID he'd been betrayed, when in reality, Madeline knew the opposite was true. He couldn't see past the mundane to the extraordinary. A heaviness settled in her heart. In that instant, she knew their relationship had changed.

"It's not because I didn't trust you." She turned from him to put items from the grocery sacks into the refrigerator.

"Yet, you didn't tell me that you thought you came from a different century. Me." He patted his chest. "The one who studies time."

She whirled on him.

"Have you forgotten that I came to see you the night of your speech?" she asked. "I was planning to tell you that night. But Antoine thought you wouldn't believe me."

"Geez…Antoine again?"

She ignored him. "Even so, I tried to tell you when you took me home that first night—"

"No you didn't," he accused. "I would have remembered that."

"But I did. I asked if it were possible for a person to come forward in time," she stated. "You made it clear that you believed it was not."

"I didn't realize you thought you had come forward," he protested. "I thought we were speaking in generalities."

She didn't reply. She just stared at him.

"As a man of science I admit I'm skeptical of the fantastical story you've told me," he admitted.

Her voice dropped, almost to a whisper. "That's exactly what I expected you to say."

"Madeline, that doesn't mean that I care less for you," he pleaded. "We've formed something special here. There's a reasonable explanation for all that you've told me. I'm sure of it."

She didn't respond. Her eyes burned. Tears brimmed her vision. She was afraid this would happen. As long as he didn't believe she was from the past, he wouldn't work to send her back. Doc said that he was the key, but she was beginning to suspect he was the lock preventing her return. He'd rather believe she'd incurred damage to her brain than the truth. But she knew better. "Kimmy believes me."

"You told Kimmy? Kimmy is a child."

"She taught me how to do things, use things. She was invaluable." Kimberly would always have a special place in her heart. Even if and when she returned to her time, she would never forget the rebellious child who was more angel than devil if only he would see. "I didn't intentionally tell Richard, he guessed because I knew something about a necklace. He *deduced*,"—her eyes flitted up to his—"That I was from that time period."

Unlike Grant who'd deduced that she'd suffered a brain injury.

She turned her back toward him. She felt alone. More alone than she'd ever felt before.

His hand stroked her hair, then traced the contours of her jaw. "I know that it is far more romantic to imagine that you're from another time," he said. "But I hope you can see the truth of what I say. People from the past simply do not walk the streets of New Orleans."

Merde! Her traitorous body responded to his touch. She turned around and buried her cheek against his shoulder so he wouldn't see her tears. His arms wrapped around her and hugged her close.

"You can tell Richard the truth tomorrow. I'll see about scheduling an MRI to see about damage to the brain."

These were not the tender words she'd hoped for. "An MRI?"

"It stands for magnetic resonance imaging and uses pulses of radio wave energy to look at your brain."

"My brain!" She felt the blood drain from her face. Her pulse rate increased. "You plan to look at my brain!"

"Not me," he said calmly. "A doctor would perform the procedure. It's a standard test. You won't come to any harm. We'll just go down to the hospital..."

"I won't go to a hospital." She backed away, shaking her head. "People that go to hospitals do not come back."

"You went to the hospital after our encounter at the Court of Two Sisters," he lightly challenged. "You look fine to me."

He knew! He knew she was there! "How did you—"

"I was in the hospital when I heard that a woman of your description was causing a ruckus." He smiled and she couldn't stop herself from smiling in response. She supposed she did cause a small ruckus that day.

"Look. The MRI isn't painful. The machine just passes over your head and makes a sound. You'd be awake the whole time."

He stepped toward her, but she moved back. He seemed so pleased with himself with his logical solutions. But she knew better.

"You honestly believe a machine will prove that I'm not from when I say?" she asked calmly.

"I'm certain of it." He hesitated a minute. "So tomorrow, you'll tell Richard the truth?"

"I'll tell him right now." She crossed to where her tote bag rested on the counter. She removed her cell box, tapped a few images on the device, another one of those modern day miracles, then strode toward the door to the patio. She placed the phone to her ear.

"Hello Richard? Oui, it is Madeline. Can you come to Professor Stewart's home to pick me up? I don't think I can stay here any longer."

Color rose in Grant's face. He stormed across the kitchen.

"Give me that phone!" He took the cell box from her hand and held it to his ear. "Richard, you don't have to come over here. Madeline will be just fine...Yes. She confirmed what you told me earlier...No. I don't believe she did. Why do you keep saying that? It's not a big splash if it's not true... Richard...Richard..." He looked at the cell box and shook his head. "He's coming over."

"I'll add a place for dinner," she said, fighting back tears. She'd begun to think of this as her home. She was safe here. "It won't take me long to pack."

He blocked her path when she tried to walk away. "I don't want you to leave," he said, his eyes big, dark and luminous.

She dropped her gaze to her feet. "This is not your decision."

"Kimmy doesn't want you to leave."

That gave her pause. She looked out into the yard where Kimmy played with the puppy.

"Look," Grant said. "I didn't mean to insult you. I was surprised to hear of Richard's 'discovery.' I just don't understand how something like this could happen. I'll need a few days to make sense of it all. Can you give me that? A few days to think this over?"

She glanced up, sad, disbelieving. "Do you think a few days will matter?"

"Maybe not," he said. "But we have to try, don't we?"

Yes. She wanted to answer. Yes. She wanted him to believe her. Yes! Yes! She wanted him to need her. She wanted him to want her. But she said none of these things because it all came down to his not trusting her.

"Madeline," he continued. "You're important to me. You're so much more than a babysitter or a housekeeper. I can't just let you go."

"Have you told Jennifer that?" It may have been mean-spirited, but she knew it was Jennifer's call the other night that had interrupted their earlier conversation.

"Yes. I have."

That caught her by surprise. She glanced up, a mistake as she caught the vulnerability in his eyes. A knot formed in her throat.

"Look. I called my grandmother this morning and asked if we could visit this weekend. Come with Kimmy and me. I'm sure my grandmother would love to meet you. The trip will give us some time to decide where to go from here."

"Aren't you afraid of exposing your grand-mère to a woman with a damaged brain?" She made what she hoped might be a gruesome face. "I might kill you all in your sleep. That's what crazy people do." She knew that was uncalled for, a "cheap shot" as she'd heard it described, but she needed to hang on to her anger or else she'd melt into tears right in front of him.

"There are many types of brain damage, many of which are mild."

He was smiling. Not that she looked to see his face. That would have meant losing that tiny sliver of control that she desperately needed. No. She heard his gentle humor in his voice, and it was almost as deadly.

"I think if you intended to murder us in our sleep that would have happened a while ago," he said. "I can't imagine a kinder, sweeter, more mentally stable person than you." His arms slipped around her waist from the back. He kissed her neck, sending tremors down her spine. "I have no fears regarding your presence, now or in the future."

Merde. She couldn't hold back the tears. They flowed down her cheeks, salting the water she'd boiled for spaghetti. She turned in his arms and pressed her cheek to his chest.

"Stay with me, Madeline," he pleaded. "Don't leave me in darkness again."

SHE MET RICHARD at the door when he arrived. He took one look at her face. "I'm too late, aren't I?"

"I told him I would stay a little bit longer. We're to visit his grand-mère and then I shall have to decide what I'm going to do."

"He doesn't believe you?"

"He thinks I have an injury and wants to have pictures taken of my brain."

"If you decide to leave him, you can always come stay with me," Richard said hopefully.

"Thank you for the offer," she replied with a soft smile. Many women would appreciate this professor's cavalier charm, but she wasn't one of them. Her heart had chosen another, and that one believed her to be damaged. "I had hoped Professor Stewart would help me find my way home, but if that's not to be then I shall need to make my own way in this century. I'll have to find my own place to stay." The thought depressed her but she could see no alternative.

"But we'll still talk, right?" Richard insisted. "There's so much I could learn from just listening to you talk about the days you spent with Queen Isabella. In fact, we could start right now."

"No," she said, holding him back. "I can not talk right now and certainly not here. Let's wait till the professor and I return from this trip and then I'll tell you all you want to know."

Chapter Twenty-One

THE NEXT MORNING, Grant, Madeline and Kimberly left for Mississippi to visit Grant's grand-mère. The trip took three hours of uncomfortable silence. Not silence in the sense of nothing spoken. No. More of silence in the sense that nothing meaningful was said.

The puppy stayed in the backseat with Kimmy giving her a thorough face wash every few minutes. Grant continued his refusal to accept that time travel was possible while Madeline no longer needed to hide her origins. She should feel happy and relieved about that consequence, but she felt neither. This was not how she envisioned her revelation being received. She'd lost her confidence that Grant was the magic key to solving her mysterious leap in time. She felt disillusioned and somehow cheated.

Unlike Richard, Maddie wasn't as convinced that returning to her former time was possible. While in her mind, it was inconceivable that a time leap could only occur in one direction, she wasn't certain that she even wanted to return if she could. Living conditions in this century, while not as luxurious as the palace, were truly better. There had been so many new inventions, new discoveries. She was endlessly confronted with gadgets to make her life easier, less demanding. She'd learned of fireless heat, candle-less lights that turned on with a switch, communication boxes that worked on magic, libraries that hadn't a need for books, music that didn't require an instrument, endless fascinating visual stories that played on a television box, less restrictive clothing…the list went on and on.

Women, in particular, had a great deal more freedom in this century. She saw on the television that women held high positions in all areas of government, business, and social programs. She saw first hand the number of women attending Tulane University, studying in all fields. If she stayed in this time, perhaps she could join them. How exciting that would be!

And she had discovered the joy to be had with a man, not that she had fully experienced all that was contained in Cici's novel. Her cheeks warmed just thinking of the intimacies she'd shared with Grant. No. She wasn't at all in a hurry to rush back to her former life, but she was adamant that it be her decision whether to return or not, and not the decision of anyone else.

So they rode in the car, past rivers and woods and small towns, each of them deep in their respective thoughts. Kimberly played with the puppy until they both fell asleep in the back. Maddie considered what would happen if this tension continued between herself and Grant. Perhaps it was time she made her own way away from the professor. That thought depressed her, but she couldn't live with this underlying conflict.

MISTY RAIN FOLLOWED them throughout the trip, dampening both the conversation and the scenery. His own depressing thoughts had difficulty escaping the thought that Madeline had mental issues concerning this time travel business. He hoped the MRI would not show indications of a brain tumor, but that was the only explanation he could imagine for her fanciful imaginings. The worry that he might lose yet another woman who meant so much to him and Kimmy combined with the depressing rain to set a dismal note for the weekend.

He turned up the dirt lane, now mud, to the grand front porch of the stately mansion that had been in his family for generations. Confronted with the evident property neglect, Grant vowed to return later to put in some needed sweat-equity. The columns required painting, some shutters needed replacement, and the piece of plywood in the attic window suggested at least one window needed repair. He'd been gone too long, and in his absence, time and weather had taken their toll.

Lucy, his grandmother's caregiver and longtime companion, opened the door and waved them inside.

"The young master is home," she exclaimed as they left the car. Grant gave her a hug and introduced Madeline. "Your grandmother is sleeping now but she'll be thrilled to know you've arrived. Why don't you all come inside for some nice cold lemonade?"

He showed Madeline the kitchen where his grandmother made her legendary pecan pie and the backyard where he used to read in the crotch of an old oak tree. He had ties here, ties of love, family and nostalgia. He sat at the familiar kitchen table determined to listen to all he'd missed while grieving his first wife's passing.

Madeline, however, worried that Kimmy and Praline had too much energy to sit quietly. The rain had stopped, but it was still too muddy to play outside.

"You can explore the attic," Lucy said. "Lots of clothes up there for dress up." She winked at Kim. "There should be some old board games as well," she added for Madeline's benefit. "If one thing doesn't interest her, another might."

"What do you say, Kim?" Maddie prodded.

"Thank you," Kim replied on cue before she cast a glance at the puppy curled in a ball, worn out from their frantic back seat play.

"Go on, you two. I'll watch Praline." Grant nodded to the puppy.

Kimmy took off up the stairs in a run.

"Ssh," Maddie counseled. "We don't want to wake your great grand-mère. Softly, mon petit. Softly."

"MISS CHARLEBOIS SEEMS very nice."

Lucy filled a plate with cookies. Her close-cropped hair had turned completely white, making a pleasant contrast to her wrinkled brown face. She moved slow but was still agile about the familiar kitchen. Little had changed from the days when he'd moved here after his parents' death, and sat at this table to do his homework. Life moved at a slower pace here, he recalled. Except he knew time raced by just the same.

"How's Gram?"

"She's getting on, you know," Lucy said, as if she alone were not. "She has her good days and bad. You know she'll be ninety-three soon."

"Ninety-three. I should have come sooner," he said, shaking his head with regret. "I've just been so busy trying to finish this paper so I can present it to the tenure committee." Plus he'd buried himself, avoiding all outside responsibilities after Carolyn's death. Maddie had helped him see that.

"She'll be awake soon and glad to see you and Kimberly." Lucy smiled, seeming to understand more than she said. "And… Madeline, is it? How did you meet her?"

Grant bit into the sweet softness of a cookie and grinned. "Oatmeal raisin, my favorite." He relayed the story of his and Maddie's unusual meeting at the Court of Two Sisters and then again when she approached him the night of his speech. "I needed a babysitter and Miss Charlebois offered to fill the position."

Lucy's eyebrows lifted. "That was convenient. I like her more than that other one."

"Jennifer?"

"That's it. She had no laughter in her life. No spark."

He'd forgotten he'd brought Jennifer here before Madeline entered their lives. Grant smiled to himself. "There was a time when I thought those were the qualities I needed. I loved Carolyn so much, I thought someone who was the exact opposite wouldn't remind me of all I'd lost." He glanced up at Lucy. "Funny, but the exact opposite occurred."

"Mmm- hmm. You're lucky you learned before it was too late. It's good to see you laugh again." She glanced to the doorway. Her soft smile spread into a wide grin. "Speak of the devil." However, she quickly sobered. "What's wrong?"

Maddie stood in the doorway wearing a pink feather boa and a funny cap that might have been popular with his great-grandmother's generation, but her face was stark white and the vitality that shimmered in the air around her had disappeared. She held a large frame by her side, a painting from the look of it.

"What have you got there?" Grant asked, concerned that a painting would have that kind of affect on her.

"Kimmy found this in an old trunk in the attic." She handed the frame over to him.

Praline stirred from her nap. Lucy hooked the dog up to a leash and asked Kim to take her outside to do her business.

"I remember this," Grant said, smiling at Lucy. He skimmed over the familiar cassocked priest writing in a journal on a table filled with beakers, potions and a collection of rocks and stones. Cages of small animals filled the space behind him, while a fireplace with roaring flames stood to the side lighting the scene. Pinchers and bellows were laid on the hearth.

"It's the old alchemist." He laughed. "Do you remember asking me about influences that lead me to science? This is one. Gram used to hang this in the front parlor. I think seeing this painting every day likely led me in that direction." Gram used to say that the painting was an ancestor. A great-great-great something, though how a priest had an ancestral line was beyond him. "I wonder if Gram would mind if we brought this back with us."

"I know him," Madeline interrupted in a trance-like monotone.

In his pleasant perusal of this piece of nostalgia, he'd forgotten Maddie's shocked reaction. Her tone caught his attention. "What?

153

Who?"

She pointed. "That's Padre Rodriquez of Queen Isabella's court. He was one of her closest advisors."

"How could you know that, Missy?" Lucy asked. "This painting was done long before you were born, that's for certain."

Madeline didn't reply. She just stared at Grant. This was somehow tied to her time travel claims. He could feel it.

An ominous tense silence hung in the air.

"I'm going to see if your Gram is awake," Lucy said. "She'll need some help before she can see visitors." She slipped from the room leaving the two of them alone.

"He was there. I saw him at the foundry." Maddie slumped into a chair. "Why didn't I consider this before? Why would an alchemist be at the iron foundry?" She glanced at Grant. "This can't just be a coincidence."

He pretended to study the painting. He'd seen it everyday of his childhood. He doubted he'd learn anything new from it now. Maddie, however, had taken something discovered in his attic and wove it into her supposed past. This was not good. Not good at all. "What do you mean?" he asked.

"I don't understand it all, but I think..." She gazed at him, her eyes bright and reflective. Her voice softened. "You're more than the key. You're the reason I'm here."

"Wait just one minute." Grant stood. "You can't be serious. You find a painting and suddenly you develop some grand conspiracy?" He tapped the portrait. "We don't know if this guy was ever in Madrid or even if this is a painting of a real person. We need to research first."

"I'm telling you. I know him." Madeline insisted. "What better resource could there be?"

"A connection that would put your Padre Rodriquez in my attic for starters," he snapped, reeling from her implication that his ancestors were responsible for her imprisonment in iron, if indeed, she ever was imprisoned.

Kim brought the dog back, wisely leaving her shoes by the door. Grant grabbed a towel to help her clean the dog's muddy paws.

"It's just a painting, Madeline," he said. "Probably a reprint. There could be a hundred of the exact same image scattered around the area."

Lucy called down the steps that his Grandmother was awake and anxious to see them all.

He extended his hand, offering to accompany her up the steps. "I'll prove it to you. Gram will tell you she bought this at some five and dime."

"COME CLOSER, LET me see you." His grandmother extended a frail arm from her position against the bed pillows, surrounded by quilts of her own making.

Grant remembered that arm when it was not so very frail. When it had wrapped around his back pulling him close in comfort when he'd lost his parents, when it patted him on the back in congratulations at the science fair, and when it grasped his arm for support as he led Gram in a dance at his wedding. Now her frailty served as both beacon and foreshadowing of the years to come. Regret pulled hard at his heart as he stepped forward. She had done so much for him through the years. He should never have let so much time pass between visits.

"You're such a handsome lad," she said once he bent down to kiss her cheek. "And who is this young lady?" she said, smiling at Kimberly still dressed in a wide brim hat. "I wouldn't have recognized you. You're growing so fast. Come give your great-grandmother a kiss."

Kimberly stood still, perhaps afraid of the bony fingers that urged her forward. Madeline stooped low and whispered in her ear. Kim nodded, then approached the bedside.

"You are the spitting image of your mother. You know that, dear? She'd be so proud of you. Just as I am."

Grant glanced at his daughter, surprised he'd not noticed the resemblance before. Perhaps if his daughter hadn't always been a ferocious hurricane of activity he would have seen Carolyn peaking out of her young eyes. Then again, perhaps he'd been—as his sister-in-law suggested—too withdrawn to notice how his daughter had grown. He smiled up at Madeline in gratitude, thanking God for that day in the hallway of The Court of Two Sisters when she burst into his life.

"And who is this?" his grandmother asked. "I've not met you before, have I?" She squinted at Maddie. "You're not that Jennifer woman, are you?" She looked askance at him. "She kept asking me about wills and things the last time she was here. Made me question her motives, it did."

Grant felt his cheeks warm. He thought he'd kept Jennifer in check but she must have slipped away from him. "I'm no longer seeing Jennifer," he said.

His grandmother patted his hand, expressing her approval. It always surprised him the number of people who recognized that Jennifer was the wrong woman for him. Why hadn't he seen that for himself?

"This is Madeline Charlebois," Grant said with his hand on her elbow, urging her forward. "She's been staying with us."

"Let me see, you dear." She stretched out her hand. "I can see you've been good for my sonny-boy." He winced at her affectionate name.

Madeline approached without the fuzzy boa or that period hat, but she brought the painting and held it behind her.

"What's that you've got back there?" Gram asked. "Bring it close. My eyes don't work as well as they used to."

"Kimberly and I were exploring the old clothes in the attic, when we discovered this painting," Maddie said. "I wondered if this gentlemen might be somehow connected to you?"

Grant took the frame from her and balanced it on the mattress so she could see, then waited for her negative response.

"Yes. Yes. I remember this," his grandmother said. "My father said my grandfather was the son of this man." She tapped the figure on the canvas.

So this would be his great-great-grandfather? How could that be? His gaze shot to Maddie who silently nodded.

"Something bad had happened causing him to fear for his family," his Gram continued. "That's why my great-grandmother and her son, my grandfather, left Spain on one of those big sailing ships. Crossing the ocean was fraught with danger then. But they made it here safely and waited for him to arrive in New Orleans." She coughed, a hoarse sound full of phlegm. Lucy handed her a small glass of water to drink.

"He had a son," Madeline said, her voice barely above a whisper. "I never knew."

Damn. It was the real deal. He thought his Grandmother had made up the fanciful tale of an ancestor to inspire his interest in science. But it was real? Could his ancestor be the slime-ball that cast Madeline into iron?

"Why New Orleans?" He asked suddenly. "I think it would be easier to sail to New York or the Carolinas. If he just wanted his family safe, why have them sail all the way to New Orleans?"

"He insisted. I don't know why." Gram sipped some more water. "But he never arrived. His boat sank in a storm. My great-grandmother went and married someone else. It was hard to be a single woman with a child to feed in those days. Our family has lived in either Mississippi and

Louisiana ever since."

"Do you remember his name, your grand-père?" Madeline asked with urgency. "His birth name?"

Gram thought a bit then shook her head. "He took the name of his new father. He wasn't more than a baby when he arrived in America."

Madeline's whole body slumped in disappointment. Clearly, she had hoped the name would link his family to the alchemist she claimed to know, the alchemist who had sent her one hundred and sixty some years into the future.

They were so close to solving the mystery. Perhaps if he had traced the family history when his Gram was younger and her memory stronger, the connection would be clear. But now, the opportunity was lost.

He wanted to offer Maddie some comfort, hold her in his arms, let her know that even without that one vital piece of evidence, the name that would tie Rodriquez's family to his own, he believed her. It couldn't be a coincidence that she knew Grant's ancient ancestor was an alchemist that journeyed from Spain to New Orleans, information that even he didn't know until today. Madeline had traveled from 1853 to the current day, though they didn't know why. Without the link he couldn't definitively prove anything relating to time travel. But he believed. He believed in Madeline. That had to be worth something.

Gram stirred. "You might find his name in that old trunk where she found the painting." Gram reached around to place both of her frail hands on his own and gazed at him with eyes that had seen so much of time.

"Did you check those old journals?"

Chapter Twenty-Two

JOURNALS!

"They were on the same boat with my grandfather," Gram said. "The alchemist must have wanted the journals hidden from someone in Spain." She yawned. "Maybe you'll find a name there. It will all be yours soon anyway."

"Thank you, *Abuela.*" Madeline kissed Gram's hand with reverence. She smiled a sad-sweet smile. "When you join your ancestors, they will thank you for all you've done this day."

Gram caught her hand and squeezed it between her own. "You'll take care of them, won't you?"

Grant wasn't sure whether she meant the ancestors or someone else. She was an old woman and prone to disorientation.

"He needs you," Gram said, or something like it. Her voice was not as solid and clear as Grant recalled.

Maddie's eyes widened. Surprise sharpened their green depths.

"I'll do my best," she said.

LEAVING THE PAINTING behind with Grant and his grand-mère, Madeline dashed up the steps with the awakened puppy on her heels to search the trunk. The very reason for her existence in this century could be in those pages. They had to be. Padre Rodriquez would not have been present at the foundry unless the queen required his presence for…what? To get rid of her once and for all?

Yes, she supposed the queen could be that heartless. All those silly hurtful games she'd played on her so long ago were just a prelude to something more permanent. But Padre Rodriquez? She always thought he cared for her. What was his part in all this?

A shiver, reminiscent of the cold she'd experienced when freed from the gates, shook her spine. The gates! The iron gates! Padre Rodriguez was rumored to work with metals. The priest must have been there to imprison her in the gates.

With sudden clarity, she stopped a foot shy of the trunk where the treasure awaited. Maddie couldn't move. Memories came rushing back, and the effort to move forward simply required too much. She remembered him now. Clearly, as if she stood before the priest again. She'd turned away from the tour group on her mission to retrieve the queen's fan, when she encountered Padre Rodriquez by one of the furnaces. An odd-shaped rock sat in his upraised palm. His eyes, immeasurably sad, bored into hers. He said "Lo siento." A blinding light flashed from the stone. Burning heat engulfed her. *Lo siento. I'm sorry.*

Padre Rodriquez had trapped her in iron.

Grant, Lucy, and Kim had joined her in the attic. Even Praline sniffed and explored the crowded space. They passed by her to discover the journals and some other items Rodriquez thought valuable. Yet Maddie didn't explore the trunk. She had no need of the journals. She already had her answers.

Something bad had happened causing this man to fear for his family. As well he should. If the queen could dispose of her protocol counselor so easily, she could do the same with his consort...*and son.* She glanced at Grant who lifted a blackened stack of old leather books from the trunk. Rodriquez did not fear for his own life, but that of his family. The queen had threatened his family! No wonder he rushed to send them out of the country, out of Queen Isabella's grasp.

That the Padre had a son did not surprise her beyond the initial revelation. The queen's court was notorious for its trysts, illicit affairs, blatant flirtations, and open innuendos. Everyone eventually succumbed, as she would have most likely had she stayed. But a son...whose seed eventually produced another son, one who became a scientist inspired to return to the studies of his ancestors. No. It could not be coincidence that she was released by his touch. It could not be!

"Maddie, come look at this. It's incredible!" Grant read from one of the journals. "Padre Enrique Rodriquez, May 1850." He glanced up. "Rodriquez. That's your man, right? He must have documented all of his experiments through the years."

All of his experiments, including the one that placed me in the gates?

Grant flipped through the pages. "I wish I could understand this. He has drawings and explanations but it's all in Spanish."

"What's this?" Kimberly upended a velvet pouch and an odd-shaped stone dropped into her hand. A large stone. A familiar stone.

"Kimmy, drop that!" Maddie said, springing into action. She

knocked the stone from Kimmy's palm causing it to tumble back into the trunk.

"What the..." Grant said, open-mouthed.

"It's just a rock," Kimmy said, pouting.

"Not just a rock," Maddie replied. "He had that in his hand. I remember seeing Padre Rodriquez raise it high in his hand the day he entombed me in iron. A bright light flashed." She shook her head. "It must have power. Dangerous power."

Grant looked at her as if she were crazy. "Entombed you in iron?"

"In the gates. In the charm gates." She pointed to the stack of leather books. "Read it for yourself. I'm sure it's all there in his journals."

"In Spanish," Grant said, a soft smile played about his lips. "It's all here in Spanish. You'll have to read it to me." He looked about the dusty room. "But not here. Let's move to better light." They carried the journals downstairs to the kitchen.

"I used to do my homework at this table." He laughed. "It's hard to believe that all that time my great-great-great grandfather's scientific journals sat upstairs buried in a trunk." He shook his head, still ecstatic over the find. Maddie wasn't as enthused. She'd finally accepted the hate Queen Isabella held for her. Perhaps the books would reveal how she could return to 1853 Madrid, but given that level of hate, did she really want to?

He pulled the bottommost journal from the stack. "Might as well start with the beginning." He slid the book across the table to Maddie.

"Better," she said, picking up the top journal instead, "to start with the end."

Lucy bustled about the kitchen to prepare dinner. Kimmy and Praline slipped outside to explore the much drier yard. Grant sat poised with a pen hovering over a blank notebook that he'd found in the attic with his old school supplies. Madeline took a deep breath and opened to the first page.

"1853, February 15..." she began.

Chapter Twenty-Three

DINNER HAD BEEN cleared from the table. The rain had stopped, yielding to heavy humid air.

After a brief interlude to catch fireflies, Madeline put Kimmy and Praline to bed upstairs. Grant sat with Gram while Lucy hovered nearby, clearing the soup bowl, offering a napkin. She recognized, as did Grant, that their remaining time with Gram would be all too brief. Thus, Grant kept the conversation away from the secrets contained in the journals. His grandmother didn't need to know about the man's experiments with fire, metal and acids and their effects on mice, rats, and birds. Instead they talked of old times, happier days, and fond memories. When the visit appeared to be taxing on Gram, Grant kissed her papery white cheek, then allowed Lucy privacy to care for his grandmother. He was glad they'd planned to spend the night and not rush the visit, brief as it was.

The kitchen's overhead lamp illuminated the pages from the old journals. Madeline translated at the table, working her way to that critical time so long ago. Grant watched the mosquitoes and bugs fly about the outside porch light, bumping into the screen door, not that Madeline noticed. She continued to read aloud. Given the state of current day chemistry and physics, the information in the journal was rudimentary at best to Grant. Nothing Madeline translated explained her sudden shift in time. Yet something had to be there. Something to threaten the alchemist's life and the life of his family.

"One of the lights plunged to Earth," Madeline said, reading about a meteor storm that the old man had decided to investigate. "He rode his horse to the area where he thought the meteor might have fallen and searched for two days. Finally, he found a large ground disturbance. He dug a small meteorite from the ground with his spade. As smooth as glass, it was as heavy as iron ore. He brought it back to his laboratory."

"A meteorite?" While interesting, he doubted that would qualify as an earth-shattering discovery.

"But this was no ordinary meteorite," Maddie continued, her eyes scanning the rest of the page. "He performed many tests on the rock until he tried an acid he'd created. Suddenly, the rock glowed red then flashed a lightning bolt." She turned the page.

"Interesting...," Grant thought about the lightning bolt at The Court of Two Sisters. Could the two be related?

"It says that he noted that a nearby iron bar became hot to the touch." She moved her finger down that page and the next, then flipped to a third page.

"What happened?" Grant asked impatiently

"He writes about his failed attempts to duplicate the reaction. He found that the meteorite only glowed when it was near a heat source but he couldn't duplicate the lightning." She turned more pages ahead. "Here it is. He has a drawing, see?" She turned the journal so the sketch was visible to the both of them. "One day, he set his cage of three pigeons on the table and the flash appeared. Two pigeons remained in the cage. The third disappeared."

"Where did it go?" He said to prod her forward, his own excitement building.

"Into the iron bar." She looked up. Shock etched in her face. "Don't you see? That's what he did to me. He used the meteorite to encase me in the molted metal in the foundry."

"How did he know that's what happened to the bird?" Grant asked. "Maybe it was sent somewhere else. What evidence does he give?" Damn! He wanted to read the pages himself. Understand the alchemist's testing. Trust his results.

"Does it matter?" Madeline sat back in her chair. "We know that's what happened to me."

Grant dropped his pen and drew his hand over his face. There was only one explanation. "He found a philosopher's stone."

"So you believe me?" Her face softened and glowed with an internal energy. "You believe that's what happened."

"It's difficult to accept," he hedged, then spread his hands to encompass the books on the table. "But amid all this, I'm inclined to believe you were trapped in those gates."

She rushed around the corner of the table and kissed him. The sizzle went straight to his groin. He pulled her into his lap to deepen the kiss, thinking that he should have admitted his belief in her earlier if this was his reward.

While his body was more than ready to accept her gratitude, his mind wasn't. One coincidence still bothered him. He pulled her back just enough to murmur in her ear. "What I don't understand is why are you free now? Millions of people have touched those gates since you were trapped."

"It was your touch that freed me." Her gaze raked over his face. "You're a descendant of Padre Rodriquez. Had you ever touched those gates before that day?"

His memory slipped to a laughing brunette holding on to the iron bars of the Charm Gates. "Come on, Grant. Grab one of the bars. Every scientist needs more charm." He shook his head, his hands firmly in his pocket. "You've enough Southern charm for the both of us."

"No," he said, his voice low and gravely. Somehow mentioning Carolyn's name with another woman on his lap felt wrong, as if he were cheating. "I hadn't. Not till that day." *The day when I said goodbye to Carolyn.*

"Then it was you." Maddie stroked the side of his face. "Your touch freed me from all those years of imprisonment."

She kissed him, but his mind was preoccupied. She pulled back, frowning. "I thought you'd be pleased."

"I am pleased that you're free," he admitted. "I wish I had touched the gates much earlier. However, that doesn't change the fact that it was my ancestor that put you there in the first place. That's not something of which I'm proud."

There was something else bothering him. He caught her gaze. "Why didn't he try to release you? Right there when the queen's back was turned. Why did he leave you sealed in iron?"

She slipped off his lap and returned to her seat, much more somber than before. She began scanning the each page until she reached the last page of the book. "Queen Isabella threatened to kill Padre Rodriquez's son if he did not do her bidding."

"So she did know." Grant swore beneath his breath. "At least you're free of her now."

"Rodriquez didn't know how to release me," she continued. "He needed to do more research. There was an explosion after the stone's flash, but the gates had already been poured. Both the queen and the alchemist escaped the explosion, many others didn't. Still, Queen Isabella had inquired as to the destination of the gates and learned they were to be shipped to New Orleans in the United States. She named them the 'Charm Gates' shortly before they left Madrid."

"How could she do that?" Grant mused. "Trap someone in molted iron and then treat it as a practical joke."

163

"You did not know the queen." The chill in her voice spoke volumes.

"On the final page, he explains he is sending his son and the child's mother along with his journals and the philosopher's stone to New Orleans so that no one could ever blackmail him into doing such an act again. He knew the gates were bound for the city of New Orleans. He wanted to be here to release me as soon as he discovered how."

"According to Gram, he never made it."

She looked at him. Her voice lowered. "But you did. You were the key. You saved me."

Her look of gratitude was so poignant that he instinctively leaned forward and kissed her. A simple kiss, a sweet kiss, a kiss of apology for what his ancestor had done, a kiss of apology for not believing her when she initially told him the truth. At least that's what he'd planned. But the moment their lips met and merged, lust consumed him.

He pulled her toward him, out of her chair, but then they were both standing, hand and arms struggling to get closer, to get more. He backed her to the wall for the stability, so he could savor her touch, her scent, her taste. He owed her so much, not only for the pains she'd suffered, but also for all the joy she'd given him. He wanted, needed to show her how much.

Of one mind, they quickly dispensed of their clothes. He kissed and stroked every inch of her flesh, determined to heat what his ancestor had frozen. "So beautiful," he said between her gasps. "So beautiful."

MADDIE TREMBLED, STANDING in another's kitchen with her back to the wall, naked for anyone to see. It didn't matter. It surprised her how much it didn't matter. She wanted him. She wanted him hard inside of her. He was the one. The key. The only one who could have freed her from the iron gates. She was meant to be his. She knew it. She felt it. She… oh my God, what was he doing?

Her back arched from her place against the wall. His finger slipped inside her while his tongue teased a spot that shifted like a pearl. Waves of that familiar titillating sensation raced clear to her breasts. Her thighs quivered. Robbed of the ability to stand up on her own, she grasped the corner edge of the wall and dug her fingers in some cabinetry. She gasped for breath while rippling sensations multiplied before they shattered taking her with them.

Grant stood, then pulled one of those foil packets from his wallet.

He hesitated, then spoke low near her ear. "Are you sure?" His words, so warm, so seductive, vibrated in her ear, releasing sensation to tingle through the rest of her body. "There can only be one first time."

"I want this," she answered. She moved her hand to his stiff shaft and stroked it to the moist tip. "I want you."

Grant rolled a thin film barrier on himself, then spread her legs further apart. She held his shoulders, biting her lip knowing what was to come. He cupped her buttocks and lifted, letting her legs wrap around him before he drove deep into her core. A sharp pinch, a resulting opening – she buried her yelp in his shoulder to muffle the sound.

He waited a moment, letting her settle about him. "Are you okay?"

She nodded, then felt the surge, the passion, the sensation and thanked the powers that be that she was in this century where a woman could have this experience with a man without fear of censure or consequences. He pumped into her, driving the sensation higher and higher till the wave crested. Suddenly he stilled, breathing heavily, holding her tight. After a few moments, he lowered her to her feet.

She could barely stand on her own. Fortunately, he supported her and kissed her neck.

"I'm sorry." He kissed her neck. "I'm sorry I didn't believe you before."

"I could barely believe it myself when I arrived. This period is quite a bit different than the one I left."

She felt as much as heard the soft laughter bubbling through his chest.

"Given what we just did, I suppose it is." He kissed her neck. "I'm glad you're here now, but we'd better get dressed before Lucy comes down to investigate the strange noises."

It was a lovely consequence of minimal modern attire that clothes are quickly disbursed and then easily recollected. The two of them were dressed in moments.

They collected the journals and returned them to the stack.

"Have to say," Grant said, placing the last one on top. "I'm glad the journals ended where they did."

Such a strange thing to say. "Why is that?" she asked.

"Rodriquez never had a chance to discover how to set you free or how to return you to your time. We found the answer to the first mystery, but we won't need to find the answer to the second."

Perhaps it was the result of the intimacy they'd just shared, but she couldn't understand what he meant. "Why not?"

His body tensed. She stood so near, she could see his eyes narrow ever so slightly. "You're here now," he said. "You'll stay."

"And I have no say in this?" His words and rigid stance surprised her. Perhaps the role of woman had not changed as much as she thought.

His jaw tensed. He placed a finger to his lips and glanced overhead as if he heard a noise. Then he relaxed.

"We'll talk tomorrow." He kissed her softly, tenderly. "I think we need to go to bed. We have a long drive tomorrow."

Yet at the top of the stairs they separated and slept in different rooms.

Chapter Twenty-Four

IT WAS HAPPENING again. Someone he loved was leaving. Not suddenly ripped from his life by a horrific car crash, but willfully, knowingly, contemplated.

Grant tossed and turned in an uncomfortable single bed tucked away in an overflow room. Kimmy and Madeline shared a larger bed in the guest room. He had anticipated making love to her in his bed back home. He'd have her thrashing all right. His lips turned in a smile. He appreciated her rush to explore her sexual nature, and he was more than willing to show her all she seemed so anxious to learn. Making up for lost time, he supposed, the both of them.

But he'd heard her plans for leaving him plain in her innocent question, so logical yet so full of life-shattering possibility: *why not?*

Why not return to an earlier century and leave him and Kimberly behind to flounder in the aftermath? Why not? Why not rip the heart out of the happy life they'd found together as a family…as a family…He pondered that a moment, for they truly were a family. Madeline teaching her classes of etiquette and languages to a group of happy, chattering girls while he worked blissfully in his office. Kimberly laughing freely for the first time since Carolyn's accident, like a young girl again, not a distraught hellion. Kimmy chasing the puppy that Madeline knew she needed. And at night…he and Madeline sharing, touching, filling the void in each other's life each night in bed. They were a family, damn it. She didn't have the right to tear it apart.

But she did have the right. In the midst of his delusion of the life they could share together, he hadn't asked her to marry him, to make the temporary babysitting a permanent assignment. Everything was perfect with Madeline in the house. From her imperfect English to her initial shy modesty which he realized had somehow faded to the point of standing naked in his Grandmother's kitchen. He squeezed his eyes tight but he couldn't shut out the image of her body pressed against the wall, waiting for him. His groin ached, with the desire to march down to her room and show her all over again why she couldn't leave. She couldn't.

She was the one. Why didn't he see it before?

She was perfect. From the way she squished one side of her mouth when she was concentrating, to her thoughtful guidance of Kim, to the sound she made deep in her throat in orgasm. He'd heard that sound just a few hours ago. That gasp that sounded as if she finally understood the meaning of life and it was utterly amazing. And he, Professor Grant Stewart, solid academic and researcher, had shown her the way.

Of course, she might have mentioned that small insignificant detail that she'd come from a different frickin' century!

How was that possible? How could she have traveled across time, across cultures and not said a word? Of course, there'd been clues. Everyone else seemed to see them. Why didn't he?

Because he was the "Professor." He was the one that said time-travel was impossible. He'd closed his mind to the possibilities, the one thing that had been pounded into his brain in undergraduate work, he'd forgotten. Always challenge the known, because when it came down to it, there were more unknowns in the universe then the knowns here on earth. And yet… he'd never considered it remotely possible…or that he would play a role in its discovery.

What kind of man would seal a woman's soul in cold iron for an eternity? And yet, if the alchemist hadn't, his son would be dead, and Grant wouldn't be around today to ponder the situation.

But he was. And she was. And he had to decide what to do about it.

The one thing he couldn't do was fall more deeply in love with Madeline. In fact, he needed to back away. He wouldn't be able to survive another devastating loss as he had experienced with Carolyn. He'd learned his lesson once and once was enough. He'd keep his heart firmly in check. No late night visits to her bedroom or her to his. No more impulsive kisses just because she looked so damn kissable. No more shared glasses of wine while they watched the news. From here on, it would be a strictly employer/employee relationship until she decided her fate. He would bury himself in his work and not give her another thought…except tonight. Tonight, all he could think of was Madeline.

THEY DIDN'T TALK the next day. If anything, they went out of their way not to talk, which is difficult when sharing a car for a three-hour ride home. Grant packed the Rodriguez journals and the philosopher's stone in the trunk, then carried the wooden case out to the car. They said their goodbyes and made promises to return soon. Kimmy and

Praline hopped into the back seat. Then Grant backed away from his boyhood home.

Maddie was fairly bursting to explain her hesitancy to stay in this time period, assuming she had a choice, but she didn't want to upset Kimberly who sat in the back. So she stared out the window at passing farms and marshland and thought about what she wanted to say to Grant when they had the opportunity to talk freely.

In truth, she wasn't sure what she wanted to do. As she saw it, consequences existed at every turn. If she stayed in this century, she would lose her family and a respected position in Queen Isabella's court. Given a second opportunity, she thought she might win the queen's favor, as she now had a much better understanding of the queen's promiscuous ways. She had a responsibility to provide heirs for the crown. As her royal consort was loath to the task, she needed to find others to do what her husband could not. Now that Madeline had experienced sexual congress with a man, she understood how devastating it would be to live without. In retrospect, perhaps she had been overly critical of the queen's numerous affairs.

And how would Madeline deal herself with the loss of Grant and his amazing fingers, lips, and very talented member? She smiled to herself even as her cheeks heated remembering last night. Even in her new experienced state, she couldn't refer to his male appendage by its proper but rather ineloquent name. Yet its function...how could she live without this fantastical, earth-shattering release? Should she return to 1853, would she become one of the compromised women of society, sharing intimacy with a man without requiring marriage? And when and if she married, how would she explain to her husband that he was not her first?

Grant flipped a knob on the radio to fill the silence with music. A news program mentioned a woman's name as belonging to some political office. A woman in politics, a seemingly common occurrence in the modern age, was not so common in the other. Unless, of course, one was royalty.

While employment opportunities for women were seemingly limitless in this century, she wondered if that would be so without a documented education or citizenship. Madeline was certain her options were less so. She would never get such a prestigious and influential position as she had held in the queen's court. But if she left...if she left...she would lose so many of the freedoms and and so many of the friends she had made in this time. She'd always assumed, that given the opportunity, she'd return to 1853. Had that goal changed?

She glanced at Grant. He looked like he hadn't slept a wink last night. She imagined he'd tossed and turned much like herself. She checked the back mirror. Kimberly was fast asleep.

"Thank you for introducing me to your grand-mère. She seems a very special woman," she said.

"She liked you as well," Grant replied. "I didn't tell her about the time travel connection. I didn't want to upset her with the thought that we were responsible for your transference."

Transference. An interesting way to describe being locked in iron.

"It wasn't done willingly," she said. "Rodriquez had no choice. But you do."

He stiffened. "What do you mean?"

"You have the choice of discovering how use the stone to send me back, or not."

"You'd go back to a queen that had you encased in iron?" He glanced at her, shocked.

"I don't know," she said truthfully, then gazed out the window. "I just don't know."

Chapter Twenty-Five

"I ASSUME YOU'VE had time to think about it."

Richard opened a water bottle. They were back at the gym at the Student center, in theory to strengthen their muscles. Grant was mainly going through the motions. He had too many concerns on his mind.

"I haven't thought about much else," he confessed, though Richard didn't know the whole story. He didn't know, for example, that Grant's ancestor was the person who placed Maddie in iron in the first place. He still remembered Madeline's reaction to that painting, and to his recent discoveries of his past. He did, however, mention the existence of journals. He just didn't mention Maddie's translation of their contents.

Maddie's translation... His research background kicked in. Madeline couldn't have been impartial to what she'd translated. Could she have modified what the words actually said to support her cause?

"You know Spanish, don't you?" Grant asked.

"Spanish, French, Italian, German..." Richard listed. "Reading the actual language first-hand helps in the tracking of rare jewels."

"You could translate something for me if I gave it to you, right?"

"I don't know, Grant." Richard settled back on the lat pull down machine. "Time is of the essence right now. Maybe you can get someone from the Spanish department." He laughed. "It's sort of ironic. You studying time and I don't have any."

Grant wasn't amused. "Maddie says the journal tells how she arrived in this century. I think it's a little too coincidental that she found a journal in my attic, don't you? If she's lying about this, then she's lying about the Moor's Tear as well."

It hurt like hell to suggest that Maddie was orchestrating a story he believed true but it was the only way to get an objective read. Maybe there was something critical in that journal that Maddie conveniently left out. Either way, he had to know.

Richard stopped his repetitions. "I don't think Maddie is lying about the Moor's Tear. She knew too many details that only someone in the industry would know."

"But if you're basing your research and paper on her perception of history, wouldn't you want to be absolutely certain that Madeline was actually from the time period? This journal will...or maybe won't...support that supposition." Grant suspected he'd stumbled upon the chink in Richard's armor.

"Can't you have Maddie carbon-dated? Maybe test her old DNA, or something? Wouldn't that prove she's from 1853?"

"You know carbon-dating doesn't work on living beings, and Madeline is definitely living." He smiled remembering last night. In spite of his plan for no late night rendezvous, he'd failed miserably. He couldn't resist bringing her to his bed. She was definitely a living, pulsating, incredibly sensitive woman.

"The same could be said of DNA," he said. "Her DNA won't prove a thing. There's no scientific proof to say she's from another time."

He could probably prove the journals were from the proper period but the content would still be construed as a good science fiction tale. No one would believe a woman actually survived the described ordeal.

"But you and I, we know it's true," Richard said. "If Maddie agrees to go back—"

"—She's already tried that." Grant let his weight crash. He took a breath to get his emotions under control. "Remember when she kissed me goodbye?"

Richard rubbed his jaw as if he felt the pain anew. "How could I forget?"

"She tried the next day to return on her own. She went back to the Charm Gates and nothing happened." He ran his hand through his hair, maddened that they were even having this conversation. "Damn it, Richard! She's not going back!"

Heads turned at the commotion. He lowered his voice. "I know you want to retrieve some diamonds or emeralds or something—"

"The Moor's Tear ruby," Richard quietly interspersed.

"—But it's too dangerous. She's here now in one piece. We don't know how traveling back in time would affect her."

"But if she wants to go back, we shouldn't try to stop her," Richard argued.

"She doesn't wish to go back."

"But if she—"

"She doesn't wish to go back," Grant repeated for emphasis. "Things will continue just as they have been. Madeline will continue to live at my house and take care of Kimberly. I'll continue to work on my paper. Things will go back to normal."

At least that's what he hoped for, prayed for. But then God had not really listened to his prayers in the past. Why would this be any different?

"HAVE YOU THOUGHT about what we talked about?" Richard's voice pooled in her ear like the snake in the Garden of Eden. Strange how that image came to her mind.

"I haven't thought about much else," Madeline replied to the phone. She hadn't gotten used to the way this tiny box could convey a person's voice across such a vast distance, but it obviously worked. No one from her past would believe her if she told them of all she'd seen and done here.

"Don't you miss your family?" Richard said.

That was a low blow. Her chest squeezed tight, as she thought of her brothers.

"What about your position with the queen's court?" he continued. "You'll never achieve that type of position here."

She knew that, but she also now knew that the queen had blackmailed another to lock her away for all time in iron. If it hadn't been for Grant, she'd be forever frozen..

"You can always return here," he said.

"What do you mean?" Did Richard know something that she did not?

"You can always come back to this time. Just take me back to 1853. Show me where the queen kept the Moor's Tear and you'll be free to return to Grant and Kimmy and your life here. You've done it before. You can do it again."

"No." She thought of the iron gates and shivered. "I don't think I can go through that again. Even if I had the philosopher's stone—"

"--Philosopher's stone?" he interrupted. "What is the philosopher's stone?"

Grant must not have told him about that. She knew the two were meeting at the gym this morning. She'd just assumed he had.

"It's the stone that made time travel possible." *If one could call being locked in iron "travel."* Maddie shivered with the physical memory. "We discovered it at Grant's grand-mère's house last weekend."

"Did Grant bring it back with him?" Richard's voice held urgency, though she didn't know why.

"He brought the journals back so I think he did."

"Journals?" He sounded surprised, but in a strange not-quite-believable way. "What journals?"

Grant must not have said anything to Richard about their discovery.

"We found some old journals at his grand-mère's house. They're probably nothing." Her gut twisted. If Grant hadn't said anything, she shouldn't either. "Look, Richard, I don't feel comfortable talking to you about this."

"Are the journals and the stone in his office?" he asked.

"I don't know. I don't go into his office, but I don't want to talk about this anymore," she insisted.

"Madeline, don't you see? You don't really belong in the twenty-first century. You're from the past, you should return to the past. If you stay, you'll never see your family again."

"But Grant…"

"What about Grant?" Richard hesitated just a moment. "He doesn't love you, you know."

Her heart dropped. "What do you mean?"

"You're the babysitter. Once Kimmy goes away to school, he won't need you anymore."

"But…" She was more than a babysitter. Grant had told her so.

"Think about it, Madeline. If Grant wants to advance in the University structure, he'll need a certain kind of wife, a wife with a documented past. Someone with at least a bachelor's degree so he can talk about his work. Carolyn had a bachelor's degree. You don't have that, do you?"

"No…" And she never would. No college would accept her without some sort of transcript. She'd checked.

"Has he told you he loved you?" Richard asked.

Her breath caught. He'd said he was falling in love, but that's not exactly the same thing. Her voice issued in a whisper. "No…"

"There you have it." Richard said. "If he loved you, don't you think he would have told you?"

She sat silent. He'd never said he loved her, but he showed her time and time again in bed, in the dark, when he brought her body to earth-shattering heights. He had to love her to do that, didn't he? But then when she'd admitted to loving him, she'd received silence in return.

"Invite me to dinner," Richard said.

"What?" The change of topic caught her off guard.

"Invite me over for dinner. I want to talk to Grant."

"But you can talk to Grant at Tulane, or you can call him on the phone."

"I want to speak with him face-to-face and I want to speak with him at your house. Invite me to dinner. Tonight."

Chapter Twenty-Six

GRANT EYED THE table with suspicion. "The table is set for four."

"Maddie says Uncle Richard is coming for dinner." Kimmy placed the last spoon on a folded napkin. Grant could remember when Kimmy refused to use or even see a napkin. She was a different kid since Maddie's intervention.

"Richard?" He raised his eyes to Maddie who kept her back toward him. He had a bad feeling about this. When she didn't respond, he moved closer and pretended to snoop at the dishes. "Richard is coming for dinner on a Friday night?"

"He invited himself. I'm not sure why. We're having spaghetti and a salad. It's easy to make." She dumped a bag of lettuce in a bowl, then chopped some tomatoes to put on top. Maddie may not have arrived with superior cooking skills but she was quickly adopting the "easy fix" method of prepackaged meals with abandon.

The doorbell rang. Grant moved to answer. He had a bad feeling about this. He held Praline and opened the front door. While he expected to see Richard, he wasn't expecting Jennifer. That raised his suspicions even more so.

"Jennifer. He ushered them in so he could let the puppy loose. "I guess we'll have to add a plate to the table."

"I'm sorry for the late notice," Jennifer said while she watched Praline sniff at her ankles. "The puppy is new."

Apparently the woman wasn't a fan of animals any more than she was a fan of children. How could he have ever been attracted to this woman?

"I was at Richard's apartment and he invited me to come along. I hope that my being here isn't an inconvenience." Jennifer smiled. "I brought wine."

She wore a business suit, but no shirt underneath, her breasts pumped up to make her cleavage a viewing pleasure. Was she at Richard's dressed like that? The thought gave him pause. And who travels with a handy bottle of wine? Before he could ask what was going on the two of them had moved into the kitchen. He heard Maddie's surprise, the clatter accompanying an additional place setting, and the kitchen door sliding open to let the dog out.

"So Richard," Grant said, keeping his distance from where Jennifer poured wine. "I saw you earlier at the gym. Why are you here for dinner?"

"Bachelors never eat alone if they can help it, you know that." Richard's teeth gleamed with his smile.

"But you weren't alone." Grant nodded toward Jennifer. "Looks to me like you already had company."

"You know Richard is one of my tax clients, don't you?" Jennifer said, instilling herself in the conversation. "I stopped by to ask him a quick question about his projected earnings this year and—"

"—I invited her to accompany me here. Just like old times," Richard finished, slapping Grant on the shoulder. "I was speaking with Madeline on the phone earlier, you know, collecting more information about the Moor's Tear. I decided to invite myself for dinner on a whim. It's much easier to ask questions face-to-face, you know."

Old times, my ass. Those two had practiced that conversation. Richard was up to something but Grant wasn't certain what. "The Moor's Tear...," he drawled, watching Maddie who seemed suspiciously quiet. How was she involved with whatever this was?

"What's a Moor's Tear?" Jennifer asked, placing the filled wine glasses on the table. "Sorry squirt. You're too young for the big-girl drinks." She plopped a plastic glass of milk by Kimmy's plate.

"The Moor's Tear is to be my salvation," Richard said before he noticed that Maddie had her head lowered to say grace. Richard stopped his chatter and pretended instead to pray.

Kim bowed her head as well, an indication of Maddie's strong influences. Silence reigned until Maddie crossed herself and passed a bowl of salad. Then Richard continued with his explanation of the significance of the necklace.

"And you discovered this how?" Jennifer asked, then winked her eye at Grant.

What the hell?

"Maddie told me," Richard said with a grin. "She has an amazing knowledge of Queen Isabella's jewelry."

"That's because she lived in the palace," Kimmy said with pride. She nudged Maddie. "Tell her."

"Did she now." Laughter sparked in Jennifer's eyes. She turned toward Grant. "How extraordinary."

Nothing managed to humor Jennifer more than when she could demean someone else. Why hadn't he noticed that before?

Madeline remained silent.

"Richard has some wild idea that Madeline managed to inexplicably travel through time from 1853 to the present," Grant explained, dishing spaghetti on his plate. While he knew the truth, he didn't want to appear supportive in front of Jennifer and Richard - at least not until he knew what they were scheming.

"Traveled through time. " Jennifer laughed. "I wouldn't mind doing that myself. I'd travel back to three weeks ago when Grant and I were still together."

The smoldering look she sent him could have ignited the placemats. Jennifer's hand suddenly landed on his knee, hidden by the tablecloth, before it began to inch toward his crotch. He grabbed her wrist then moved the roving appendage back to her lap. So that was her agenda. Good. He could deal with that easy enough.

"If I could control time," Madeline said with a downcast gaze. "I'm not certain that I'd choose this present."

Grant's ears picked up on her words and her morose tone. His lips slanted down. He thought she was happy. Didn't she like it here? "Why's that?"

"Everything is fast here. Fast food, fast cars,—" she glanced at Jennifer's cleavage "—fast clothes. I believe I'd prefer a slower time with more civility."

"I'm in favor of that," Richard said, lifting his glass in a toast. "To civility."

"That's an interesting observation," Grant said, directing his statement toward Madeline. "If I could travel in time, I wouldn't. I wouldn't want to miss Kimmy-bear growing up." He smiled at his daughter.

"You wouldn't travel back to before Carolyn's accident?" Jennifer asked. "Wouldn't you want to warn her?"

A silence descended. Grant sat stunned. The possibility of preventing Carolyn's death hadn't occurred to him. In fact, he rarely thought of Carolyn these days.

"I know I'd travel back to 1853," Richard said, breaking the awkward silence. "I'd want to see the Moor's Tear for myself."

"I think it's Kimmy's bedtime." Madeline turned to the child. "Are you finished? I can read you a story while your daddy speaks to his friends."

"Velveteen bunny?"

"Again?" Maddie winced. "Come along then. We can manage a chapter or two."

"Come on Praline," Kimmy called the puppy inside before they both scrambled up the steps.

His friends? Richard specifically came over to speak with Madeline. He could speak with Grant at Tulane. What was going on? He was on his own and he feared deep in dangerous waters.

"DOES EVERYONE KNOW the secret now?" Kimmy looked at Maddie with big blue eyes so reminiscent of her father's.

"Not everyone, sweet." Maddie brushed Kimmy's hair. "The mothers and daughters that come to our language classes don't know and we don't want to tell them," she cautioned. She'd seen Jennifer's caustic reaction to Grant's attempt to downplay Kimmy's outburst. "They wouldn't believe us. Sometimes—" she laughed "—I'm not so sure I believe it myself."

Though her comment was meant to soothe Kimmy, it wasn't far from the truth. The more she stayed in this time, the more her memories faded. Sometimes she wondered if she'd dreamed the queen, and the explosion, and her long period in iron. Even if Rodriquez's journals supported what she knew to be true, the incident had taken on a dream like quality. How long before the faces of her past disappeared completely?

"Shall we read?" Maddie opened Kimmy's favorite book to the first page and began to read how a loved toy rabbit dreamed of becoming a living breathing animal. Praline hopped on the bed, circled, then settled down. She read quietly, stopping to show Kimmy the pictures, even though Kim knew them all by heart. She read:

"Real isn't how you are made,' said the Skin Horse. 'It's a thing that happens to you. When a child loves you for a long, long time, not just to play with but REALLY loves you, then you become Real."

"That's what happened to you," Kimmy said, her voice drowsy with sleep.

Maddie stopped, closing the book slightly. She kept her voice light, not wanting to disturb the relaxing atmosphere. "What do you mean?"

"You used to be like my dolly, all dressed up." Kim yawned, then snuggled into the pillow. "Now you're like that. You're Real like the bunny."

Maddie smiled and continued reading, not wanting her young charge to wake from almost asleep due to the lack of her voice. She changed her tone to the higher-pitched one she used for the rabbit's dialogue.

"Does it happen all at once, like being wound up,' the Rabbit asked, 'or bit by bit?'

'It doesn't happen all at once,' said the Skin Horse. 'You become. It takes a long time. Generally, by the time you are Real, most of your hair has been loved off and your eyes drop out and you get loose in the joints and very shabby. But these things don't matter at all, because once you are Real you can't be ugly, except to the people who don't understand."

Maddie closed the book and watched Kimmy's chest gently rise and fall in sleep. She placed the book on the nightstand and noticed the doll Kimmy had brought to the hospital that first day. She picked it up, remembering that day when she first met Kimberly. Little did she realize how much her life would change as a result.

The doll still wore the fancy flounced dress with her hair in a tight coif, tucked under a flower-laden hat. Though she wasn't an exact image of Madeline on that day, she could understand how Kimmy may have been confused. She set the doll back down and rose to leave the room.

That's when she caught her reflection in Kimmy's mirror. Her hair, no longer pulled and twisted in a tight coif, hung limp at her face, the result, she imagined, of cooking in the steamy kitchen. She wore a casual shirt and a pair of comfortable jeans, not the fancy cumbersome 1853 gown that she'd tucked deep in a closet. She'd made a complete transformation. *But now you're Real like the bunny.*

Could it be true? Had she become a woman of the current century and not the one of long before? Had she become Real? If she had, it was due to the love of Grant and Kimmy. Perhaps God brought her forward to this time for them. Padre Rodriquez was just the means to do it.

She thought she heard a light step going downstairs. She hadn't heard Grant slip upstairs, but he probably had come to check on Kimmy, then decided not to disturb the two of them. She smiled, thankful for the blessings she'd been given to live with this family, one she considered hers.

And now it was time for her to go downstairs to entertain their guests.

RICHARD STARTED CLEARING the plates. "Why don't you two take your wine out to the front porch. I'll take care of this. It's the least I can do."

"Excellent idea!" Jennifer stood with her glass and looked back at Grant over her shoulder. "Coming?"

He wouldn't discover what was afoot without playing along. He stood with his wine glass and followed Jennifer to the front porch.

"It's such a lovely night," Jennifer said. "You're so lucky to live where you can enjoy it."

"Why are you here, Jennifer?" Grant said, leaning on the railing. "And don't give me that hokey story about circumstance."

"And here I thought I was being obvious," Jennifer said, her teeth gleaming in the dusk. "I want you back." She stepped closer. "Richard thought you might be having second thoughts about your flighty French Pollyanna. She may be fine for reading children's books but a scientist in your position needs someone more...adult." She rubbed her breasts against his chest, while she tilted her head, inviting him to kiss her.

He stepped away. "I'm sorry Richard gave you false hopes. I owe more to that French Pollyanna then you could possibly imagine. In fact, if she'll have me, I plan to..." He squinted his eyes at a light near the edge of the porch. That hadn't been there before, had it? He pushed his wine glass into Jennifer's hand and went down the steps to investigate.

A tall votive candle, the sort sold for voodoo rituals, sat in front of the porch surrounded by mardi gras beads, stones, a contraption that displayed a wire corset topped by hooks, a small African mask, and piece of paper that bore the letter "X" written three times. "What the..."

"It's a voodoo altar," Jennifer said. "I've seen shrines like that in the cemeteries."

Grant had seen similar items left at the burial sites of Marie Laveau, the so-called "Mother of Voodoo," but that was mainly for tourists. He'd hunched down to study the items left. Was that the dried rooster leg he'd tossed on the lawn last week? Someone must have found it and propped it up in the back.

"I bet she did this," Jennifer continued. "She and that voodoo priest that came to your speech."

"Antoine."

"That's him," she said. "She probably told you they'd stopped practicing their voodoo ways but they obviously haven't."

"Antoine and Maddie didn't do this," Grant concluded after his objective consideration of the items left. "They wouldn't have left the triple X markings and there would have been more Catholic symbolism if Maddie had been involved." He blew out the candle and stood.

"What do you mean?" she asked, innocence personified.

"I think you and Richard are responsible for this makeshift altar. I don't know why, but..."

Jennifer glanced toward the open door then unbuttoned her suit jacket exposing her lacy bra. She raised her voice. "You know why. I love you, Grant." She rushed into his chest and plastered her lips to his. His arms went around her to steady her and pull her back.

He broke the kiss, but heard a gasp to his right.

Madeline stood at the open door with her eyes wide and her mouth agape.

Chapter Twenty-Seven

A LUMP SETTLED in her throat. The earth may have spun on its axis many times since she was in Madrid, but some things never changed. No wonder Grant had seemed so distant since their return from his grand-mère's home. She turned and retreated to her room, locking the bedroom door behind her. Grant could deal with his friends. *His* friends, she reminded herself, as she couldn't say she had many friends of her own.

There was Doc and Cici, of course. Cici's words replayed in her head. Be careful Maddie. Sometimes a man chases the challenge and not the prize. Once they get what they want, they move on to something else.

She'd foolishly defended Grant but it appeared that she was the fool. He'd enjoyed her sexual favors and now planned to get the same from Jennifer. Of course, she reminded herself, she'd enjoyed granting those sexual favors, but that was a different matter.

A woman needs to be self-sufficient, because the only person you can depend upon is yourself.

That much, she supposed, hadn't changed since the nineteenth century. She'd had to depend on herself to keep calm in the midst of Queen Isabella's tricks and challenges. She had to depend on herself when she was plopped into a futuristic time period for which she was unprepared and uneducated. But she'd learned how to find shelter and substance.

He doesn't love you, you know.

Richard's voice spoke in her mind. Had she been so obvious? Yes. She thought she'd found love. She thought she and the professor were meant to be, that he was the one meant to rescue her and that she would somehow rescue him back. Foolish, foolish girl. She swiped at the tears streaming down her cheeks.

Through the open window, she heard car doors slam. A few minutes later a soft knock sounded at her door.

"Maddie? Can I come in?" Grant asked softly so as not to wake

Kim.

She didn't answer. She knew the tears would start again if she tried to speak. Why did she ever agree to stay here? She should have asked Beth if she had room.

"It's not what you think, Maddie," his harsh whisper slipped under the door. "Jennifer means nothing to me."

She must have meant something for him to have his lips fastened to hers, his arms on her hips.

The doorknob tried to turn but the lock held. Even if it hadn't, the chair she'd wedged beneath the knob would have kept him from entering. Some things learned from the nineteenth century still had validity.

"Maddie?"

She clasped her hands over her ears to chase away the plea in his voice. "Go away," she said. "I was asleep," she lied.

Silence. One heartbeat, two, three...

"We'll talk in the morning then." She heard the sadness in his voice, the resignation. She doubted it even approached her own.

He doesn't love you, you know. She put her hands over her ears, but she couldn't drown out Richard's words that sounded over and over again.

Visible beneath the door, his feet remained. After a few more moments, he turned and left.

WAS HE LOSING his mind? Or just Madeline.

He sat alone in his office the next morning with a model of the starship Enterprise dangling overhead for company. Grant stared at his article on tesseracts without seeing a word. What was wrong with him? He raked his hand through his hair. Why couldn't he concentrate?

Because you screwed things up, he answered himself. A mental image of Maddie's smiling face slipped into his memory, her hair lifted in a breeze, her eyes lit with an internal fire that had a special sort of smolder whenever she looked his way. A bulge formed in his pants while a yearning filled his heart.

Stop that! Didn't he decide he didn't need that sort of frivolity in his life? No one would ever get so close to him that their departure would rip him in half.

And yet - that's exactly how he felt. As if his heart had been ripped out of his chest. He'd gone and done it. He'd fallen madly in love with another woman and she had abandoned him, just like Carolyn.

CHARMING THE PROFESSOR

What was wrong with him? No one knew better than he how much it hurt to live a life without laughter, a life of fear of meeting another woman who could steal his breath away just by being near.

The bobble head doll mocked him with its permanent smile. Who was he kidding? He loved Madeline. Loved her with his head, his heart, and some very responsive parts of his body. He shouldn't be hiding in his office in a bid to avoid falling in love. It had happened anyway. Nothing had made that clearer than seeing Jennifer and realizing that he had no interest - even when she fell out of her suit in her desperate plea to lure him back. Desperate! And here he had the perfect woman living in his house and he was avoiding her. What kind of an idiot does that?

Well, he wouldn't do it anymore. He got up from the desk. Richard was right. Padre Rodriquez had given him the golden ticket, the big splash, with his journals and philosopher's stone. He glanced to the spot where he'd placed the stone - the now empty spot. The hairs lifted on the back of his neck. How did that happen? Did Madeline move it? Did Kimmy?

He went downstairs to ask. Kimmy played alone on the floor quietly building a structure in Legos.

"Look Daddy, I'm making a palace!"

"That's great, honey." He looked around the empty kitchen. The TV played an educational show in the next room, but otherwise all was quiet and still. Even Praline lay curled up in a sunbeam. "Where's Maddie?"

"She left. She said she had to meet Uncle Richard about something."

"Did she say where she was meeting Richard?" He doubted Richard would be in his office at Tulane on a Saturday morning.

Kim squinted up at him. "I think she said her sister's court. Is her sister a princess, too?"

"The Court of Two Sisters?" Christ. That can't be a coincidence that she was meeting Richard at the same place as...

"That's it!" Kim added a block to the castle's turret. "She left you a note."

"Quick!" He grabbed Kim's hand and whisked her off the floor and unto his hip. He snatched the folded paper off the counter as he ran to his car.

"Where are we going?" Kim asked, her voice rippling as it had on Gram's lumpy drive.

Like a ripple in time, Grant modified. The philosopher's stone, the Charm gates, Richard...it all fit!

185

"We're going to stop Madeline from going home, that is, if we're not too late."

AS RICHARD HAD requested, she'd retrieved her court garments from the far reaches of the closet - another one of those modern day advancements that she'd miss when she returned to 1853 Madrid.

Lacking a lady's maid, she'd asked Cici to help her dress for the return trip. This wasn't a journey that she anxiously anticipated, but she couldn't argue with Richard's logic. She belonged in 1853. She didn't belong to this crazy, fast-paced, world. She'd been silly to ever contemplate it.

While she was grateful to Grant for freeing her from the iron prison, she just had to accept that he didn't love her. To continue to live in close proximity to him was too painful to consider. Her throat tightened. Yes, she was doing the right thing for both of them. He'd be free to marry that cold conniving Jennifer woman, and she'd be free to…well, she'd be free. That would have to do for now.

Cici pulled tight on the strings of her corset. "This is not as easy as when I dressed you the last time. Girl, you put on weight?"

She wasn't sure. "My waist isn't used to the constraint as it was before," she replied. She grabbed the doorknob and braced herself. "Now try."

Cici managed a slightly tighter fit before tying off the strings. Now Madeline just had to tie on her petticoats and be laced into her dress. She'd sold her beaded reticule, hat, ear bobs and other jewelry after her visit to the Lady of Guadalupe chapel. All she had left was her cross necklace, a jeweled comb, and her bracelet, a gift from the very same jeweler who fashioned the Moor's Tear into a necklace for Queen Isabella. It fastened loosely about her wrist and dangled a small blue stone.

Her shorter hair refused to be fashioned into her former coif, so she left it as it was. She didn't take her tote bag as if would stand out where she was going. She did, however, slip a ballpoint pen in the valley of her breasts. No more need for a sharpened quill or a bottle of ink.

"Keep this for protection." Cici handed her the gris-gris bag that Doc had prepared for her a long time ago. "You just never know what you're gonna meet on the other side."

While Madeline tucked the red sack into her corset top, she was uncommitted as to the item's power. It certainly hadn't protected her from a broken heart.

Doc accompanied her to The Court of Two Sisters where she was to meet Richard. Madeline bid a silent goodbye to each building she passed, a salute to the city she'd learned on her repeated rounds with Louis and his mule.

She said her goodbyes to Doc on Rue Royale and entered the hallway that led past the Charm Gates, to the inside restaurant. She waited for Richard on a seat in the dark interior at a bar lined with brass tags of the patrons. Many of those patrons breezed past her, unseeing, as they marched up to the Maître d's station. That was fine with Madeline as she gazed longingly at their casual attire. She chided herself, remembering her impression of those tee shirts and shorts when she'd first arrived in New Orleans. Perhaps when she returned to 1853, she'd travel to New Orleans and wait for Grant's ancestors, but she knew she would not. Revisiting would bring back hurtful memories.

A family entered the restaurant with a small child about Kimmy's age. She clutched a much-loved toy rabbit. Maddie instantly recalled reading The Velveteen Rabbit to Kimmy. The story about the toy struggling to become real. *You're like that,* Kimmy had said. *You're Real like the bunny.*

Richard bustled in dressed in a business suit with books and a knapsack. A wide brimmed hat was pulled low over his eyes making him difficult to recognize, but once he approached his emerald eyes were unmistakable. She should have known a man with eyes like that would be interested in jewels.

"Sorry, I'm late," he said. "Choosing what I might need in 1853 proved more difficult than I'd anticipated." He patted his knapsack. "I'm surprised you're not taking any 'marvelous wonders' back."

She shook her head, while nervously twisting her bracelet around her wrist. One couldn't fit people in a reticule and everything else were just "things."

"Are you ready to go home?" Richard asked with a nervous laugh.

"One thing bothers me," she said, remembering Grant's discourse on the arrow of time. "How do you know we'll arrive where I started? I read Padre Rodriquez's journal. He describes how to capture a person's essence in iron, but not how to direct its travel or how to release it." She shuddered at the thought of being encased in iron once more.

"That's true, but I'll have you as a rudder." Her face must have shown her confusion. "A boat needs a rudder to direct it where to go.

You, a woman of 1853, will direct our travel to that year just by your existence. When you were first placed in the gates you had nothing to steer you to your destination, but I have you."

"But I tried to go back myself by touching the gates. Why do you think this time will be any different?"

He smiled. "Because I have the stone." He removed a black stone from his pocket

Her heart dropped and gooseflesh rose on her arms. The stone had powers not to be trifled with. "How did you…?"

"Grant foolishly left it out on his desk. When Jennifer and I came over for dinner last night, I snatched the stone while Jennifer distracted Grant."

Then Grant hadn't been truly interested in Jennifer. It was part of a plan to turn his head.

"Plus I have the magic words from the journal, we'll be okay."

He looked around the bar, rubbing a finger on the brass plates. "The Court of Two Sisters and I go back a ways. Actually, I could say the same about most of the establishments in the Vieux Carre. It's a bachelor's paradise. I'm going to miss this place."

"Perhaps we shouldn't do this," Maddie said, feeling the weight of her reluctance to go back. "It's risky."

"Nonsense." Richard waved her doubts aside. "I don't intend to be gone very long. I just want to grab the jewels and come back to finish my paper." He tossed the stone in the air than caught it again in his palm. "If this works, I might have a host of places to visit."

"It doesn't work that way," Maddie said, suddenly afraid of Richard's ambitions. "You can't control the travel that precisely."

"Oh, but I will. I have a whole arsenal of 'rudders' at my disposal, but none quite as attractive as you or that has your knowledge of the period." He grabbed her hand. "Let's go. It does no good to stay here. Time to get this show on the road."

Her feet followed behind, while her mind spun in turmoil. Was she mistaken in her thoughts that Grant didn't really love her? Was the Jennifer incident just staging? As they approached the gates, her ears buzzed at a much higher rate of vibration then when she had come on her own. It was the stone! It had activated the gates.

She glanced back to the glass door that separated the hallway from the restaurant. The little girl stood there, watching with sad eyes, clutching her toy rabbit. Kimmy! She didn't want to leave Kimmy!

"No. I can't do this." She tried to pull her hand out of Richard's grasp. "It's too late," he said. "You're coming back with me." He held the stone high in his other hand.

She braced herself, and using all of her strength, pulled her hand free, but he quickly grabbed her wrist.

"Sorry Princess. You're coming with me."

Chapter Twenty-Eight

RICHARD CLOSED HIS eyes and mumbled some nonsensical words that she'd recognized from the journal. Had he recognized the language? She thought the words were Latin but the meaning hadn't made sense.

"You can't do this," Maddie said, playing a bluff. "You don't know the words."

The stone started to glow.

"But I do," Richard said with a sly smile. "It's not the words. It's the sound, the notes. The alchemist tried to describe them the best way he could. But as you can see." He glanced back at the glowing rock. "I know what I'm doing."

"You're not going to do it with me!" Madeline struggled in earnest, trying to pull her whole body out of his grasp. The vibrations in her ears sounded louder. She could already feel a chill settle deep inside. If she touched the gates she'd be lost. "No! No!"

Richard tugged her wrist closer to the gates. "Touch them, Madeline. Come back with me."

"Madeline!" Grant's voice boomed in the small hallway. "Don't do it!"

But the stone still glowed and the vibrations turned painful in their intensity. Dizzy and nauseous, with a bone-chilling cold settling deep in her stomach, she watched helplessly as Richard forced her palm closer and closer to one of the iron rungs.

Suddenly, Grant's strength added to hers as she resisted Richard's grasp. Grant tugged her arm in one direction while Richard pulled her wrist in another. Her wrist threatened to shatter from the pressure. Grant pulled her toward him with so much sudden force that Richard, caught off guard by the change of direction, twisted in front of her. His back fell against the gates.

"Madeline!" he screamed, his grasp clutching at her gloved wrist as Grant chopped at his hold. Richard's clutching fingers grasped her bracelet, the loose chain slid over her hand. The gates sucked Richard into their depths, absorbing him whole inside their resolute stillness. She fell backward against Grant, pushing the two of them to the opposite wall. Richard was gone.

The vibrations stopped immediately. The dizziness and nausea faded as quickly as they had arrived.

"Are you hurt?" Grant asked, his lips close to her ears. Odd question as he had taken the brunt of their fall against the brick wall. She should be asking him if he was all right. She struggled to stand, unsteady on her feet. Grant instantly had her waist, holding her so that an inadvertent slip wouldn't send her back in time with Richard.

"I'm alright," she assured him. "The danger is past."

"How can you tell?" Grant asked, not releasing his grasp of her.

"The vibrations have disappeared." As had the dizziness and the nausea, but she didn't mention those. She backed slowly from the gates. "I can just feel it. The danger is past." Though she wasn't about to tempt fate and touch the gates to be certain.

"Richard!" Grant yelled at the wall and the mocking message from Queen Isabella. "Richard, can you hear me?"

Silence.

"I left the gates when you touched them," Maddie reminded him. "Maybe the same thing will happen if you touch them again."

"It's worth a try," Grant said. He took a deep breath, then grasped the gates with both hands.

Nothing happened. Richard didn't reappear. The gates did not scream. Neither Grant nor Richard were thrown to the opposite wall of the hallway. Richard remained gone.

"It's not working. Perhaps my touch only worked before because I'm the descendant of the man who initially trapped you." Grant leaned his head against the gates. "He's gone. I've trapped my best friend in iron."

"You didn't do it," Maddie reassured him. "Richard had the stone. He trapped himself." He had sounded so wretched. Maddie's heart broke all over again. She twisted her hand about her wrist, then realized something was missing. She gasped, earning Grant's glance.

"My bracelet!" She looked about the floor and couldn't locate the gold links or the blue stone. "It's gone!"

She remembered that moment of release, right before she and Grant had tumbled across the hall. She had felt as if a rope connecting her to Richard had broken. She wrapped her hand about her wrist, tracing that last connection. "I think...I think Richard took it with him."

191

"Took your bracelet. Why?" Grant straightened.

Why indeed. It could mean nothing...or it could mean Richard wasn't trapped in iron after all.

"He said that I was a rudder, a time beacon. He thought by taking me with him, he would go back to the moment I was cast into the gates. Once we went back together, he planned to take the Moor's Tear and return to this time. I wonder..." She rubbed her wrist, devoid of the dangling charm. "I wonder if my bracelet would serve as the rudder he needed?"

"You think he made it?" Grant looked at her hopefully, then at the gates with respect. "He's not trapped inside?"

A man and a woman entered the hallway from Royal Street. Other than a cursory glance at Maddie's authentic costume, they passed the two of them and the charm gates as if nothing out of the ordinary had occurred.

"I don't know." She looked at the gates. "I suppose we may never know."

He turned her around to face him, forcing her to look into his eyes.

"You're wrong," he said empathically. His hands gripped her arms.

Her throat thickened. What was he saying? After saving her from entering the gates with Richard, did he plan to toss her into the gates alone? Already, she imagined ice forming in the marrow of her bones.

"I beg your pardon?" Her voice shook.

"You're wrong about the things you said in that note."

Relief passed in an audible breath. She patted her heart. "I thought you were threatening to put me in the gates."

His eyes narrowed. "Why would I do that? I don't want you to leave. I don't want you to ever leave." He glanced about the hallway. "Besides, you have the philosopher's stone."

"I don't have it," she protested. "Didn't you see it glowing in his hand?"

"I only saw that Richard was trying to force you to touch the gates and you...Thank God. You were resisting." He scowled at the floor. "I don't see the rock on the floor. Do you think he still held it when he went in?"

She nodded.

"Then he has the means to come back to us...I hope. I wish I'd had more of a chance to study the stone's properties. Then I'd know if passing through the iron might affect its ability to guide translocation through time." He looked back at the gates. "So much for my big splash."

"Where's Kimmy?" Maddie paused.

"Don't worry." He pulled her closer, as if afraid to let her go. "She's safe at home."

"You left her alone!" Her eyes widened. Kimmy was too young to be by herself.

"No." He smiled. "Jennifer is watching her."

"Jennifer." Her voice slumped. She tried to push back. "I should have known."

"Yes. You should." Grant said, gently guiding her chin toward his. "You should have known that you mean everything to Kimberly and me. Before you entered our lives, I was lost. It was as if I were the one trapped in iron, not you. After Carolyn died, I thought I could never find another person to love. And if I did, I was afraid of ever loving another again, and then losing them as I almost lost you just now. Had you gone into that gate, I believe I would have tried to follow. I can't live without you, Maddie. You are the light of my life."

"Then why is Jennifer at your house?" she asked suspiciously.

"She came to apologize. Apparently, Richard planned the entire evening last night so he could steal the philosopher's stone. Jennifer was supposed to seduce me so I'd be sufficiently distracted."

"You appeared sufficiently distracted to me," she murmured.

"I won't say that I didn't enjoy her attempt, but even she realized that I wasn't interested in what she offered. This morning, she came over to apologize, not to me, but to you."

"To me?"

"She was jealous of you, of your life, of your compassion. She thought she could hurt you by stealing me away. But after her little stunt last night, she realized it was a pointless experiment. When she saw your face, your shock, your hurt, she realized this wasn't a game. She didn't like herself in that moment, so she came to apologize."

"Oh." Perhaps she wasn't as unfeeling as Maddie had supposed.

"She met us outside on the way to the car. Kim had mentioned your note and I realized what you intended to do."

"And you came to stop me." She smiled, love for this man filling her heart, making her light-headed.

"You're the only woman for me, Madeline. I can't let you go. I love—"

He didn't manage to finish as her lips found his with a passion. They

193

stood just inside the street entrance to The Court of Two Sisters and kissed as if they had all the time in the world.

"Ahem."

Grant glanced up to see the Maître d standing in front of them.

"May I find you a table for two, Monsieur?"

He glanced down at Maddie. "Would you like to stay here for dinner?"

"No." She smiled. "I want to go home and get out of this dress."

He grinned. "I can help with that."

"Home," she repeated. "That has a wonderful sound."

They left by the swinging door and stood on Rue Royal amidst the ever-present tourists and revelers traversing the street.

"Some day I'd like to eat at The Court of Two Sisters," Maddie said. "I've never gotten beyond that bar and into the courtyard."

"Then we shall," he said, patting her hand where it rested in the crook of his elbow. "After we're married, we'll come back and—"

She stopped walking. "What did you say?"

He smiled. "I read your note. You said that your ways may be old-fashioned but when two people love each other, they should get married."

She blushed. "That was this morning. I'm no longer old-fashioned. Now I'm thoroughly modern."

"You don't want to marry me?" His face crumbled with disappointment.

"Eventually." She said. "But first I want to go to college and earn a degree, and then maybe run for political office, and learn to cook well and drive a car. As I'm to stay here I must learn to drive a car, and Grant--" She turned to look at him. "--If I'm going to stay in this time then I need to earn my own money, like Jennifer. But not doing what she does. Maybe I can open a school for young girls…a charm school."

"Madeline," his warm voice interrupted her rambling.

She looked up at him.

"I love you."

She smiled, feeling that her destiny brought her to this time and to this man. The Virgin Mary, Ezulie-Freda, Legba, and Saint Jude, all had told her that he was the one, the key to finding her home. She just hadn't realized that "home" meant the twenty-first century. But she knew that now. Knew it to the very breadth of her soul.

"And I love you too," she said. "Let's go home."

Epilogue

THIS HAD TO be Hell.

Thick bubbling liquid like lava flowed past him, flames licking the surface, yet he himself didn't burn. *The stone,* he thought, clenching his hand around it. The stone protected him from the fire, but not the heat, he realized, feeling his internal temperature rise. He quickly gained his feet in the shallow trough and climbed out to chaos.

Screams rent the heavy smoke-filled air. Chunks of masonry lay scattered about. He was surrounded by evidence of some sort of explosion. But where? He stuffed the stone and Madeline's bracelet in his pants pocket then stumbled toward a doorway in search of answers and air that didn't burn his lungs. He made it to a courtyard outside the flames and smoke, only to be hit on the back of the head. He fell to the paving and the world turned black

Cool soft hands stroked his face. He tried to open his eyes, but they wouldn't budge, likewise his lips refused to ask the myriad questions that leapt to his brain. *Where am I? What year is it? Who are you?*

A sweet floral scent reached his nose verifying that his visitor was a woman. She bent low, her hair tickling his cheek. She was listening for signs of his breath, he realized. An angel of mercy. If only he could see...

"This one's dead," she yelled in Spanish. "Put him on the cart."

No! He wanted to scream. *Not dead!* But his lips wouldn't move.

Hands suddenly tugged at his pockets, searching the contents. *I'm being robbed. They'll take the stone!*

But rather than remove his valuables, the hand added something round and heavy to the inside pocket of his jacket. Then she left. He heard her footfalls on the pavement, only to be replaced by a heavier tread. Rough, unsympathetic hands slipped under his armpits while another pair of hands grabbed his ankles. Sagging like a bag of flour, he felt them lift him and toss him unto a cart of other sacks of flour, which he suspected from the smell was anything but.

"That's her!" A man yelled in the distance. "Stop her. Thief!"

But the cart rolled on in search of other bodies and, he supposed, his early grave.

My God! What have I done!

Thank you for reading CHARMING THE PROFESSOR, the first book of the Charm Gates time-travel series.

I'd love to hear your thoughts. You can connect with me in many ways.

The easiest way to hear about new releases is to sign up for my newsletter. If you do, you'll receive a free short story as a thank you. Every month, I do a book give-away of a book from my to-be-read pile. Every newsletter subscriber as an equal chance to win a book. To sign up for my newsletter, click here: http://eepurl.com/mweWX\ Or like me on Facebook, https://www.facebook.com/Donna-MacMeans-152106361521316/timeline/ That way you get the latest news on new releases.

You can also contact me through my webpage at www.DonnaMacMeans.com I guarantee a response.

You have the ability to make or break this book and the series. If you liked the book, please consider posting a brief review on Amazon and/or Goodreads. Recommend the book, lend it or share it with your friends. Word of mouth is extremely important. Reviews, good or bad, show that the book has been read and allow for advertising that wouldn't be possible otherwise. So please do me the favor of a short review.

With deepest respect to the film CASABLANCA,
I hope this is the beginning of a beautiful friendship

What's True, What's not

If you've read my other books, you know I love to incorporate true events in my stories. This book is no exception.

Queen Isabella II of Spain was not a popular ruler. She came to the throne as a child and was forced to marry her double first cousin for political purposes when she was sixteen. The marriage was not a happy one. Rumors persist as to her children's true paternity. She was forced into exile in 1868.

The Court of Two Sisters is a wonderful restaurant in New Orleans, and yes, the restaurant is home to the Charm Gates. Many years ago, my good friend, Sherry Hartzler, and I stumbled upon the Charm Gates by accident. The hallway where the gates currently stand was under renovation. Nothing was in the hallway except the gates and the sign mentioned in the story. Today, that hallway looks much different, but the Charm Gates still exist at the end of the entrance off Rue Royale. The restaurant's website is http://www.courtoftwosisters.com . I highly recommend a mimosa with brunch.

Our Lady of Guadalupe Church is also a real church a few blocks from the restaurant. It houses the International Shrine to St. Jude, the patron saint of lost causes. You'll find it across the street from the cemetery where Marie Laveau, the famed Voodoo Queen, is said to be buried.

I'm sure you are familiar with the passage from The Velveteen Rabbit. Thank you Magery Williams for penning this classic.

The Moor's Tear necklace is pure fiction, but you can read more about it in the prequel to this novel, which you can find on the next page. It will make another appearance in the sequel.

Thanks for reading CHARMING THE PROFESSOR. I hope you enjoyed the reading as much as I enjoyed the writing. Watch for the next book in the Charm Gates Time Travel series, a book I'm tentatively calling, CHARMING THE THIEF.

ABOUT THE AUTHOR

Award winning author Donna MacMeans made a wrong turn many years ago when she majored in Accounting. Balancing books just can't compete with crafting plots and inventing memorable characters. A licensed CPA, she writes seductively witty Victorian historical romances and historical and contemporary paranormal romances in what can only be described as her dream job.

Her books have won many awards including the prestigious Golden Heart from Romance Writers of America, and the Romantic Times Reviewers Choice Award for Historical Love & Laughter, as well as many regional contests. She consistently receives high praise and glowing reviews.

When her fingers aren't on a keyboard or adding machine, she loves to dance. In fact, she met her husband of forty+ years on a dance floor in Cleveland, Ohio. She paints in acrylics, does counted cross stitch, and periodically creates desserts with copious amounts of alcohol. A member of the popular Romance Bandits group and Great Escape Books, she is always approachable and loves to hear from her readers.

Other Books by Donna MacMeans

Victorian Romances:

The Chambers Series
The Education of Mrs. Brimley (2006 Golden Heart winner)
"Lord Hairy" in the Tails of Love Anthology (short story)
The Seduction of the Duke
Redeeming the Rogue

The Rake Patrol Series
The Casanova Code
The Whisky Laird's Bed
Scotland Christmas Reunion (short story)
To Bait a Rake - Coming soon

Victorian Paranormal:

Charm Gates Time-Travel
The Moor's Tear (Prequel short story)
Charming the Professor
Charming the Thief (coming soon)

Bound By Moonlight (Romantic Times Critic's Choice Award for
Historical Love and Laughter)

Paranormal Contemporary Romance:

Smoke and Mirrors (short story)

Made in the USA
Coppell, TX
05 December 2021

67159151R00121